By Any Other Name

by

Kayla Danoli

Copyright

Publisher: Eaglemount Books, Queensland, Australia

Cataloguing-in-publication data
Creator: Danoli, Kayla, author

Cataloguing-in-Publication details are available from the National Library of Australia
www.trove.nla.gov.au

ISBN: 978-0-6489423-1-3 (paperback)
ISBN: 978-0-6489423-2-0 (digital)

Cover design: T A Marshall, Mackay, Queensland

This novel is a work of fiction. All characters and events are the product of the imagination of the author. While some of the characters might remind you of people you know, they are fictitious and any resemblance to anyone living or dead is purely coincidental. Although some locations also may seem real and familiar, most places referred to in this work constitute a collage of places the author has known. But they are fictitious, and any resemblance to an existing location is coincidental.

Contents

Chapter 1

"Someone wrote: *caches of old newspapers are like graves; you shouldn't open them.* The same might be said about DNA test results: *best left unopened.* That's how I counselled myself in a half whisper as I threw today's mail onto the back seat. And, I should have realised the journalist in Kate would not let my conversation with myself slip by unnoticed.

"Lisa, what's that all about? No, don't fob me off. There's a whole lot of emotion at the root of that comment. I want to know why and what it is. From the way you carried the mail to the car, it looked as though you thought it might explode. We need to have a long talk. You are so uptight. I was beginning to wonder who the strange woman was collecting me from the airport this evening. It certainly isn't the Lisa I know; not the one I came here to support. So, talk to me … please.

"What are you on about? I've been talking to you." Kate's withering look made me look away. My question was unnecessary. I knew what Kate meant. Kate Langdon is persistent and, as a journalist, is a skilled interviewer to boot. Resistance was pointless.

"You haven't been talking to me. Since I arrived, I've had nothing but a few stilted comments. I need to know what's going on, so I might help you cope with whatever it is."

After parking the car in the garage, I had a brief moment of introspection before the pulsating silence curtailed it. Instead of scrambling out of the car, I sat there gripping the steering wheel and staring straight ahead. As Kate reached around to unclip her seatbelt, she said, "Let's go inside and settle down with a drink. Come on, we can't sit in the car all night. We should go and be comfortable."

While I knew Kate was right, we should sit down and talk it through as we did with every other problem encountered during our long friendship, this time I needed to work-up courage first. I negotiated a postponement until after Kate showered and we had eaten. Unpacking a few things and showering took Kate no time. On joining me in the kitchen, she spotted the two steaks resting on a board on the bench.

"Wonderful…! I have been looking forward to a great home-grown steak. But… There are only two… Is Tremayne not joining us for dinner? Silly question; I can see there are only two steaks. Is he off on one of his 'jaunts' again? Where is it this time?"

"I don't know. No, don't ask. Wait until after dinner." As soon as we settled into comfortable chairs later, Kate began the interrogation.

"Right, I wanted to know about your comments when you collected the mail, but I think I'd prefer to hear about Tremayne first. You didn't say much but I detected something was amiss there. He was away when I was here last time. That was almost six months ago. Hasn't he been back since?"

"He came back about three weeks ago."

"And he's gone again already? Where is he supposed to be going this time?"

"As I said, I don't know … but then, I never did know where he went. You know how everything was on a need-to-know basis. Anyway, after a while, I realised I didn't want to know."

"Because you didn't care…?" I shrugged. What was there to say? "…And, I don't suppose he gave any indication of when he was likely to return?"

"He won't be returning?"

"Eh …? Why not? Why are you sure he won't be back?"

"A few things happened, and I've had enough. He planned to head off again, but I threw him out instead. That's it; all over, done with and finished. There's nothing more to say."

"At last…! I've never made any secret of the fact I didn't like the man, and couldn't understand what you ever saw in him in the first place. Nevertheless, I am concerned for you, and how you are coping with such a major event. As for 'there's nothing more to say', there is plenty more to say."

"I'm fine. Life became easier once I threw him out. I didn't have to worry about where he was, what he might be doing, when he might return. I could get on with my own life. It wasn't easy, but it was the best thing I've done."

"It looks like I've brought the rain with me, and it's getting heavy."

"That bit of breeze behind it will have us soaked if we stay out here on the deck much longer. Maybe we should adjourn to the lounge room." As Kate settled into a lounge chair, I remembered a phone call I should make. "I might give my harvesting contractor a quick call to confirm they won't be harvesting here tomorrow – not after this rain anyway."

My phone call became two, and both took longer than expected. When I returned to the lounge room half an hour later, Kate was slumped, sound asleep in her lounge chair. Goodness knows how many hours in the air she clocked up by the time she arrived back in Australia, changed planes at Brisbane, and flew north along the coast to meet me at the airport. After shaking her awake and seeing her to her room, I promised we would resume our conversation first thing tomorrow.

*****

This morning dawned fresh and bright, but leaden clouds still hung low over the distant coastline. Rain was heavy for most of the night, causing me some concern about the creek running along the boundary of my property. My neighbour rang to see if I needed a hand with anything. I assured him I was okay. His call was enough to bring a tousled-haired Kate out to the kitchen in search of coffee.

Armed with our preferred breakfasts and coffees, we took ourselves out onto the deck. After a few sips of coffee to kick-start her day, Kate asked, "I love how everything smells so fresh and clean after the rain. I don't suppose there is much we can do, but what's on our agenda for today?"

"First thing, I'd like to go down to check on the creek."

"Oh good; we can have a swim."

"No one will want to swim after all the recent rain. The rain had kept the creek high for a couple of weeks now. After last night's downpour, I needed to check the cattle had feed and water. And, I might need to move them from the paddock on the creek bank to higher ground. After that, the day is ours. We can take the two quad bikes and do a run along the creek bank to check for erosion while we are checking everything else."

"Sounds great; let's get this breakfast stuff cleared away and head off." Minutes later we were kitted out for what might be a muddy ride, and on our way to the shed.

After opening the door of the appropriate shed bay, I froze. "There should be two," I muttered to no one in particular. "There should be *two.*"

"Two what...? Lisa, what's wrong? You look as though you've had a shock."

"There should be two quad bikes parked in here, but there is only one."

"Oh yes, I remember. They usually are parked side-by-side in here. When did you last see them?"

"I'm in and out of the shed all the time, but not necessarily down this end of it, but I haven't used one in a few weeks. I don't know when I last saw them, but it was a while ago."

"While I know it's stating the bleeding obvious, is it possible Tremayne has gone off on one of them for a spin around the farm or something?"

"Yeah, that would be a logical explanation, except for two things: it would be so out of keeping with the man. He only ever rode the bikes once or twice, and he was never interested in going for a 'spin around the farm'. The other thing is, he is not supposed to be still here. Don't ask right now. Just accept he was supposed to be gone by the end of the month, and that was two days ago. Never mind, we still have one bike. We can both go on that one if you're up for it."

My main mission didn't take long to complete. The ground wasn't too boggy and the cattle were fine. Then I drove down to the creek and started back along the bank. There was a good flow in the creek and it was lapping the banks. "I see what you mean about no one wanting to go swimming after rain," Kate said. "The water even looks cold from up here."

Apart from some minor erosion in a couple of places along the opposite bank, there was nothing serious or needing attention. We came to the main headland which, running between two cane paddocks for most of the way, ran straight back to the house. I turned onto the track and started back towards home. We hadn't gone too far before we were off the bike and on foot.

About fifty metres along and off to one side of the headland, cane had been flattened. A narrow strip of flattened cane ran at an angle back in towards the centre of the paddock. As I walked over to inspect the damage, Kate asked, "What happened here? It's a bit of a mess – looks like a herd of elephants ran amok. Last night's rain wouldn't cause this damage would it?"

"No, and even a cyclone doesn't cause damage in such a pattern. Damn, I can't see where it ends. It sort of circles back around on itself a bit."

"I suppose that means there is nothing for it but to scramble over the cane to see where the damage ends, and determine how much damage has been done," Kate said.

She was right. The only way we will know what happened and the extent of it, is to follow the trail to its terminus.

Chapter 2

I could see muddy tracks over the fallen cane. Was it possible they were made by the other quad bike? They looked like quad bike tracks but, if Tremayne hadn't left and was on the other bike, what the hell was he doing to create this much damage? "We are not going to get answers standing out here wondering about it. Let's go and find out what happened in there." Kate announced. She came around and walked up to join me at the start of the flattened cane.

"Stop, Kate. We're not going in there. Now that we're up close, I can see there is more than one set of tracks across that cane. There is what I think are quad bike tracks, but there also is another set of wider tracks probably made by a larger vehicle of some sort."

"What if Tremayne took the bike and something happened to him? Maybe he had a heart attack, or fainted, or something else made him run off the track and into the cane. Shouldn't we at least take a look?"

"Don't go in there, Kate. This mess wasn't created by a quad bike running off the headland. I don't know what we might find in there, but I do know it's not safe for us to go in there alone. I need someone here with us. This might take a few minutes. I'm calling Connor to see if he will come over."

Connor was slow to answer, but said he would be over straight away. I told him where we were and we would wait for him at the site. I heard him galloping his horse towards home as I ended the call. The good news for Kate was that we would be waiting in that hot, humid spot between two cane paddocks for a little while until Connor arrived. She remained unhappy we hadn't traipsed into the paddock to investigate the full extent of the damage. "If we went in and had a look, you might not have needed to call Connor. If you are so concerned about what might have happened here, we could just call the police. I don't understand your logic."

"Over the last twelve months, quite a few farmers in this area have found drug plantations established in the centre of their paddock. Sometimes they're not found until the cane is burnt prior to harvest. This could be a similar situation. I admit, it would have to be rank amateurs who did this. Professionals would have been careful not to leave any tell-tale signs to indicate what happened. I will call the police … when I know more about what happened here."

Twenty minutes later, Connor, in the Rankins' four-wheel-drive farm vehicle, roared up to us. I didn't need to explain the situation. One look was all it took for him to arrive at the same opinion as I had. "You pair stay out here and keep an eye out for unwanted visitors while I take a look in there. It should only take a minute or two but, if you hear me yell, get on that bike and flatten it all the way home. Call the police. Now, stay out here. This shouldn't take long."

Kate scrambled back on the bike. She looked pale and tense. I felt more than a bit nervous myself. "Kate, are you all right? You don't look so great."

"As a journo, I've covered stories in some hair-raising places. Somehow, sitting here in the middle of a cane farm, I feel more exposed than I have in a long while. The implications of what we found here didn't dawn on me until Connor said his piece. Now, I just want him back out here telling us everything is all right."

"His being in there alone doesn't sit comfortably with me either. Something tells me, when he returns, his news will not be good. I don't know how far the damage extends, but it shouldn't take him long to reach the end of it and establish what happened."

My words didn't seem to reassure Kate – or me either for that matter. I climbed back on the bike with her. We sat perched on the wretched machine for what felt like an eternity. In reality, it probably was only a few minutes before I heard footsteps crunching across the cane. I scrambled off the bike and went to wait for Connor to reappear.

One glance at his face sent my stomach into spasm. The set of his jaw, and the fact he wouldn't look me straight in the eye, told me his news was not good, but I had to wait to find out what that was. "Lisa, get on the bike and go back to the house. Do it now. I'll follow you back. We will talk there."

"Connor, what…" His look silenced the argument I was about to launch. "Okay, we'll meet you back at the house."

"This does not look good," Kate whispered as I climbed on and started the bike.

Nobody mentioned any need to hurry, but I pushed the machine to its limit all the way home. I needed to know what Connor found, and he was determined not to say until the three of us were seated in my lounge room. Even then, he appeared to struggle with it.

"Lisa, I can't find the right words; don't know what the right words are. So, I'm just going to dive straight in. Brace yourself please." I nodded and encouraged him to go on. "I followed the trail a long way into the paddock. At the end of it … At the end of it, I found a damaged quad bike and Tremayne. I'm sorry. He's dead. I've called the police. They should be on their way here by now. I don't know what else to say, except I'm pleased you have someone with you at this time. I will be here as well for whatever you need."

When Connor delivered his 'punchline', Kate gasped and rushed over to sit on the arm rest of my chair and wrap her arm around my shoulders. "My God, not another death; Lisa, you don't deserve this. You've had more than enough to deal with over the last few months. From the moment we saw the damage, I knew you were concerned it was something serious, but I never expected anything like this. Fate can play a mean hand. Why Tremayne…? If he'd left by the end of the month as you stipulated, he would have been gone at least two days ago, and maybe this wouldn't have happened."

"We don't know when it happened… or do we, Connor? Was there any indication?" Connor shook his head.

"That's something for the police to determine. They should be here soon. I'll take them straight to the site when they arrive. Kate, I think coffee with a drop of something in it might be good about now."

"No, I don't want anything. Maybe after the police have been, a drop-of-something might be good. But, Connor you and Kate should have one now if you need it." Consensus was none of us wanted coffee or anything else at the moment.

About twenty minutes later, the police arrived. Connor met them and led them down to the site. Half an hour later, Connor returned and was talking to someone as they came up the stairs. "Lisa, this is Detective Inspector, Dan Taylor. He will lead the team investigating Tremayne's death." Out the corner of my eye, I saw Connor give Kate a look and jerk his head towards the kitchen. She understood and they both exited the lounge room.

"I hope Mr Rankin has gone to organise coffee," Inspector Taylor said. "I could do with one and I suspect you need one too." I was grateful he didn't hesitate, but went straight on to tell me what they found in my paddock.

"Mr Rankin identified the body in your paddock as that of your husband, Mr Tremayne Bancroft. Did you see the body?"

"No, Connor … Mr Rankin, followed the damage into the paddock, while Kate and I stayed out on the track. It wasn't until we returned here to the house that he told me about the body and that it was my husband."

"Right, so you can't confirm the identification at this time?" I shook my head. "There was a damaged quad bike at the scene. Is it likely to belong to this property?"

"It's possible. I own two identical quad bikes. When my friend and I went to take the bikes out this morning, one was missing. I don't know when it disappeared. It could have been at any time during the last fortnight, but probably within the last few days."

"That's probably close to the mark. Our experts will confirm the timing, but my guess is within the last two or three days. What were your husband's movements over the last week or so?"

Here we go. Things are about to become embarrassing and complicated. Still, I suppose the truth must out at some point in time. This is probably as good a time as any. I cleared my throat, stalling for time to marshal my thoughts into some logical order which made sense and didn't complicate matters too much. "As daft as it might seem, Inspector, I can't tell you much at all. I'll go back to about three weeks ago when my husband returned from one of his overseas jaunts."

"If that will help, but before you do, please explain 'overseas jaunts'."

"My husband claimed to be a foreign correspondent, a journalist covering international issues and events. It involved frequent periods of time away from home, some, if not all, spent at various places overseas. About three weeks ago he returned from one such sojourn. Within a few days, several discussions relating to private and personal matters occurred. Those discussions turned sour and resulted in the breakdown of the relationship."

The inspector gave me a questioning look – or was it a confused look? I knew my statement required clarification. "In plain language, I threw him out, but allowed him to stay in the other cottage on the property until the end of the month while he sorted himself out and found somewhere else to live."

"Did he move into the cottage?" I deemed a nod was sufficient to answer the question and the inspector continued. "It seems he didn't comply with your deadline. What can you tell me about his movements while domiciled in the cottage?"

"Almost nothing; yes, it sounds strange, but things have been a bit hectic here over the last few months. It included sorting out any number of things with banks and solicitors. I've spent quite a bit of time in town, as well as trying to keep this place running. I don't recall seeing my husband at all once he moved into the cottage – not even driving on or off the property. I can't say I even noticed lights on in the cottage at night."

"So, you don't know whether he took you up on your offer to stay in the cottage for a while, or if he left the place immediately after you threw him out?"

"No, as I said, I don't recall having seen him after he moved out of this house. But, my friend, who arrived to spend a bit of time with me, pointed out that the end of the month had passed, and suggested we should check everything was left okay in the cottage. We were to do that later this morning."

"What happened this morning? You mentioned you had things to attend to on the property."

After explaining about checking on the cattle and the creek before we came across the damage to the cane paddock, I thought my session with the detective was finished. There was nothing else I could tell him about today, or the previous two or three days. Kate popped her head in to ask if we would like our mugs refilled. My hope of being finished with the detective was dashed when he said 'yes please' to a second cup. For the few moments while Kate delivered fresh brew, I allowed my mind to roam free. Damn! It found something more which might be of interest to the inspector.

"I don't know if this is relevant or not…" He assured me everything was relevant at this stage of the investigation. "We had a lot of unseasonal rain over the last couple of months. It caused havoc with harvesting schedules. Then, the rain a couple of weeks ago further delayed operations. My cane should have been harvested a week ago. Thanks to the rain delay, and a few problems at the mill, the harvester was due to return here earlier this week. Then, the rain a couple of nights ago caused a further delay, resulting in harvesting not starting here today."

"I'm sure that is important to your operations here on the farm, but I don't see how it might interest me."

"It might, if you knew that, had there not been a further delay and harvesting commenced here today, the paddock containing the body would have been burnt last night in preparation for today's harvest."

"O-oh … So, if it hadn't rained, we would now be investigating a crime scene where much of the evidence had been incinerated before we arrived?"

"I don't know whether that's useful or not, but I thought it an interesting coincidence."

That was my last card, but the inspector was showing no signs of leaving my lounge room. Salvation arrived when a couple of his officers came looking for him. The forensic people had arrived and wanted to speak to him. This caused a dramatic sigh of resignation and profuse apologies for having to rush away. Then it was my turn to heave a sigh – of relief.

After seeing the police officers out, Kate and Connor joined me in the lounge. On his way past, Connor clapped me on the shoulder. "How are you holding up? I suggested leaving talking to you until tomorrow, but Taylor insisted it was best done now, before people had time to forget details."

"Standard practice I think. It's as well to have it over and done with."

"How do you feel? Would you like to lie down for a while?" Kate asked.

"I don't know how I feel. Nothing seems real. I know what's in the middle of that paddock, and understand that Tremayne is dead, but nothing is computing. I'm unable to comprehend what it all means. Maybe when we know what happened, I will understand, and it will hit me."

Connor wasn't impressed with my response and asked Kate if she would be sticking around for a while. "Don't worry Connor. I'm not going anywhere. I think I'll be here for quite some time to come."

My attempt to elicit more details from Connor went nowhere. "I can't tell you any more than I already have, Lisa, because I don't know anything else. None of us will until the police share the outcome of their investigation with us … and that's unlikely to be today."

"You're right," Kate agreed. "They will play it close to their chests until they have something definite to tell us." Debating the mysteries involved in the police conducting an investigation was curtailed when a young police officer appeared. Taylor had sent him to collect Mr Rankin. There were a few things Taylor and the forensic people wanted to discuss with Connor.

"It's almost lunchtime, Connor," I said. "When the police are finished with you, come back here for lunch with us. We'll wait for you."

As soon as Connor left, Kate became serious. "Lisa, we know you chucked Tremayne out, gave him until the end of the month to be off the property, and the end of the month has come and gone. Do we know what happened between then and now?"

"Like what…?"

"Let's see: is his stuff gone from here? Did he move into the cottage? Did he move out by the end of the month? Was he still living there when this 'thing' happened? Did he hang around in the hope you would change your mind and take him back? Is his…?

"Whoa! Too many questions…"

"Well, you are going to need answers to them, because the police will be asking them sooner or later … and it might be handy to know the answers beforehand."

"I agree. We should check out the cottage. We'll send Connor home as soon as lunch is over, and then we will investigate."

As if on cue, my phone chirped. It was Connor. "Sorry; I can't keep our lunch date. Something has come up on our property. I'm going home to give Dad a hand." A part of me was disappointed. I like Connor's company. But, mostly I was pleased we didn't have to wait until after lunch to visit the cottage.

"Connor is not coming for lunch. We can check out the cottage now. I'm sure there will be nothing to find there. Tremayne didn't make a fuss when I told him to go, and I'm sure he had no intention of hanging around," I told Kate.

"Right, let's go." As we clattered down the stairs together and strode out towards the cottage, Kate said, "I love that cottage. I still can't believe how you turned that ugly cane cutters barracks building into such a glorious home. There's not even a hint of the original building evident in it now, and it became such a well laid out and comfortable place to live." I chuckled at the memory of that transformation process and all it involved.

"In spite of the fact that it was hard work, and sometimes felt like a hopeless project, I really enjoyed the challenge of turning the old barracks into our home. All through the project, it was always referred to as *The Barracks*. Then, as soon as the work was nearing completion, almost overnight, it became *The Cottage*. I loved living there. It was my place; somewhere I had created, and just the way I wanted it to be. It was a wrench when Mum's condition reached the point where I needed to be close to her 24/7. The only way for that was to move into the big house to care for her."

"If I were living there and had to move out, I think it would have broken my heart. I'm pleased it's been looked after and hasn't deteriorated in spite of not being lived in for quite a while." Kate strode out resolutely. Her long legs made it hard work keeping up with her. As we marched up to the front door, she said, "There are no obvious signs of inhabitation out here. Shall we go inside?" She waited a couple metres back as I marched up to the front door.

My solid knock on the door received no response. As I began pounding it again, Kate asked, "Why are you knocking? There's nobody in there to answer the door. ...Unless you think he might have moved in a lady friend." I stood there for a moment with my fist poised to thump the door again – and feeling a total fool.

"Don't be silly. Even Tremayne wouldn't be foolish enough to do that."

I tried the door. It wasn't locked. My stomach was doing flip-flops. My instinct suggested caution. Why was I so nervous? I had every right to be there, and to confirm the place was vacant. I opened the door and stood aside to latch it back.

Kate continued past me, and took a couple of steps inside before coming to a sudden halt.

With the door dealt with, I looked around to see Kate, hands on hips, surveying the living area. "That's about what I expected," she snarled.

I rushed to stand beside her and followed her example to see what upset her. "What...? What are you carrying on about?"

"I'm not surprised. The lazy sod didn't clean up before he left. No respect... He knows how you feel about this place, but still left it in a mess."

"Well, at least we know someone has been staying here recently."

Chapter 3

A pile of dirty plates and other bits and pieces stacked on the sink grabbed our attention. I yanked open the fridge. Not a lot to see: two cans of beer, half a bottle of milk, and what looked like a bowl of leftovers from a Chinese take-away meal. Those flip-flops in my stomach stepped up their pace.

"What's in the fridge?" Kate demanded. I gave her an inventory of its contents. "Dirty dishes, stuff in the fridge… It appears whoever was here hadn't moved out. Was it Tremayne?"

"Dunno, but the beer is his brand," I called over my shoulder as I headed down the hall to the bedroom. I passed the bathroom, then doubled back to look inside. "…This does tend to answer one question." Kate rushed up to peer over my shoulder.

She shook her head. "He hadn't moved out, had he?"

My stomach had tightened into a huge lead ball. I tiptoed towards the bedroom. "Let's see what awaits us in here," I whispered.

"Lisa, why are you sneaking about and whispering? Do you think he has someone stashed in the bedroom, or that Tremayne's ghost is waiting for us in there?" Kate asked with a jerk of her head towards the bedroom door.

"Probably not; but I don't know do I?" I heard her murmur *oh, for God's sake…,* but I chose to ignore it.

The door was partially ajar. One deep breath to steady myself, before shoving it open and peering inside. I didn't need to go any further. From the doorway, I could see Tremayne had been here. Odd bits of clothing were strewn about the floor. A pair of trousers hung off the end of the bed – which remained unmade. One of the wardrobe doors was open. A few shirts on hangers were visible. "Well, here's your answer, Kate. There's nobody in the bedroom, and I think it's safe to say Tremayne hadn't moved out."

"You are sure the stuff is Tremayne's?" I nodded. "Okay, but where are you going now?"

"I just want to check something. It won't take a moment." I left Kate standing in the hallway and made my way to the interconnecting door to the garage. It wasn't locked either, so I opened it a fraction and peered inside. Even in the gloom of the garage, there was no mistaking Tremayne's vehicle parked inside. I closed the door and made my way back to Kate. "I now have my definitive answer: Tremayne was staying here and hadn't moved out before his untimely demise. I suppose I must let my solicitor, Justin Farley, know what's happened and find out what I'm supposed to do next."

Kate grabbed my arm and dragged me to and out of the front door. "Close the door. We'll have a long talk about what needs to be done next after we've had lunch." I almost had to jog to keep up with her as we crossed to the house and galloped up the stairs. There was almost no conversation until we were seated on the deck with our lunch.

At first, we ate in silence but, at one point, I noticed Kate shaking her head as if to rid herself of a troubling thought. "What is it, Kate? What is bothering you?"

"Nothing hangs together." I felt my eyebrows crawl up my forehead in surprise. My feeling was that we had gone quite some way to establishing what happened in the lead up to today.

"Don't look at me like that, Lisa. Think about it. Tremayne's reaction was way out of keeping with the man. For him not to burr up when you threw him out was strange. I expected at least a monumental argument, if not something much worse. Then, to continue to hang about… Why? If he understood anything about you, he would know you wouldn't change your mind. And, from what I saw in the cottage, he wasn't preparing to leave. It looked more like he was settling in to stay."

"I don't know what to say. I can't argue with any of that. But, I thought we were going to talk about what I needed to do now he's dead."

"…And we will, but first, there's something more important I need to ask you. Lisa, are you ill, I mean seriously ill?"

"Ill…? God, no, there's nothing wrong with me. Why did you ask me that?"

"It all goes back to when you collected the mail when I arrived, and the comment you made. You dumped all the mail on the hall table, but later took most of it through to the office. All except the one envelope that remains, forlorn and lonely, on the hall table. Yell at me if you want, but I checked the envelope. It's from your GP. So, if you are not ill, why did your GP send you a letter?"

"Argh… it's a part of a much bigger story."

"Is that the story of what's been happening here since I went overseas?" I shrugged and then nodded. "So, talk to me, Lisa. Tell me what is going on. What I've come back to. I can't help you cope if I don't know."

If only I could explain everything to Kate. Therein is the problem. I don't trust myself to open up. Even if I felt so inclined, I wouldn't know where to start. "Kate, it's complicated. For the last few months, I've felt stranded in some parallel universe … or, as though I'm having a nightmare from which I can't wake up."

"Just talk to me. Don't worry about any of it not making sense."

Tell her, the little voice in my head demanded. I obeyed. "My problem is where to start. I don't know when I lost control of my life, or how to get it back. All I know is that my life is in a downward spiral … And I suspect, taking my sanity with it."

"All the more reason to talk to me; let me help you sort it out. As for where to start, let's go back to the last time I was here. It was the few days prior to my departure for overseas. Do you remember?" Unable to speak, I nodded. "Good; start talking."

"You were taking six months off to go tripping around Europe, and came here for a few days before you left. And, you invited me to go with you, even for just a couple of weeks. The whole time you were here, you kept at me to go with you. I couldn't. You knew that; knew about the situation here, but you kept at me anyway."

"Of course I did. Even back then you looked frazzled. Yes, I understood about your responsibilities and your obligations here, but I was concerned that, without a break, you would go down in a heap. I now believe that occurrence is imminent. So, let's start unwinding you shall we?"

"Not going with you was the right decision. A few days after you left, Mum had a mini stroke. Her dementia had almost become too much for me to manage. The stroke sealed it. She went into care in a top-class place down south Dad knew about. They had a vacancy. Maybe a 'backhander' might have helped such a convenient vacancy occur."

"I knew you moved back home because your parents were becoming too old to manage everything on their own, particularly your mother. She was integral to running this place, as well as being a wife and mother. When you gave up teaching for full-time work on the property, I knew your mother's condition was deteriorating. How did she settle into the care facility?"

"We were amazed at how well she settled in. But, my parents had never been separated more than a day or two during their married life. So, within about a week, they both started to fret. That didn't last too long. Dad lost weight and looked poor. You commented on it when you were here. At first, I thought it a consequence of everything happening with Mum. When it became worse, I persuaded him to go to a doctor. He had leukaemia. The sort people sometimes develop late in life. It was well advanced. The prognosis was for no more than a couple of months."

"Yeah, I remember how poor he looked. When I asked him about it, he just laughed it off."

"That's what I would expect of him. As soon he was diagnosed, he rang Mum's care facility and arranged to join her. About a month later, Mum passed away after another stroke. At least they had time together before she went. I rented an apartment close by to spend time making sure Dad was okay. Then, about six weeks later, he too was gone."

"My God, why didn't you tell me? You knew I would come back straight away. You didn't have to deal with all that on your own…. And you would have been dealing with it on your own. Tremayne was never going to be much use to you at a time like that."

"I didn't tell you because I knew you would come back. Tremayne wasn't around at the time. I think he already was away when you were last here. It was just as well anyway. I was able to deal with everything as it happened, without worrying about him and his needs. He did return in time for Dad's funeral, but only stayed a couple of weeks before taking off again."

"…And then he came back about three weeks ago?" I nodded. "I've always loved spending time here on the property with you, but I don't think I've ever asked you about the history of the place. When did the Soldarno family first start farming here?"

"My grandfather took up the first bit of land a few years after he immigrated from the old country. Over the years, he, and then my father, bought up the surrounding small farms to end up with the property we have now. In the beginning, my grandfather grew vegetables, bananas; anything he could sell to make a bit of money to build a home and bring the rest of his family out to Australia. A bit later, they introduced a few cattle, and gradually built up the herd. But, in those days, sugarcane had become king. So, the next move was to build up the area they could put under cane. When Grandad died, the place passed to my father, and now it's mine … and it still has sugar cane and cattle."

"I understand that, as the only child, the place passed to you, but are you going to be able to run it by yourself?"

"I don't anticipate any problems. I wasn't just my parents' only child and their only daughter. I also was their only son. I've always helped Dad on the farm. Over the last twelve months, as my father's health declined, I took on more of the running of the farm. I'll see how things work out. Whether I need a farm hand of sorts to help with the place is a decision for the future. So far, with all the help I've had from Connor Rankin from next door, it hasn't been too hard to manage."

"Connor is Bob Rankin's son, isn't he? I remember him being around when we were kids, but then he seemed to disappear. I didn't realise he was back on the farm next door until the last time I was here. While he was away, I remember you and your father gave Bob Rankin a hand to muster his place on occasion. It's good Connor's been able to spare the time to help and support you now. This is a hell of a big property. You have a mammoth job ahead of you if you try running the place on your own … Not that I thought Tremayne would be much help to you. He seemed allergic to dirt."

"He wasn't from a farming background. He was a city boy. Although he was happy to travel all over the world, I don't think he was ever comfortable – not truly comfortable – being stuck out here on the property."

"When you two first hooked up, I remember you were teaching in the city. I'm sure he had no inkling he would end up stuck out here on a farm. He was supposed to be a foreign correspondent or something when you met him, wasn't he?"

"Uhmm … He was a reporter of some sort back then. It wasn't until he started going away for periods of time that I found out he was a foreign correspondent. I don't know whether he freelanced from the outset, or if he turned to freelancing after we moved back up north to be near my family … Or if he was freelancing at all. If he wasn't freelancing, I don't know who he worked for."

"Okay, let's leave that for the moment and return to your story. Tremayne was away for a while, came home about three weeks ago, and then you chucked him out. Is that right?" I nodded and Kate continued. "It's a bit indelicate of me, but what happened to make you throw him out? You put up with him for this long, in spite of the fact we thought you were mad, and then, all of a sudden, you throw him out."

"Things changed, Kate. Everything changed during the six months you were away. Both my parents died. As an only child, I inherited everything. But, 'everything' includes complete responsibility for running not only this place, but everything else I inherited as well. No matter how much I thought I was doing before Dad died, it wasn't a half of it. Dad continued to control the Soldarno business empire. I didn't even know about some parts of it – but I do now. That would be irrelevant except, Tremayne was astute enough to work out what all the changes meant."

"He worked out you were now a wealthy woman in your own right, and somehow that caused the problem? Why would your changed circumstances make any difference?"

"I've never talked to anyone about this. Although Tremayne was always dashing off to chase some story, he didn't have a regular income. When I moved back here to care for Mum and help run the place, Dad insisted on paying me. I was at odds with the idea of being paid. It wasn't costing us anything to live here, not even for food. Nevertheless, he insisted on paying me a wage of about a thousand dollars per week. I split my pay three ways. In the interests of domestic harmony – and to protect Tremayne's male dignity I suppose – I paid him a weekly allowance."

"What…? You paid your useless lump of a husband a weekly allowance?"

"Now you know why I didn't tell anyone. That's exactly the response I expected if people knew. So yes, in effect, I paid him an allowance of about three hundred dollars a week. I put an equivalent amount into our joint account. The rest of it was mine, but I sometimes delved into that to buy bits and pieces for this place."

"Just as well your father didn't know about it. He wouldn't have been impressed with your paying your husband an allowance, and he would not approve your spending your money on this place. What sort of things did you pay for?"

"Nothing significant; I just contributed to what I considered the cost of my personal use of farm resources."

"You said you contributed to a joint account. I assume you both could access the account for specific purposes."

"We both could access the account to pay for things like occasional holidays, or to buy big-ticketed items which we both used – like a TV."

"So, what happened? Did he get greedy? It wouldn't surprise me. The man always wanted to appear more than he was. Your allowance wouldn't have facilitated the life he fancied for himself."

"Greed is what it amounted to. He demanded more money; said my 'changed status' meant I could afford it. What he considered a reasonable weekly amount, was more than I was paid. Well, that was never going to happen. So, he insisted I sell up – everything – and we could move to live in 'civilisation'."

"If 'civilisation' equates to 'city', which city?"

"He never mentioned anywhere specific, just a city somewhere down south."

"You weren't going to entertain that, even for a moment. So, how did that discussion end?"

"Thinking back on it, he didn't think I would agree. So, when I dismissed that idea, he came back with an alternative. As my husband, he was entitled to be a joint partner in everything … And wanted that put in place immediately. No, don't ask. Of course it wasn't going to happen. I'm not fool enough to have believed for one moment that he was entitled. I just laughed at him. Probably wasn't the wisest thing to do at the time, given tension was building between us. Then, he played his trump card. If I didn't agree to one of the two options he put forward, he would move out and sue me for half of everything."

"What sort of fool was the man? He didn't have to belong to Mensa to work out such an approach would bring down your red mist in a flash. Sorry, do go on with the story."

"Yeah, the red mist came down, and that's when I told him to get out. I made it clear he would get nothing, and wouldn't have a leg to stand on when I could prove I had been keeping him for all this time. Then, when I realised he had nowhere to go. I relented a little. Told him I wanted him off the place and gone as soon as possible, but I was willing to let him stay in the cottage until the end of the month to get himself organised. If he were still here then, I would have him removed."

"You were taking a risk. I have him tagged as someone who wouldn't hesitate to resort to violence if things weren't going his way. How did he take your ultimatum?"

"He just seemed to accept it; stormed off to collect a few of his things and went over to the cottage. I hadn't seen or heard from him since. Earlier, you said, as a result of everything that's happened, there were things I needed to do. What do I need to do?"

"Okay, let's go through them quickly before we do something about dinner. The first thing to do is to close down that joint account. Unfortunately, he might already have cleaned it out."

"I did that first thing the day after I chucked him out. What else should I do?"

"Good; the other thing you should do is to make sure your future is secure. You've always said you know nothing about Tremayne's background. You need to make sure family members aren't going to come out of the woodwork and claim half of everything you own."

"My solicitor, Justin Farley, lodged a separation document, and sent a copy of it by registered mail to Tremayne's post office box in town. Making decisions about my future wasn't all that difficult. I realised there hadn't been anything between us for a long time. Oh, things were cordial enough. There weren't any blazing rows or anything like that. I don't know how to describe the relationship. Perhaps 'détente' is the best I can come up with now."

"I am impressed … And I apologise for selling you short when I assumed you had not been clear-thinking enough to put those measures in place. Anyway, let's take a break from all that and make a start on preparing dinner."

Connor drove up just as we came in off the deck. Kate giggled. "Seeing as how he missed having lunch with us, should we invite him to stay for dinner?"

Chapter 4

A few minutes after Connor arrived, Inspector Taylor drove up and parked beside him. After going down to let the two men in and bring them upstairs, Kate took herself off to the kitchen to rustle up dinner. I was surprised at Taylor's arrival so late in the day.

"I planned to be here earlier to follow up on a couple of things, but other cases had me pinned down in the office. Can the pair of you spare me a few minutes now – and do you feel up to it after the day you had?" Connor and I assured him we were happy to talk now. After I led the two men out onto the deck, the Inspector wasted no time getting down to business.

"Miss Soldarno, this morning you indicated checking out the cottage was on your agenda for today. Did that occur?"

"Yes; and my husband's belonging are still there. There's no evidence of him packing up to leave, so I don't think he took my deadline seriously."

"Did he often go for a ride around the paddocks? ...Maybe down to the creek for a swim or to go fishing?"

"No. Tremayne wasn't interested in the farm, and wasn't interested in fishing. I don't recall him ever going for a swim in the creek. After the recent rains, that would be impossible anyway. The creek is about ready to flood and is flowing swiftly. Look, Inspector, I have no idea why Tremayne took one of the quad bikes for a spin. He has never done that in the past."

"Okay, there is one other avenue I'd like to explore, if you can spare me a little more time." As he was about to tell us what that was, Kate poked her head out.

"Connor, I know you're staying for dinner but, Inspector Taylor, are you interested in joining us for dinner?"

"Thank you. I'd love to."

I struggled to prevent my groan escaping. "Should you let Mrs Taylor – or anyone – know you won't be home for dinner? I'll fix us drinks while you make the call if you like." He assured me there was no one he needed to call. Okay, so he is a bachelor; good to know I suppose.

"Thanks for the drink. Now the other thing I wanted to ask you about is whether you've noticed any strangers hanging about in recent weeks … Maybe not even strange, but people who you would not normally see around here."

"No-o, I don't recall… Oh, there was one – a bloke – but that was a while ago, just before Dad went into care. He drove up to the shed and spoke to Dad. I don't know what it was about. Dad never mentioned it later, but I don't think it went well. Because I observed it from up here, I didn't hear what was said, but Dad didn't seem too happy about it. In the end, I could tell Dad was angry, and his actions suggested he told the bloke to get off the property."

"Was the bloke driving a grey SUV?" Connor asked.

"Yeah, a silver-grey coloured thing."

"It might be the same bloke who spoke to us. We were mustering a few head in the paddock beside the road when he pulled up and started asking questions. It was obvious he was trying to give the impression he was lost and wanted directions, but his actions suggested something else."

"What about his actions?" Taylor asked. I noticed he had moved forward on his chair and seemed excited by Connor's comments.

"He seemed to be checking us out; looking to see if there was anyone else around as well. We didn't like the look of the bloke, or the way he behaved. So, we moved all the stock out of the paddock and brought them up closer to the house where we could keep an eye on them. We thought he might be scouting for duffers. We never saw him again."

"What about you, Miss Soldarno, did you…"

"Inspector, it might be easier for both of us if you call me Lisa."

"Okay, thank you, Lisa. Do you recall ever seeing the bloke again?"

"Nah, but I did keep an eye out for him for a while after his visit. I didn't like the look of him – and I could tell Dad didn't either. O-o-h, wait a minute … I did see a similar vehicle recently. On my way home from town, just around the bend before you get to our gate, a similar vehicle passed me going the other way. At the time, I had the feeling it might have come out of our driveway – but it was only a feeling. I didn't *see* the vehicle come out of here."

"Was anyone here at the time?"

"No, there was no one at home. Dad had passed away and Tremayne was off overseas somewhere … and I was in town."

Kate came out to announce she would be serving dinner in a few minutes. The Inspector chewed his lip during a moment of indecision, before deciding to share something more with us. "Before we eat, I think you should know, I'm having difficulty understanding how you weren't aware your husband had gone for a ride on one of your quad bikes. That aside, the forensic boys don't believe your husband's death was an accident. I can't give you any more details at the moment, because I don't know anything more, other than they have flagged it as a suspicious death. I'll keep you posted, but it might take a while before we know anything definite." I felt a moment of discomfort. Was I imagining it, or did the inspector give me a searching look as he spoke?

As soon as we finished eating, Connor – bless him – started making noises about my difficult day and how I needed time alone to deal with everything. It took a few minutes for Taylor to get the message, but it was quite early when they both left. Kate took it on herself to walk the two men to their cars. I'm sure she knew it wasn't necessary, and I was equally sure she had an ulterior motive for doing so.

Silence, glorious silence and solitude cloaked the deck. Short-lived though it was, I savoured every moment of it until Kate returned. "It was kind of you to show the men to their cars. Did you do any good?" I asked as soon as she reappeared.

"Did I do any good…? I don't know what you mean."

"Yes you do. You were hoping to pick up some information by way of asking a couple of well thought out questions."

"Yeah, but the gentlemen were not as forthcoming as I hoped. Both were cagey. Anyone would think they were used to being interviewed."

"Perhaps 'questioned' is a more accurate word than 'interviewed'." Kate gave a wry smile. "So, come on. What did you find out? Don't think about fobbing me off. I've had enough of people being considerate today."

"Okay … I wanted to find out the cause. Did Tremayne have an incident, or was it something else. And, information about his injuries might be useful in understanding what occurred. I received no straight answers, but did pick up a couple of things; they don't believe it was natural causes or a problem with the bike. I took that to indicate foul play. But, that doesn't tell us anything new after you spotted those extra tyre tracks. I did press them about the nature of Tremayne's injuries … said, if I couldn't give you that information, you would raise hell until they let you see the body."

"Cheeky, but probably correct; maybe that would make me feel something about what happened. Regardless of how thing were between us, I know I should feel something – grief, loss, anger, something – but I don't. All I feel is confusion about how I *should* feel."

"You left out 'relief'." Kate cut me off before I could protest. "Tremayne's demise does simplify moving on with your new life. As for your feelings, maybe what you're experiencing is shock coupled with a lack of comprehension about what happened. Don't try to find the 'right' feelings. Relax, leave it alone, and let your feelings sort themselves out in their own good time."

After a few moments silence, Kate tentatively continued. "Lisa, I don't know if this is the right time, but I want to follow up on something I asked you before."

"That's ominous, but it might be good to change the topic of conversation. So, ask away."

"That envelope on the hall table; the one from your GP … are you expecting bad news and are not game to open it?"

"No, nothing like that. It probably contains the results of a whim I indulged in. It won't be bad news, but its contents are irrelevant now."

"Was it about Tremayne? Has he been ill?"

I know when to give in, and this was just such a time. "I'm sure it's about a DNA test I arranged a while ago."

"Why the sudden interest in your DNA?"

"Not my DNA, Tremayne's … and that's why the results are now irrelevant."

"Are you happy now you have me intrigued? Don't leave me hanging in suspense."

"It sounds a bit weird but, after Mum died, I realised it wouldn't be long before Dad joined her. It started me thinking. I am the last of the Soldarno line. There's no one to come after me; no grandchildren. When the time comes, what will I do with this property and everything else I own? On the off chance he survived me, I never considered leaving anything to Tremayne. For various reasons, from early in the marriage, there was a mutual agreement there would be no children. I'm sure Tremayne never changed his stance on that one. In my case, as time went by and I realised the truth about Tremayne and the marriage I was in, it served to confirm the 'no children' decision was the right one to take."

"At first, I wondered why children didn't appear. You're a teacher. You love kids. I know that, as a teacher, at the end of the day, you can send them home to their parents. But you have a genuine affinity for children. One I don't share, I must admit. Then, as your marriage progressed, I felt some comfort in the fact there were no children. But, how does this relate to Tremayne's DNA?"

"I also realised I wasn't getting any younger. Neither of us is, and I don't need to tell you that."

"While I don't think about age, you are right. Time is slipping by. Our next birthdays are our BIG birthdays. The one when we officially join the ranks of the middle-aged."

"Yep, and I realised that, if I wanted to do something about continuing the Soldarno line, I had to get a move on. I remained unsure about bringing a child into the world. The same niggling questions that bothered me for years still remained. On many occasions, I endeavoured to learn more of Tremayne's background; to know his family history, and know about any conditions that might exist in his family's line.

A couple of serious conditions existed down through several generations of my family, but seem to disappear in the last two or three generations. My concern was that those conditions might reappear in my offspring and, if combined with prevalent conditions in Tremayne's family history, might result in serious complications. For whatever reason, Tremayne would never discuss his family. His parents' names are on our marriage certificate, but that's all I know. He said he had no siblings, but I don't know if that's true. Is there family I should be advising of his death? I don't know. What I'm saying is Tremayne, his life and his family history, are a blank to me."

"Are you suggesting there might be something in his background he didn't want you to know about … maybe something embarrassing or criminal in his family history he was ashamed of? I understand you would want to know those details before going ahead with having a child."

"That's why, on my last visit to my GP, I discussed the possibility of a pregnancy and she assured me I was healthy enough to go ahead with it. When I explained my lack of information regarding Tremayne, she suggested a DNA test. It might not tell me who his parents were, but it would pick up any markers on his chromosomes likely to cause problems. A DNA test sounded the right way to go, but getting a sample was the problem."

"Can't they take samples from toothbrushes, or hairs from brushes and combs, or fingernail clippings and the likes, if a person is reluctant to provide a proper sample?"

"Yes, I think so. But, we had a ready-made opportunity. The next time Tremayne came home from one of his trips away and went for his usual blood test, my GP would ask for a DNA screening to be carried out."

"How often did Tremayne have blood tests done? Were they a regular occurrence?"

"They were. Some years ago, when he began spending more time away more often, I insisted. The first day he was back home, he had to have a blood test. After all, he's a bloke, and God knows what they get up to when they're away from home … And who knows what they might bring home from strange places? He had to have the test, and I needed the results before I had anything to do with him."

"He agreed? I can't believe the Tremayne I knew agreed to such an arrangement."

"He raised little argument when I brought it up, and went along with it without complaint afterwards. Getting back to your interest in the unopened envelope, I'm sure it's the results of the DNA test my GP sent away after his blood test about three weeks ago. As I said, it doesn't matter anymore."

"I don't know much about DNA, and I don't imagine you do either. Nevertheless, I think you should at least look at the results. As you say, they can't make a difference to your life now, but they might satisfy your curiosity."

"You are right. I probably am being a bit silly about it. All notion of a child went out the window along with my marriage. Once that happened, it didn't matter if the tests showed everyone in Tremayne's family had two heads and six fingers on each hand. It was of no consequence. I might take them back to my GP and ask her to interpret them for me … after I have a quick look at the results."

Kate fetched the envelope. I ripped it open and studied the contents, which were completely bewildering. My wonderful GP took the trouble to attach a note explaining in simple layman's terms not only how to read the results, but pointed out a couple of unique markers on his DNA sequence which would assist in finding familial matches. There was nothing in the results to cause concern from a pregnancy point of view."

"So, nothing scary in the envelope after all... When you carried it from the mailbox the other day, you looked as though you expected it to explode. Now you have the results, will you take it any further; search for close familial matches?"

"Not likely. As I've said, it's irrelevant now. There are plenty of other issues to take care of in the next little while without worrying about any possible relatives he might have. It's still early, but I think I might turn in for the night. Maybe everything will seem more real in the morning."

*****

Kate was still in bed, and I was lingering over my breakfast when Connor drove up to the house.

"I went down to check on the creek and the stock in that paddock close to it. Everything looks okay." I invited him up for a coffee.

"Connor, I didn't have a chance to ask you yesterday, but what did the police ask you about when they spoke to you alone at one stage?"

"I think they were curious about why you called me when you first came across the damage to the paddock. You know the sort of questions they ask: were we close? How well did I know the deceased? Had there been any trouble here lately? That sort of stuff. They were questions they could have asked you, but chose to ask me instead."

Kate joined us while Connor was speaking, and promptly added her thoughts to the conversation. "Yeah, it's strange, but not unexpected. Lisa should expect the same questions in the near future. The questions probably are designed to establish a picture of who Tremayne was and what his life was like in the lead up to what happened. Such questions are just part of the investigation. Did the cops discover anything interesting? There were plenty of them swarming over the site. Did you pick up on anything they were thinking?"

"If they found anything, they didn't share it with me. Sorry, Lisa, I don't know how the investigation is going. I couldn't get a feel for it, but that paddock is likely to remain a crime scene for some time yet. And, Kate, because you are here, the Inspector will eventually ask you a lot of questions too."

"That will add to his frustration. I don't know any more than you do."

"Lisa, I did pick up on something the Inspector said," Connor added. "Nothing specific, but I heard him tell someone it might have been four days ago. Then, later, he suggested to me it was three days ago. You might have a better idea of the timing."

"Sorry to disappoint you, but I have no idea at all. I didn't even know if he was still here on the property. …And, it doesn't bother me how long they are poking about down there, as long as they do a good job."

"Was he about to go off again?" Connor's disgust at Tremayne's frequent absences was evident in his tone. "He'd only been home a blink. I'd pay good money to know where he went and what he got up to. I don't know how you put up with it. Not too many other women would tolerate it."

"I would be one of those 'other women'," Kate said. "Still, this is not the time for a character assassination, and it's not an appropriate time to question Lisa's sanity – or her taste in men."

Conversation reverted to topics of no consequence before Connor made noises about going home. Then he dropped his bombshell. "If you'd rather I stayed with you for a while, I'll tell Dad to call the young bloke from down the road to give him a hand. I haven't told him what happened here. I'll do that later if it's all right with you, Lisa."

"Don't hang about here, Connor. I'm fine. You have a property to look after. Go and help your father. Besides, Kate is here, so there is no need to worry about me." Although he remained reluctant, between Kate and I, we managed to convince him to go home.

"Connor seems like a top bloke," Kate commented as he drove away. "You could do a lot worse for a neighbour."

A call from the harvesting contractor halted any further discussion of Connor. I managed to put the contractor off for a week – without divulging why – and confirmed he would be harvesting a different paddock from the planned one when he came next time.

It appears Connor continued to occupy Kate's mind while I spoke to the harvesting contractor. She continued the topic as soon as I returned.

Chapter 5

"Lisa, Connor and Tremayne were such different people. How did they get on?"

"They never had much contact. Connor only came over when we needed help with mustering or the likes. Since Dad died, he's been here helping out a lot more … and keeping an eye on me. I don't think Connor had much time for Tremayne. As you said: two different people, with different sets of values and standards."

"He seems like a top bloke; a nice bloke. What's his story? I suppose he's married. All the decent ones are."

"He's not married. I don't know much of his background. He went away to boarding school. Then graduated from university with honours in whatever he studied, before working in his chosen profession. His father was getting older and hoped Connor would come home to take over the farm, but he wouldn't pressure Connor into giving up the life he made for himself. When his mother died, Bob, his father, struggled. She looked after the cattle side of the business. After her death, Bob had to pick up everything. …And he was lonely. Connor started coming home for long weekends and whenever else he could. Bob was excited when he told us Connor was coming home for a while. No one knew how long he might stay, but it seems to be working out."

"Was his homecoming a recent thing?"

"Uhmm … at least four years ago, or maybe a bit longer. Just prior to that, I heard he was getting married. I don't know what happened, but he's still single. He's a good farmer, and a whizz at the management side of things as well. I don't know how Bob would cope if Connor decided to leave again."

"By the way, what are your plans for the future? Now your father is gone, how are you going to manage this place on your own? I know I've asked the question before, but have you given it any thought?"

"…Still working on that one. There are a couple of possibilities. I'm not sure about either of them. I need time and space to think it through." The conversation was straying into territories where I didn't want to go.

A couple of exaggerated yawns and an announcement that I was 'out on my feet' did the trick. Within twenty minutes, I was in bed and asleep.

*****

"Detective Inspector Taylor seems to be haunting the place. He's just arrived again," Kate said as she came in from the deck. "I've lost count of how much time he's spent at the crime scene over the last three or four days." She stopped mid-stride when the doorbell rang. "…Seems like he wants to talk to you this morning." I grimaced. Pleasant though Inspector Taylor always was, his visits had lost their appeal. I still harboured a concern about the look I imagined he gave me at dinner that night.

"Inspector, do you have time for a coffee?" Kate asked as she showed him through to the lounge room.

"I'd love one … oh, that is if Mrs Bancroft can spare me the time of course."

My smile was more strained than sweet. "I think two coffees are in order please, Kate. …And, Inspector, I never went by the name of Bancroft. I didn't change my name. So, I am still Lisa Soldarno."

"My apologies; I wasn't sure. No offence meant. I just thought… Well, we didn't discuss precise names earlier, did we?"

"No offence taken; just clarifying the situation. What brings you here today? I'm sure it wasn't Kate's coffee lured you out here again. So, how is your investigation progressing, and how can I help you?"

As Taylor began his progress report, I thought I heard a car pull up. He tried to create the impression of good progress being made but, in effect, said nothing. After the first sentence or two, I only half listened. My interest was in footsteps coming up the stairs. They were followed by a few whispered words in the kitchen. The Inspector ended his report, and I took advantage of the situation.

"Excuse me please, Inspector. Kate, do we have a visitor?"

"Only me," Connor announced. "I came to see how you were going. I'll come back later."

"No; come through and join us please, Mr Rankin," Taylor said. Once Connor was seated, the purpose for Taylor's visit today became apparent.

"Earlier, you both mentioned a suspicious stranger in a grey SUV. Do you recall seeing him more than that one time?"

Connor shook his head. I was about to do likewise when a memory flash to the surface. "Inspector, there was one incident, but it would have been maybe seven or eight months ago. I know it was before we put Mum into care, but I can't associate it with anything else to help determine the likely timing."

"Don't worry about the exact timing for the moment. Just tell me what you remember."

"It was mid-morning on a week day. I went out onto the deck and was surprised to hear raised voices. My mother was asleep. The only other person around was my husband. Tremayne sounded … angry … no, more like upset and defensive. Then another voice predominated. He *was* angry – *really angry."*

"Is it possible it was an argument between your husband and father?"

"It wasn't Dad's voice I heard. Anyway, Dad was down south looking into suitable care facilities for my mother at the time. Later, I asked Tremayne about the argument. He claimed no knowledge of any argument or incident."

"So, between that incident and when you saw your father appear to order an unwelcome visitor off the property, were you aware of any other similar incidents?"

"Well, maybe; I'm not sure. I was working in the office and couldn't hear clearly, but I heard a conversation going on downstairs somewhere close to the house. My father was having stern words with someone. I wouldn't say he was angry, but he sounded 'stern'. It was a 'pointed' conversation."

"Do you know whom he was talking to? Could it have been your husband?"

"No, most of the time, Dad just ignored Tremayne. Anyway, Tremayne was off somewhere at the time."

"What does 'off somewhere' mean? It sounds as though you didn't know where he was. Might he have come home without your noticing he had returned?" The question wrong-footed me. What I said sounded quite clear to me. Connor jumped in to explain.

"Her husband had gone off on one of his frequent 'jaunts'. He hadn't just slipped into town. God knows where he was when this happened. It's possible he wasn't even in the country."

"Did he often go overseas?" Connor rolled his eyes. I felt obliged to rescue the situation.

"We weren't privy to where Tremayne's work took him but, yes, on occasions, he went overseas. Most times, I only worked that out from inferences in conversations after he returned."

"When did this particular incident occur?"

"Don't know exactly, but it was after the incident when I heard Tremayne arguing with somebody."

"Do you know who your father was talking to?"

"No, I didn't see who was there, and it could have been anybody; harvesting contractor, someone from the mill."

"What about later when you saw him arguing with somebody over near the shed, could you describe the man he was talking to?"

"Only sort of … I didn't get a good look at him, and only had one brief glimpse of his face in profile."

"Just describe what you can remember please."

"Here goes… He was neatly dressed in jeans, with a buttoned shirt tucked in and he wore sunglasses, which he hadn't removed while talking to my father. Olive skinned, or a reasonable tan I think. At least, he didn't seem fair … and his hair was dark, as was his beard."

"He had a beard? Can you describe it?" Inspector Taylor looked surprised by my mention of a beard.

"Maybe 'a beard' wasn't an apt description. It was more like a five o'clock shadow on steroids. The sort of facial adornment young blokes are wearing these days. Trimmed close to the skin all over, but styled to leave strategic bits of skin exposed. His hair was well trimmed too, and I think it might have had a bit of a wave to it. I don't think there's much else I can tell you about him."

"So, his hair wasn't long – over his collar for instance – or unkempt-looking?" I shook my head. "Tell me about the vehicle."

"I would if I could. I only glimpsed it part way down our drive. It was a grey 4x4, and sounded gutsy. That's all I can tell you." Connor confirmed my description of the bloke was the same man who they spoke to when they were mustering near the road. He gave Taylor more specific information about the vehicle the man was driving. Then Taylor turned his attention back to me.

"What did your father say the argument was about?"

"I let it cool down a bit before I asked him over drinks that evening. He was evasive and, when I pressed him for an answer, he concocted a story to shut me up. He said it was *one of those agricultural agency salesmen trying to unload another of their useless products on me.* I knew it was a crock, just as Tremayne's answer was, so I let it go by. It was unlike Dad to fob me off like that. Before you ask, no, I didn't pursue the matter again. It was a lost cause and, as I didn't see the bloke again, I assumed the issue was resolved." There was that look on the inspector's face again. Did he believe me? I wasn't sure, and I felt my stomach squirm.

"Inspector, perhaps I can add something to this," Connor offered. "I've been thinking about that bloke I saw. It was not close. He got out but stood beside the car. He was swarthy looking. I guess Asian – maybe Indonesian, or Filipino perhaps. His eyes were very dark and his heavy eyebrows were black. His most noticeable feature was a wicked scar running from the corner of his left eye halfway down his cheek towards his nose. Probably an old scar acquired some time ago, it had healed and lost any redness."

"Did you see him again anywhere at all after that first encounter?"

"Maybe; I can't be sure. But, I think I saw the same bloke talking to Tremayne sometime after that. I remember Lisa was away at the time; down at the care facility with her mother I think. One of her cows was due to calve and I promise to keep an eye on it while she was away. I was in the paddock with the cattle when I saw Tremayne come down to the creek on one of the quad bikes. I looked away from moment or two to do something and, when I looked back, Tremayne was standing on the track along the creek bank talking to some bloke. I can't be sure but, from that distance, it looked a lot like the man Lisa and I described to you."

"Was he driving the same vehicle as previously?"

"I don't know what he was driving, or how we happened to be on the track along the creek bank at just that precise time. I couldn't see a vehicle anywhere. It's a long hike on foot from the road and, as the creek was swollen and fast flowing at the time, I doubt he swam across. And, no, he didn't look wet, if that's what you were going to ask me."

"Is it possible to drive onto the property and down to the creek without anyone who lives here being aware of it?"

Connor pondered the question for a moment before delivering his answer. "It is possible, if you know the property well and you're prepared to drive along the headlands. I suspect only someone who lives or works on this property knows how to do that. There are a couple of ways to get to the creek, but they both go past this house. At the time this occurred, nobody was at home. Anybody aware of that fact could drive onto the property and down to the creek without any concern about being seen or stopped."

"Did you draw any conclusions about the meeting between Mr Bancroft and the other man? I mean did it look like a friendly meeting; was there an argument?"

"Hard to tell; I didn't hear any shouting or see any violence. Thinking back on it, I don't think it was a friendly meeting. It's hard to explain, but I think it had something to do with the stance of the two men as they faced each other. They both looked 'tense', but don't ask me to explain what I mean by that."

"Since then, have you seen the man anywhere around here or in town?"

"No-o, but I might have seen his vehicle on a couple of occasions. It could have been just a similar car, but I'm not familiar with one like that from around here. I saw it out on the main road, not on either of our properties, and I didn't see it go onto anyone's property either."

"Thank you both. Your information is helpful, but I should go now and let you get back to whatever it is you have to do."

"Not so fast, Inspector; perhaps you would share your investigation's progress with Connor while he's here." I saw Taylor start to shake his head. I wasn't about to give up so easily. "Can I assume you haven't found any evidence to suggest it was anything other than foul play, and that you are still treating my husband's death as a murder investigation?"

"Your assumption is correct. While it is a murder investigation, we have yet to come up with a motive. I hoped talking to you today might trigger a memory of something out of the ordinary, and not necessarily from just the last few weeks. Come to think of it, I'm still not aware of what your husband did. Why it was necessary for him to make such frequent trips away … And not tell even you, his wife, where he was going

Connor sniggered. "Join the club. You're not the only one who couldn't work out what he was up to. There are two others sitting here who were just as much in the dark as you are."

"Thank you for your insight, Mr Rankin, but it is not helpful. Miss Soldarno, can you shed any light on why your husband was away so often?"

"I'm no more help than Connor. I believed he worked as a foreign correspondent. I don't know whether he worked for a particular media firm, or if he was freelance. We did have a… We discussed his work a couple of years ago. His comments were obtuse, but there was strong inference he worked for some sort of security organisation.

He didn't mention ASIO or any of the other obvious ones, and refused to be drawn on whether it was any of those. I tried a direct question: was he employed as an intelligence officer? I didn't get a straight answer. I don't remember his exact words, but they amounted to a denial of sorts. It left me confused and a bit miffed about the whole conversation. I tried a different question. I asked if being a foreign correspondent was just a cover for the real work he was doing. I got a long, hard look in response, but no answer. I suppose I took that as confirmation, and never mentioned it again."

"Did you wonder about it? Weren't you concerned about what he might be doing or how risky it might be?"

"No. I knew I had all I was going to be told. It was pointless to pursue it further. Anyway, if I'm honest, with time, it ceased to be important. My life was hectic here at home. Between running the farm and concern for my parents, sometimes not having Tremayne around to add to it all was a blessing."

"I will make a few discreet inquiries to see what I can find out about your husband's recent past. I have a friend – who you might call a 'mattress relation' – in the Federal Police. As a starting point, I'll ask him off-the-record what he knows about Tremayne Bancroft. Of course, he might know nothing. In which case, I would need to go through official channels to establish if there were any connection." There it was again. I sensed the inspector was keeping some doubt he held under wraps.

"If you find out anything about my husband – no matter what it is – please share as much as you are able with me. It would be nice to know what I lived with for all those years."

"No promises; let's see what we uncover first. You've given me a few things to look into and, you never know, some of it might turn into actual leads for my investigation. There is something you should be aware of. In a murder investigation, the spouse always tops the list of suspects. Your claim that you didn't see or hear your husband about the place after you chucked him out, strengthens your position on the top of the list. I'm not suggesting anything; just saying that is a fairly standard situation."

The place was plunged into silence when Kate walked Taylor to his vehicle. Connor and I sat silent, each of us lost in our own thoughts. "Geez, this place is like a morgue," Kate quipped as she settled into one of the lounge chairs. "What would you like to do next? We could have a very late morning tea of coffee and cake, or we could write off the rest of the morning and have an early lunch. Which would you prefer?"

"God, where has the morning gone?" I checked the time. It wasn't much before twelve o'clock. Lunch seemed the best option. Connor also checked his watch before scrambling up out of his chair.

"I should be going. I've taken up too much of your day already." I laughed and motioned for him to sit down again.

"You haven't taken up my time. I'm pleased you are here. You told the inspector things I didn't know; things which might prove important to his case. Stay and have cold meat and salad for lunch with us. Who knows what else we might be able to remember over food and a glass of chilled white wine?" It didn't occur to me until much later that I should have asked whether Connor had something pressing to do at home rather than accommodating me by staying for lunch. But, he didn't appear in a hurry to leave, and I did enjoy the lively and insightful conversation the three of us shared over the meal.

His parting comments did give me pause for thought as I spent the afternoon in the office trying to catch up on paperwork: Stay alert, Lisa. Keep your eyes peeled for strangers, or anything unusual happening around the place. I have an uneasy feeling about all of this, and I'm not convinced Tremayne's death is an end to it.

Those comments were a distraction looping through my mind for the rest of the afternoon. It didn't matter how often I replayed them, I couldn't be sure what Connor was suggesting. I felt he knew something, but didn't want to share it with me. I found that hard to believe, as Connor and I are close. He knows how confused I am by what's happened. So, I can't believe he wouldn't share with me something he knows about what happened to Tremayne … Or why. Maybe that's the key: it's not the what but the why that's important in this case. I wonder if Taylor shares that thought. The next time I encounter him, I might float the idea past him to see how he reacts. And, damn it, I should try to find out if I'm going to have to prove my innocence in all of this.

*****

Floating anything past Taylor had to wait. It was almost a week later before I heard from him again. As luck would have it, Connor was here when the inspector arrived. We came back to the house for a mid-morning coffee break after checking on a couple of calves born during the night. Kate met the inspector and escorted him to the deck where Connor and I were.

"Inspector, you must have the nose of a bloodhound," Kate said as they made their way up the stairs. "Even from your office, you seem able to smell when coffee and cake are on the go out here. I assume you are not averse to having morning tea with us?"

"Black with one sugar please, Miss Langdon, and a wedge of that delicious looking chocolate cake would go down well."

While I wasn't feeling antisocial this morning, I didn't feel up to further interrogation by the inspector … and I remained somewhat miffed at his comments about my topping the list of suspects. Nevertheless, I tried to make him feel welcome. In spite of my best efforts, out the corner of my eye, I saw Connor trying to suppress a grin. He moved to deflect the anticipated new barrage of questions. "Inspector, I hope your visit isn't a waste of time today. We've been wracking our brain about the whole situation surrounding Tremayne's death. The only thing we are sure about is that we have nothing more to add to what we've already told you; absolutely nothing more."

"Thank you for your concern, but I haven't come today in search of further information. Today's visit is to tell Miss Soldarno her husband's body is available for release to the undertakers. I leave it to you to make those arrangements as soon as is convenient for you."

"It will be good to get the next part over and done with, much better than having it hanging around waiting to be dealt with. Maybe once the funeral is over, I'll be able to move on and focus on what I'm supposed to be doing around here … Instead of constantly wondering about how, who, and why. Argh, I know the funeral will not be an end to it. It won't be over until you bring your investigation to a successful conclusion. By the way, how is your investigation progressing?"

"There is only one word to describe it: slowly. I've no new breakthroughs to share with you. While I have a lot of feelers out for information, nothing has come in since I last spoke to you. Anyway, cases aren't solved sitting around drinking coffee and eating cake. I'll be off, but keep in touch should anything exciting develop."

Moments later, Inspector Taylor was gone, and Connor was on his feet as well "I should get going too. There are probably things I need to attend to at home… And I believe you now have a funeral to arrange. Let me know if you need a hand with anything."

While Kate cleared away the morning tea things after walking Connor out, I had a few moments of contemplation. I knew I needed to talk to the undertakers, but I still had a problem. I still didn't know how I felt about Tremayne's death. Somehow, it seemed almost hypocritical to be arranging his funeral, when I still didn't know how I felt about his being gone from my life forever.

The best part of an hour went by before Kate decided it was time to come and spur me into action.

Chapter 6

Choosing an undertaker was a no-brainer. It made sense to stick with the same one as ensured my parents' funerals went off without a hitch. I called them and they said they would collect the body from the morgue the next day. The degree of surprise my call generated intrigued me.

Tremayne's death was not common knowledge. With the recent demise of local newspapers, including this community's, now there was no way for people to find out. Still, it seemed curious the police had not released the information. I called Inspector Taylor on the pretext of advising him the undertakers would be in touch tomorrow. Then, I moved on to what I really wanted to ask him.

"Inspector, I was surprised when the undertakers claimed no knowledge of Tremayne's death. It seems information about it hasn't been released. Is this standard procedure, or should I read more into it."

"We do not issue a press release whenever we retrieve a body. When we had a local newspaper, there were local reporters. Little happened in the community that they weren't aware of – through whatever channels. If they learnt of the discovery of a body, they haunted the police station, and its senior officers, until a press release was forthcoming. So, simply put: no paper equals no reporters, equals no information released to the community. Feel free to rectify the situation if it doesn't suit you."

"It suits me fine, and I would prefer it stayed that way. I have instructed the undertakers not to release any mention of my husband's death. I intend the funeral will be a closed, private affair."

Having promised to finalise arrangements with the undertakers tomorrow, I felt compelled to devote some thought to the matter. The only definite idea I had was for the event to be closed to all but a handful of invitees. Tremayne wasn't well-known here. No one else, other than the post mistress, knew him. She only knew him because he maintained a mailbox at the Post Office and occasionally went inside to collect a parcel. No, I was determined it would be private. Outside of a handful of close friends who might be interested in attending, any others would be no more than looky-loos out for whatever gossip they might pick up.

As I sat on the deck trying to focus on Tremayne's funeral, my eyes slid along the track to the site where his body was found. Maybe staring at that place will help me get my head together, I told myself. It only took a minute or so to realise that was a load of rubbish. After all, how much was there to organise? This would not be a gathering of thousands of wailing friends and associates.

It would be a cremation, pure and simple; no frills or fuss. Just a few words from the undertaker before the casket disappeared through the curtain. Then, those attending would adjourn to the restaurant further along the street for a drink, and maybe a light lunch. That wasn't so hard. Why was I concerned about it?

Kate came out wearing a concerned look. "I don't want to begrudge you precious time alone, but is everything all right? If something is troubling you, maybe I can help sort it out. Is there anything you want to discuss with me?"

"I was trying to sort out Tremayne's funeral. Then, I realised I had nothing to do. It was all straightforward."

"What have you decided?" I shared my mentally outlined plan, and how I only had to call the undertakers to arrange the cremation.

"Have you decided on a date?"

"It will be a soon as the undertakers have a spare booking for their chapel.

"Did Tremayne make a Will?"

"A Will…? How should I know? Anyway, they're supposed to be confidential until a reading after the funeral. Does it matter if he had a Will at this point in time?"

"Sometimes they contain the deceased's instructions for what happens after their death. It might stipulate whether to be buried or cremated, where to be buried or their ashes scattered, and whether they wanted a full church funeral or a graveside service. The other reason to check on the Will, if there is one, is to find out about beneficiaries. It would contain the names of those who were to benefit from his estate. They should be advised of Tremayne's death and given information about his funeral."

"Wouldn't the executor or the solicitor who drew up the Will be responsible for that?"

"Yes, but we don't know who the executor is, or even if there is a Will."

"We could go through his papers for a copy. First, I'll check if he left any papers here in the house, before going through his belongings in the cottage. He did take a box of personal papers and other stuff to the cottage. There might be a copy in that box."

"Okay, but it might be worthwhile calling Justin Farley too. He might have acted for Tremayne, as well as being your family's solicitor. Even if he didn't, he still could organise a search on your behalf. I know you think it unnecessary, but I urge you to talk to Justin before doing much more."

"I just want this thing over and done with. I could just go ahead with the cremation and plead ignorance afterwards. After all, we don't know what's in his Will, because we don't know if there is one."

As I finished speaking, Kate reached over and grabbed my phone from where I left it on the end of the table. She hit the call button before handing it to me. "Stop mucking about and make the call."

She made sense. I should make the call. I also wanted to avoid complications. Simple was good but, somehow I knew, once I called Justin, my plans would be scrapped and the funeral would develop into something different. Nevertheless, in the interests of harmony and common sense, I keyed Justin's number.

His ever-efficient receptionist, Amy, told me Justin was seeing a client out and would be with me in a minute. While I held the line, Kate produced a notebook and pen from a pocket of her shorts, and scribbled something. As I heard Justin's footsteps coming to the phone, Kate shoved her note in front of me. "What's this about?" I asked as I skimmed the note.

"They're questions you need to ask Justin. Don't skip any. Ask him to find answers to all of them, and impress on him how some information might be urgent."

Justin's phone rattled in my ear, refocusing my attention on my quest. "Lisa, Amy said your call was urgent." In compliance with Kate's instructions, I asked all the questions on her list. He didn't groan in despair, but said, "I've noted all of that and I'll get onto it straightaway. You're right to be querying some of those details in view of your complicated situation. I'll get back to you as soon as I locate any information."

Updating Kate on what eventuated with Justin, I told her, "He didn't give me any indication of how long it might take to round up any of the information, but I'm going to proceed as though there will be no surprises forthcoming. I'm convinced I should go ahead with the simple event I planned, and worry about anything from Justin when and if it arrives before the service. Do you have any other obstacles to throw in front of me?"

"Right… Then get on with it, but there are a couple of things you haven't addressed yet." My frustration was approaching a dangerous level. I snapped at her to tell me whatever these new complications might be. She shot me a savage look and was silent for a couple of heartbeats – probably attempting to control her temper before answering.

"What if the undertakers say they can hold a service tomorrow? Have you let his family know what happened? Can they arrive in time?"

"Notifying family isn't a problem. There isn't any. Maybe I should qualify that: he has no family as far as I am aware. God knows, I asked him about family on many occasions. The most I got out of him was that he was the only one left. I suspected something sinister or embarrassing in his background made him so reluctant to talk about his family, and which prevented him sharing anything about them with me. The only thing I'm sure about … Damn! And now I'm not sure about it at all. I was about to say I was unaware of any contact between Tremayne and possible family members during the whole time I knew him. What I can say with certainty is that I will not make life difficult for myself by trying to find relatives."

"Fair enough; if you don't know about them you can't round them up in the next few days. That eliminates the need for delay to accommodate the arrival of people. Now, have you thought about the casket, and when are you going to do something about it?"

"Argh… I'd forgotten about that. Would it hurt if I put it off until tomorrow?"

"I don't know if it makes much difference to the undertakers, but I thought you might like to tie up all the loose ends. A quick trip to town this afternoon could have everything in place by tonight. I'm not trying to rush you, but you seem to want this over as soon as possible. You have little to do: choose a date and time, choose a casket, organise flowers and music if you want them, and run through with the undertakers how you want things to happen at the service. That's it; nothing much to do. So, why are you still here? Get yourself into gear. Go into town and take care of those things. Then, all you have to do is sit back and wait for the appointed time to arrive."

"Yeah, I know you're right. Can I just…"

"No you can't. Whatever you are going to say would only amount to procrastination."

"It must seem that way I suppose. The realisation that Tremayne is dead hasn't sunk in yet. It just feels like another one of those times when he's away."

"Is that the truth? I suspect it's deeper than that."

"The truth…? I still don't know what I feel; how I should feel. I don't feel anything – not sadness or grief, not relief, not disbelief. I should feel something. But I don't, and that seems wrong. It feels wrong to be arranging his cremation without appropriate feelings to support and guide the decision-making. I've felt more grief burying a favourite farm dog."

"This is getting maudlin, and that might not be a good thing. I'm taking you into town to finalise those arrangements. Then, you can come home and get drunk, or fall into a black hole of guilt or whatever, but the arrangements will be in place."

Kate was right. I followed her down to the car and we drove in silence to the undertakers. After shooing me into the office, she made herself comfortable in the reception area with a pile of ancient magazines. About an hour later, I went to find her. "Are you right to go?" I asked as she looked up at me.

"I don't know if I can tear myself away. While sitting here, I've learned so much about the love life of everybody who is anybody, and I haven't finished this last magazine yet. There's bound to be more gossip I need to know about, in the bit I haven't read."

"How inconsiderate of me; I could leave you to finish reading it while I check the mail and buy some bread."

"Remove your tongue from your cheek now, Lisa, and prepare to be raced to the car. I'll drive. Where do you need to go, and what is this business about checking for mail? Your mail is delivered to the farm."

"Yes, farm mail and my personal mail go in the mailbox at the farm gate. I found a spare key to Tremayne's post office mailbox. I need to check if there is anything in it. There's no point in maintaining the box now he's gone. I'll close it down and have anything that turns up in the next little while redirected to the farm. I should close down his bank account too in case there are any automatic periodic payments set up on it."

"As only a few people know Tremayne is dead, you might encounter a few problems trying to do that. The way things stand at the moment, only Tremayne can issue instructions about his mailbox, and only he can operate on his personal account. Once he is 'officially dead' – that might mean once there is a death certificate – the executor of Tremayne's estate will be able to do those things."

"I suppose I'll have to wait to see what Justin Farley finds out. If there is no Will, he might have to take care of such matters. If there is a Will, I'm probably the executor anyway. But, I'll leave it until after the funeral and, if there is one, until after the Will is read, before I talk to the postmistress and the bank … unless someone else is appointed executor. In the meantime, I'll continue checking his mailbox whenever I'm in town for as long as it takes to sort out his estate."

The afternoon was gone by the time we arrived home. "I think the sun is over the yardarm, or whatever the saying is. Should we adjourn to the deck for a drink before dinner?" Kate asked. We took a bottle of red wine with us and Kate poured the wine before collapsing onto a chair opposite me and opening the conversation. "So, did you manage to sort out everything for the cremation?"

"Hang on a minute. It looks like I missed a call this afternoon – from Inspector Taylor no less". He left a voice message, and I listened to it twice before sharing its details with Kate. "The inspector will call in this evening on his way home from 'a job'. I suppose that's what it is to them: a job. While we tend to think of it as a crime scene, a murderer, or whatever, to a copper, it probably is just another job. Anyway, he said he'd be here around six o'clock and asked to let him know if it didn't suit."

"…Might be a bit late to call him back now if it doesn't suit. Did he say what it was about?"

"No, but if he doesn't take too long about it, I don't suppose the timing is a problem. If it looks like he's settling in for a long session, please go into the kitchen and start banging pots and pans about. Maybe he'll get the message to leave. ...That sounds like a car now."

Kate showed a somewhat more dishevelled Inspector Taylor onto the deck. "This is just a quick update visit," he announced. "Your husband's body has been released. Your quad bike remains impounded and might be held for a while yet, as the tests they need to carry out on that take a while. The coroner's and the forensic reports are in. Both of those confirm your husband's death was murder. I know there's no surprise in that statement, but it's now an official murder investigation."

"I assume you are simply following procedures, and I shouldn't read any more into your visit than that?"

"Yes. Have you arranged a funeral yet?"

"This afternoon; I arranged the cremation service for the day after tomorrow. It will be a private affair and should be over in about twenty minutes. God, when I say it like that, it sounds so heartless. Maybe three family funerals in less than six months have numbed my emotions. What I meant to say was, only about five people will attend the simple, no-frills affair."

"Are no family members coming?"

'Not that I'm aware of. Tremayne always claimed he had no family; no living relatives. Justin Farley is searching for any people who should be advised of Tremayne's death. So far, he hasn't found anything to contradict Tremayne's claims. As the lead investigating officer do you need to attend?"

It's not a requirement, but I usually do. If I'm free and you have no objections, I will attend."

"If the reports confirm it was murder, do they say how he was killed? I still don't know the nature of his injuries. While I accept it had something to do with the bike, I have no clues beyond that."

"This is only a preliminary assessment, and it could change if further evidence is uncovered. It appears the quad bike your husband rode was shunted from behind, pushed off the track and driven into the middle of a cane paddock at high speed.

Your husband was thrown from the bike and landed a couple of metres away from the damaged machine. The other vehicle involved continued into the paddock, passed the capsized bike, and ran over your husband while he was lying on the ground. It's possible he was unconscious – or dazed – from landing heavily, and perhaps was incapable of taking evasive action."

"The flattened cane should have cushioned his landing, and offered some protection when he was run over. The effect shouldn't have been as harsh as being run over on a hard road surface, should it?"

"That's a reasonable assumption … if he were run over only once. Our investigation of the site leaves no doubt the vehicle ran over him several times before reversing out of the paddock and exiting the property."

I sat too stunned to say or do anything. Kate rushed over and threw her arm around my shoulders. While I could accept the vehicle accidentally running over him, I struggled with the image of Tremayne being run over intentionally and repeatedly. Why? Why would someone find it necessary to do that to my husband? Whom had he upset so badly? Although Tremayne was supposed to be a journo, a foreign correspondent, I had never seen or read anything he wrote. Maybe it had something to do with his other 'occupation'; the intelligence work he inferred he was involved in. I shared my thoughts with the inspector.

"Perhaps it's worth thinking about, but it's getting late and I should be going."

Kate showed him out and then ran back upstairs. "Interesting how he had to hurry home after you mentioned Tremayne's intelligence gathering activities, don't you think?"

I did notice a raised eyebrow as she asked the question, but I was too busy dealing with my own thoughts to answer. Those thoughts would keep me awake most of the night.

*****

This morning had me at a bit of a loose end. I felt I should be doing something, but had no idea why I should, or what it might be. Everything was organised for Tremayne's cremation tomorrow. The only thing on today's agenda was having Connor and his father over for morning coffee. Their invitation was so I could invite them to tomorrow's service and explain how things would be. So, with nothing to do until they arrived around 10:30, I took myself to the office to deal with things neglected over the last few days.

Kate was turning this morning's coffee with the Rankins into something more than I envisioned. I heard a cake being mixed, and then smelled its aroma filling the house as it baked. A while later, I smelled something savoury wafting out of the kitchen. Something with tomatoes; yes, she was baking a batch of her favourite tomato tartlets. Guilt enveloped me for a brief moment. I remembered that, as the hostess, it should be me out there slaving in the kitchen. I reassured myself with the thought that, if Kate were not busy in the kitchen, she would have nothing else to do this morning, whereas I had plenty to keep me occupied in the office.

Bob Rankin, always a stickler for punctuality, pulled up outside my front door at exactly 10:30. Connor inherited his father's trait. He's another one who always turns up on time for everything.

Chapter 7

It was pleasant out on the deck. The smell of freshly burnt cane and the sound of harvesting operations in full swing drifted across on the light breeze from the Rankins' farm. While the rest of us were relaxed about life in general, including the reason for the morning tea, Bob had resurrected his most solemn personality for the occasion. It began to rankle and was putting a dampener on the gathering.

"Bob, thanks for your concern, but I am okay. Tomorrow is no more than a formality to bring closure to an unfortunate situation. I didn't intend you should suffer a morbid interlude. If it helps, maybe you should adopt the modern way of looking at such occasions: a celebration of his life, of who Tremayne was and what he achieved."

"I suppose I'm old school, and was brought up to believe such times were solemn occasions. In Tremayne's case, I can't be positive about his life, or admire what he achieved. I never got to know him well enough to have a wealth of happy memories of shared times together, or have any knowledge of his lifetime achievements. If I am honest, my feelings are for you, and how I might help you through this time."

After his father finished speaking, Connor added his honest and heartfelt comments. "You didn't get to know him because you didn't like him; couldn't stand the man any more than I could. Not that it concerned Tremayne how we – or anyone else – felt about him. He never had time for any of the locals, including us. I consider Lisa's reaction is honest, and appropriate for the life she had with him. Yes, he was her husband. But, she is not going to miss him for long, if at all. He was never here; was never a part of her life, and never showed any interest in being a part of it."

"Son, regardless of all that, it is not good form, or good manners' to speak ill of the dead. We brought you up to behave better than that."

"The most important rule in my upbringing was: always tell the truth, always be honest. Lisa is sharing her honest feelings, and I am being honest about Tremayne's death as well. Lisa is better off without him. He was a millstone around her neck; never helped her and never showed any interest in this place or her life. In some ways, I suppose it might have been just as well. That way, it was easier when he spent so much time away from here."

"Apologise at once, Son. That is no way to speak about the man in front of his grieving widow."

"No, Bob, there is no need for an apology. Everything Connor said is true. I have spent the last few days trying to conjure up 'appropriate' feelings for what happened… without success. Maybe it just hasn't sunk in yet, but I'm more inclined to believe it is because what happened broke no strong ties between us. There might have been a time in the early days when things were better, but we were never really close. I have no significant or emotional shared moments to reflect on."

Kate slapped her hand hard on the table. "That's enough of this. Okay, I never liked Tremayne either; could never understand why Lisa married him. Nevertheless, this conversation is inappropriate at this time. How about we all shelve our 'honesty' for a while and talk about other things?"

"Thanks, Kate," Connor said. "We were out of line. Now, changing the subject for a few moments, Lisa, the harvester is due to cut here tomorrow. I can take care of that for you or, if you would prefer they didn't come here tomorrow, I could organise that too."

"Thanks, Connor. I would appreciate that. I would prefer they didn't harvest tomorrow. But, I still don't want people knowing about Tremayne. So, everything should proceed as normal, with one exception. The paddock they were to harvest this time is the crime scene. I think it best if we leave that one for a while, and harvest the paddock opposite the intended one." Connor promised, as soon as he went home, he would call the contractor, and would come over tonight to make sure they burnt the correct paddock for tomorrow's harvest.

Bob leaned forward on the table. "At the risk of incurring Kate's wrath again by mentioning the cremation service, what is the running order for tomorrow?"

"Oh yes, we haven't discussed it yet. The service is scheduled for eleven o'clock, and shouldn't take more than about twenty minutes. Only the four of us, the undertaker, and maybe Inspector Taylor, will be there. Once it's over, I hoped we might all go for lunch together. I booked the small alcove at the restaurant further along the street from the chapel. While it won't be a wake as such, I thought we should do something. Lunch might be a nice way to send him off. If the pair of you can spare the time, please come to lunch with us." Both Connor and Bob confirmed they would join us.

"Great; I think lunch might be the highlight of the day. Geez, I just noticed the time. It's almost today's lunchtime. Will you both stay and have lunch with us?" After putting on great show of reluctance to put me to any trouble, they both accepted the invitation.

While Connor went off to call the harvesting contractor on my behalf, and Kate retreated to the kitchen to make lunch, Bob began a conversation about how I thought I could manage to run the place on my own. It was obvious he subscribed to the notion that such an undertaking was impossible for the 'little woman'. I tried re-educating him gently – really I did. But there came a time when it was clear that approach was not working. I became fed up with his nonsense. The clincher was his statement: *Now both your father and your husband are gone, there is no one to help you here. You will have to sell up, or watch the place being run into the ground.*

"Your concern is touching, Bob, but based on a false assumption. Let me correct you on a couple of the points you raised. Your first erroneous idea if that, now Tremayne is dead,

I won't be able to manage without his help. My husband didn't know the first thing about the farm; never helped with running it in any way, and had absolutely no interest in the place. So, simply put, his passing makes no difference to me when it comes to running this place." Bob went to interject, but I cut him off. I was a long way from finished yet.

"Furthermore, I ran this place single-handedly before my father died. After my mother had to go into care, my father wasn't around much. Then he became ill and couldn't work. For more than six months now, I have run this place on my own … and that's how it will continue. My role was never just to take care of the housework and the office. I have been out in the paddocks being a farmer. I do not share your concerns for the future of this property, and I will not be selling out any time soon."

"I didn't mean to upset you, or criticise your ability. You are quite capable, but running a place like this is a big job, with no chance of taking time off. I know from my own experience. Granted, my place is larger than yours, but I was finding it hard going until Connor came home. Now, it's a doddle for the two of us to manage. Perhaps, your next husband should have at least a bit of farming experience."

It was a struggle not to point out that, with my late husband's official farewell not until tomorrow, I was not looking for a replacement yet. Nor will I be for some time, I don't think. Bob is a top bloke and the best neighbour anyone could hope for. But, his 'fatherly' chat with me was both out of keeping with what I knew of the man … and not appreciated. I suppose I should be grateful for his concern, so I bit my tongue and a truce was established – or perhaps it was a détente.

After an enjoyable long lunch, the Rankins went home a little after two o'clock. As we waved them off, I let an unintentional sigh escape. Kate heard it and giggled. "I bet you are relieved. From the kitchen, while I prepared lunch, I watched the red mist coming down as the local sage doled out much sound advice. I'm impressed. Apart from one bit of an outburst, you behaved well."

"Bob isn't usually like that – such a misogynist, I mean. He would be the last bloke I expected to tell me I couldn't run the place."

"Well, he did suggest you should consider selling up. Do you think he was laying the groundwork for buying the place himself if you did sell?"

"If I did sell, I'm sure he would be interested, but I don't think his comments were designed to nudge me in that direction. Bob is all right. Like Connor, he is one of the good guys."

The rest of the day was spent playing the waiting game. For some inexplicable reason, I seemed unable to focus on anything until the funeral was over. It was ridiculous. Up until about an hour or so before the service, life could be going on as usual. I was still pondering the situation when the harvesting contractor's men arrived to burn the cane in readiness for tomorrow's harvest. I decided to join them. On my way to the shed for the quad bike, Connor intercepted me.

"Where do you think you're going," he demanded. "I told you I would look after tonight's burn. Go back upstairs and behave like a wife in mourning. At least try to create an illusion for those who don't know how you really feel."

"What do you mean by *how I really feel?* Would it be a more credible performance for the contractor's blokes if I stood on the deck weeping and wailing? I'm not without grief ... just not overcome by it."

"Of course you're not – overcome by it, I mean. Now, go back upstairs and have dinner or whatever, while I go and organise that mob of blokes. You are welcome to watch the fire from the deck, if you must, and if you have nothing better to do."

Although still prickly from my encounter with Connor, I stomped back upstairs, only to find a smirking Kate at the top of them. "Those Rankin men appear to have your measure at the moment. No; there's no need for a tantrum. Connor was right. At this time, it would be inappropriate for you to be down there organising the men. You should focus on behaviour more suited to the occasion. Stay up here and keep out of the way. Let Connor take charge down there … unless you think he is not capable."

"Of course he is capable, more than…"

"Good to hear. Now shut up and come and give me a hand to prepare dinner. You've seen cane fires before. You don't need to watch this one … and someone has to peel the potatoes and finish shelling the peas."

Earlier, I wasn't interested in food, and questioned Kate's choice of a baked dinner tonight. Now, sitting out on the deck with a glass of wine as I watched the men extinguish the few remaining embers from the fire, the aroma wafting out of the kitchen had my stomach rumbling. Like cows plodding their way to the milking shed, the men made their way to where they left their vehicles. One by one the vehicles departed, until only Connor's remained ... and he was making his way up the stairs.

When reached the top, he spoke to Kate in the kitchen. "My boots are dirty, so I won't come any further. I just wanted to let Lisa know how the burn went."

"Well, take your boots off, and go through to the deck to tell her. Here; take a glass of wine with you. Is Bob expecting you home for dinner?"

"No, Bob's not home. Some committee or other he belongs to has a meeting in town tonight."

"So, why not stay for dinner? The roast I cooked is big enough to feed an army. We could do with some help to dispatch it."

"Thanks, but Lisa might prefer to be alone tonight."

"You know her better than that. We both would welcome the company. Now, get out of my kitchen, get your boots off, and go tell her about the fire."

The exchange between my most favourite people in the world still had me smiling when Connor stepped out onto the deck. He was chuckling to himself. "What's tickled your sense of humour?" I asked, perhaps with a bit more tartness than intended.

"Oh, apologies, I was being disrespectful. This is not a time for such levity."

I couldn't work out whether he was serious, or just being sarcastic. "Rubbish… for those of us still around, life goes on as normal. The sun will come up in the morning, men will work in the paddocks, and we will be dealing with whatever life chooses to throw at us on the day. So, what were you chuckling about?"

"…The guard dog slaving away in your kitchen this evening. I suspect she could run an army single-handedly. It's good she was here at this time. She is so protective and supportive of you. Those of us who care about how you're coping can breathe a little easier knowing Kate is keeping a close eye on proceedings."

"I'm sure she sees it as repaying something that happened a long time ago, and when my parents and I were there for her."

"You have been close friends for a long time. Although you both went your own ways after university, it didn't diminish the friendship. I do have a vague recollection of some major event in Kate's life."

"Her parents were killed on their way to our graduation. Their light plane went down when a sudden storm blew up just this side of the range. Kate was disappointed when they didn't make the ceremony, but assumed something had happened on their property to prevent them attending. We didn't have mobile phones in those days. It was later that night, when we were all out to dinner together, that the police found her and broke the news. Apart from being my best friend, my parents thought of her as a second daughter. The news was devastating for all of us. We stuck to our original plan; took the next year off to travel and generally bum around. Although she hasn't said anything, I know she has been upset since she arrived this time to discover she wasn't here when I lost both of my parents."

Our depressing conversation ended abruptly when Kate marched out onto the deck and announced, "Dinner is served – in the dining room tonight. I decided it was time to reintroduce a little refinement into our lives. Quick and easy on the deck is okay most of the time, but not tonight. Besides, we have a guest.

We should honour him with a beautifully laid table and fine wine in crystal glasses."

On our way into the dining room, Connor nudged me in the ribs and murmured, "At least someone thinks I'm worth the effort…" I shot him an 'oh-really' look. We both dissolved into giggles before pulling up short at the sight of the table.

Kate had excelled herself. Mum's best stiffly starched damask table cloth and napkins were on the table. The best crockery, cutlery and glassware were set. Lit candles along the middle of the table cast a soft glow over the setting … and, where did that small posy of flowers come from? In hindsight, such fuss and bother seemed a little ridiculous but, at the time, it was wonderful, and made a threesome dinner party feel quite grand.

As the adage says, all good things must come to an end. That included our intimate little dinner party. Conversation was light and lively. While the setting tended to encourage hushed tones, nothing maudlin ruined the ambience. We remained at the table until well after ten o'clock, and the night only broke up then because Connor mentioned wanting to check his pumps before turning in for the night. He assured me he would be over at four o'clock the next morning to ensure everything was okay when the harvesting contractor started work. Then, Kate and I walked out into the crisp moonlit with Connor to see him off.

By the time the dishwasher was loaded, it was well gone eleven o'clock. Kate and I took our nightcaps out onto the deck. The night had an incredible stillness; a peacefulness about it. Our only light was from the big moon in the clear sky. An almost imperceptible night breeze drifted the sweet-smoky smell of freshly burnt cane in our direction. Kate sighed wistfully. "What a glorious night; I had almost forgotten how magical nights like this could be. My six months away were in overcrowded cities, or poverty-stricken villages in the jungle. It is so good to be home."

"Yeah, it's good to be able to remember nights like this when you are in the middle of the monsoon season and have a cyclone breathing down your neck. Kate, this is your home … or, it can be if you want it to be. But, there is no pressure on you to stay here. Regardless of where you travel to, or choose to work, you will always have a home here. Nothing has changed."

"The Soldarno family has always been so kind to me, even before my parents died. And, since that tragic plane crash, this has been my home. Your parents made that quite clear to me at the time. I've always felt free to return whenever I felt inclined. In many ways, it has been a healing sort of place, and it remains so, in spite of what has happened this time. Have you given the future – your future – any thought yet, Lisa?"

"There isn't anything to think about. My future is here. As it has been for the last few years, it will continue to be henceforth. I love this place and I'm not going anywhere else. And, no, I haven't thought about marrying again. I'm not sure I was cut out for it in the first place, and I'm a long way from being prepared to consider giving it another go. What about you? Aren't you expected back at work soon?"

"My original plan was to return to work in about a fortnight's time. There has been a slight change to those arrangements."

"Don't put your job – your career – in jeopardy because you feel you need to stick around to keep an eye on me. I'll be fine. Life will continue as normal, and the Rankins will make sure I don't get into too much trouble while I'm about it. You are a journalist … an amazing writer. You need to write; must write."

"Oh, I will. I just won't be going somewhere else to do it. I'll be staying right here, at least for the immediate future anyway."

"Please explain. There is not much happens around here to keep a journo occupied or interested."

"There are a couple of major international conferences in Cairns during the next few months. I'm to cover them. The job also involves a lot of pre-conference interviews with organisers, visiting speakers, and the community, to gauge their views on the issues being discussed at the conferences. From that, I am to produce quite a number of long articles and opinion pieces. In addition, in my spare time, I am to work on tourism material for the region. My company was engaged to produce a range of material, and can't believe their luck to have someone already on the ground to do it."

"Are you saying you will be able to continue working from here?"

"That's correct. It will mean spending the odd day or so away from the farm from time to time, but I will be based here. I haven't got my head around everything yet, so I can't give you more details. We both need to settle a bit after all that's happened before we discuss it further. In the meantime, it is getting late, and we need to be functioning well tomorrow – which isn't too far away now. I suggest we call it a night."

I had no argument with Kate's suggestion. Earlier in the night I thought I might have trouble sleeping. By the time I fell into bed, I knew I would be asleep within minutes.

Chapter 8

Dark clouds threatened an unpleasant day. Kate voiced her concern when she brought her breakfast out onto the deck. "Argh, no... We don't need rain; not today. Do you think it will hold off until after the service?"

"What impact can it have on the service?"

"I don't suppose it matters if it's not a nice day, as long as it is dry. We don't want a wet day for Tremayne's send off."

"Whether it rains or not won't make any difference to the service. The whole event happens inside the chapel. Nobody is going to get wet … except perhaps on the way to the restaurant afterwards."

"So, you don't care if it rains today?"

"Ye-es, I do care whether it rains or not. I have half a paddock of burnt cane waiting to be harvested. Left standing for too long because it is too wet to harvest is not a good thing. So, no, I don't want it to rain today."

Kate's interest in the weather intrigued me. A graveside service in the rain is not something anyone would want, but a service and cremation under cover in the funeral chapel makes rain irrelevant. Although neither of us made further comment on the subject, I continued to mull it over as I munched my way through breakfast. It wasn't until I was halfway through my coffee that a glimmer of understanding crept in.

"Kate, is there some superstition associated with rain during a funeral? Whatever it is, it won't hold true today. Rain will not make one bit of difference to the day ahead."

"Well, I don't think it is superstition. These days, funerals are supposed to be about celebrating the deceased's life; celebrating the wonderful life they led and how it enriched the lives of those around them. The sun shining down on the day sort of signifies God's approval and support for that assessment."

"In that case, it's likely to start bucketing down at any minute. What was there to celebrate about Tremayne's life? Don't get me wrong. There might have been something worthwhile in there somewhere. I just don't happen to know about it. He worked so hard at keeping his life hidden. I feel I don't know anything about my husband of twelve years."

"There's something else. Funerals often attract hitherto unknown family members or relatives. It can't happen in Tremayne's case, as so few know about his death. Word won't have spread to any such hidden connections."

"Is that a reprimand? Are you criticising me for not announcing his death and preventing people from emerging from the woodwork to attend his funeral? How was I supposed to do that when there isn't a local newspaper?"

"What about the major tabloids? Perhaps an announcement might have been placed in the Cairns, Townsville or Brisbane newspapers."

"That's a tad presumptuous. For someone significant or well-known, placing ads in those papers might be okay. Nobody knew Tremayne in any of those places, so why would I bother? Let me correct that. I'm not aware, he was known in any of those places. If he were, I didn't know. Anyway, it is too late to fret about it now."

"Lisa, it's none of my business, but I can't help wondering if we will ever know about Tremayne's life; what he did or where he went. It's hard to believe, someone's life can be such a closed book in this day and age."

I saw little point in sitting around discussing the unknown, and I had finished my coffee. Heaving myself out of my chair, I gathered up my breakfast things and left them in the kitchen on my way to hide in my office until time to get ready to go to town. Nevertheless, Kate's comments haunted me. Had I done the wrong thing; deliberately acted in a way that prevented possible family, friends and associates, from fronting up at the service today? I don't believe I did, but doubts nagged me. While I told myself 'what's done is done', I remained uneasy and couldn't quite manage to erase the doubts. It had me on edge, and decidedly prickly by the time we left for the service.

Nothing untoward happened at the funeral chapel. Only those invited were in attendance. Detective Inspector Dan Taylor arrived and took a seat at the back. The brief service went as planned, and the casket slid silently through the curtain on cue and as expected. Part way through the service, Kate leant over and whispered to me, "Are you all right? Do you need a glass of water or something?"

"No, I'm fine, and I don't know what you're on about. Shhh … Whatever it is, leave it until after to ask me about it." Good old Kate; she can read me so well after all the years we've been friends. All through the service, I sat rigid and focused.

The service was brief, lovely, and probably quite moving, but I still couldn't feel the grief I believed I should. There were funerals in the past at which my family wanted to be represented. I did that on their behalf, without even knowing the deceased at all. Although sombre occasions, I didn't share the grief of the family and friends. I was there simply out of respect. The fact I felt pretty much the same way today bothered me. After being married to the man for more than twelve years, shouldn't I feel something more?

No matter how hard I tried, I couldn't conjure up the feelings. It was when the casket started its slow, soundless slide towards the curtain that I felt anything. Whatever that feeling, it was tinged with relief. Perhaps I did feel something for the man after all. Then, it was over. The undertaker was wrapping up the service.

With his assistant trailing along behind him, the undertaker came to stand in front of me. With heavy solemnity, he clasped my hands in his, and again expressed his condolences and best wishes for the future. Then he stepped back to allow his assistant to come forward to present me with the floral arrangement previously adorning the casket. I did my best to appear grateful, in spite of feeling slightly revolted. *I did not want those flowers.* Again, Kate understood. She reached over and took the flowers from my hands. "Let me carry those. I'll slip out and put them in the car."

Then, I was shaking hands and thanking people as they made their way to the door and out onto the steps. I hung back a little as the others moved outside. Whether out of deference, or because he wanted to speak to me, Inspector Taylor remained near his seat until the others left. When I was alone, he came up to me, shook my hand, and said quietly, "I would like to come and talk to you – soon. This isn't the right time to ask you, but please give me a call when you feel up to discussing a few things."

"Come out to the farm tomorrow. I have nothing scheduled, so whatever time suits you will be okay." Then he was on his way to his car.

As the undertaker closed the chapel's doors, I heaved a sigh relief. It was over. I felt as though a weight was lifted off me. I was finished beating myself up about lacking the appropriate feelings for the occasion. A couple of niggling thoughts still lingered in the back of my mind: Did Tremayne mean so little to me, his loss caused no grief? In the future, would the realisation he was gone hit me hard? No answers required today, I told myself.

An ice bucket containing a bottle of French champagne awaited us in our restaurant alcove. We were the only diners at that time, so staff was attentive – perhaps a little too attentive. I caught the Maître D's eye and hoped he understood my signal to 'back off a bit'. The champagne was opened and glasses filled the moment we were seated. Just about every one of us proposed a toast of some sort: to Tremayne, to my health, to all our futures, and to every other possible inconsequential thing.

That interlude over, lunch was served. I had ordered an uncomplicated menu …and then began worrying it might be too light and simple, and would look mean. That wasn't the case. The dishes were simple, but the restaurant did them proud. Lunch lingered on until a bit after two o'clock when Bob and Connor needed to check on their farm.

On arriving home, coffee was our first priority. While I faffed about making it, Kate went to the car. She returned as I was about to take the coffees out onto the deck. "What should I do with this?" she asked. She was holding the floral arrangement from Tremayne's coffin.

"Whatever you like; I don't want it."

"Okay, I have an idea." She pulled the arrangement apart and dumped the flowers with long enough stems into a vase. I could live with that.

After a few sips of our coffee, Kate dealt with what had nagged her since the funeral. "It was decent of Inspector Taylor to attend. I sensed he was doing more than expressing his condolences on his way out. Has there been a development in his investigation?"

"Not that I am aware of, but he did ask to come and talk to me. I told him I was free tomorrow. He didn't seem particularly excited, so perhaps there hasn't been anything new. Nevertheless, he did appear anxious to talk as soon as possible."

"…And, he didn't think it inappropriate to mention it at that point in time? No doubt, he will turn up in time for coffee – or lunch – tomorrow."

"Whatever time he arrives will be fine. Relax, Kate. My sensibilities have not been offended by his talking to me about it at the funeral. If tomorrow's visit helps discover what happened here, then bring it on. I'd be happy to talk to him right now … except you wouldn't allow it; not today." She responded with a disgusted sniff.

Around six o'clock, while on his way home from my paddock, Connor called at the house to report on today's harvesting operations. Now my day of 'mourning' had ended, I insisted there was no need for him to look after things for me. Everything would return to normal tomorrow. He was equally adamant he would continue to keep an eye on things for a bit longer. His visit ended on that note.

After watching an ancient movie with a weak plot line, Kate and I turned in for an early night. Having done nothing all day, I wasn't ready for sleep, so I finished a book I had been trying to read for weeks. It was two o'clock when I turned off my light.

*****

"I wish I knew when to expect Inspector Taylor today," I told Kate over breakfast. Today already was looking like more time spent just hanging around waiting.

"Make a start on something. Five minutes later, he is bound to arrive. Was there anything pressing to do today?"

"Nothing urgent … I hoped to sort out a few things with Justin Farley. I don't know whether he has found a Will by Tremayne. Submitting an application for probate, and generally tidying up Tremayne's estate, are high on my list of priorities. I would like them to be high on my solicitor's list of things-to-do as well."

"So, there's nothing there for me to help with."

Until Taylor arrives, I'll fill in time in my office. You might consider baking a cake or something. His bloodhound nose seems to know when coffee or food is happening here, and it brings him running."

"You seem a bit uptight about his visit. It might be nothing more than a routine meeting or follow-up. As I have nothing better to do, I'll follow your suggestion and bake a cake." My denial about being uptight fell on deaf ears.

Not long after going to my office, I heard a car pull up. "Please let it be Inspector Taylor," I murmured to my empty office. It appears someone was listening.

Kate raced down to let him in while I nudged the coffee machine into life. I was taken aback by Taylor's demeanour when I went to meet him. I shot Kate a questioning look. She responded with a shrug, but the look on her face was a giveaway. She was tense – or upset – about something. I felt my innards start to squirm, but hoped it didn't show. "Inspector, thanks for coming. Is coffee on the deck okay?" He gave a curt nod. "Should Kate be part of whatever you've come to talk about?"

"Maybe it wouldn't hurt for Miss Langdon to sit with us. No doubt, you will want to discuss matters with her later, so it probably is as well she hears what I have to say."

My innards regrouped and set about developing into a lead ball in the pit of my stomach. So far, there was nothing to suggest his visit was for a friendly update on his investigation. There followed the usual brief period of faffing about as everyone loaded their plate with cake and stirred their coffee. Taylor seemed impatient to begin. I gave him his cue. "So, Inspector, what news do you have? If it is about progress with your investigation, I hope it is good news."

"I don't know that I would describe it as 'good'. Earlier, you mentioned your husband intimated some of his work was intelligence related, but didn't indicate which agency he worked for. Australia doesn't have many to choose from. Since then, I've had a suspicion what happened here might be connected to intelligence work involving your husband. To explore that line of thinking, I spoke with a couple of contacts I have in the right places. In the first instance, I wasn't seeking information about what he was involved with. At that point, my interest was in confirming he worked for one of the agencies, and which one."

"Good; Tremayne's veiled comments always have intrigued me. Were your enquiries successful?"

"…Successful in that they answered the basic question. This may come as a shock. The initial response from my contacts was that they had never heard of Tremayne Bancroft. Although they were quite definite, they did agree to dig deeper to see if there was any evidence to suggest someone such as your husband might have been involved in some way – under a different name perhaps, or under deep cover. Both now have come back to me with negative responses."

"It sounds as though you're telling me my husband never was involved in any way with any of the Australian intelligence agencies. That can't be true. Is it possible he was involved with another country's similar agency? After all, he was a foreign correspondent and spent a lot of time roaming around overseas."

"After my contacts' responses, I went through official channels to ask exactly your question. I received my answer just before Tremayne's funeral. It was the same answer as I received to my earlier questions. It is now clear your husband never was involved in intelligence work for any agency of any country at any time. While I know that will come as a shock, it also narrows our possible lines of investigation into his death. Of course, we will follow up on anything he worked on recently as a foreign correspondent. It is possible something he discovered made someone unhappy."

"That's not quite what I'd expected to hear. I can't believe it. What I construe from what you've told me is that my husband's work, which took him away from home frequently, was as a journalist or foreign correspondent. If I stop to think about it, there should no surprise in that. After all, that's what I understood him to be from the outset. But, somehow, that doesn't fit with what I saw – what I knew – to be the case in more recent times. Regardless, I understand how drawing a blank with the intelligence line of enquiry has left you few other avenues to explore. Are you able to say what they might be?"

Taylor kept his eyes riveted on his empty coffee mug while he considered my question. After a few heartbeats, he shook his head and slowly lifted his eyes to meet mine. He gave another feeble shake of his head and a shrug, before returning his eyes to his mug. Throughout Taylor's performance, out of the corner of my eye, I monitored Kate, for her reaction to Taylor's comments. I saw her squirm at the inspector's non-verbal response to my question.

She eased forward in her chair and clasped her hands tightly on the table. "Lisa, perhaps we have to accept not only Tremayne's background is a mystery, but that he was an enigma. Inspector, I suggest it might be a waste of your time trying to investigate Tremayne's work as a journalist. I'm sorry, Lisa, but I knew that not knowing anything about Tremayne's family or his work was eating at you. In spite of having been around him for so long, he remained a stranger to both of us. I decided to investigate his work; what pieces he wrote, where they were published, that sort of thing."

"Why would you bother with that?"

"I wanted to put together something to help you better know the man you were married to for so many years. I thought it might help you deal with what happened."

"What a nice gesture, but it wasn't necessary. From here on, it is all about moving on – not looking back. What did you find out anyway?"

"If only that were the case – the 'not looking back' bit, I mean. Right… what I discovered is along much the same lines as the inspector's results. I got onto a few of my colleagues who know just about everything there is to know about our industry. It went like: I spoke to a man, who knew a man, who spoke to another man. Inspector, you know how the system works. My world operates in much the same way as yours." Taylor gave Kate a knowing nod.

His non-verbal response was polite and understanding. My reaction was one of rising frustration. "So, Kate, sometime today, will you share with us what you learned from your chain of informants?"

"Okay… No one knew anything of Tremayne Bancroft working in the industry. For an idea of when Tremayne might have been working as a journo, my contact searched archives for articles by him, but couldn't find any – not even in overseas archives. I did ask him to search again, this time to look at 'mystery' foreign correspondents or similar."

"Mystery correspondents…? What are they?"

"Sometimes, people in 'informed' positions write under a pseudonym to 'leak' sensitive material to the media. In most cases, they have to maintain deep cover for the sake of their own and their family's safety. In some instances, people in the know within the industry have an idea who the correspondent is. In other cases, nobody knows. Nevertheless, even in the latter case, the writer is identified as a 'mystery' person whose identity, and even clues to their identity, remain unknown. I knew I was pushing my luck, but the 'mystery' brigade was the last hope of finding out something about Tremayne's work as a journo. I'm sorry, Lisa. I failed. All the search did was prove nobody by the name of Tremayne Bancroft – or anyone who might be identified as him –worked as a journo anytime during the last twenty years."

My head spun. I pushed my chair away from the table to stand up. My legs wouldn't respond. A wave of nausea swept over me and I felt in danger of falling off my chair. "No…no, this can't be true," I heard myself moan as I dropped my head into my hands and propped my elbows on my thighs to support it. I don't know how long the feelings of light headedness and nausea lasted, but I suspect it was close to a minute.

Feeling sufficiently in control again, I sat up to find a glass of water set in front of me. I hadn't noticed Kate fetch it. Inspector Taylor cleared his throat as I gulped down about half of the water. Kate asked me at least twice if I was all right.

"I'm okay. Sorry about that. All you discovered – or couldn't discover – about my husband knocked me off my axis for a moment or two. One thing is now certain. My quest for information has officially begun. *Who was that man I was married to for more than twelve years of my life?* I intend to find out, even if it's the last thing I ever do. And, I think my quest begins in Justin Farley's office."

Chapter 9

Inspector Taylor looked sombre and stony-faced when he arrived, but confused when he left ... or was he dejected? It was obvious his visit did not go as expected. He was leaving with more questions than when he arrived. As soon as he left, I snuck off to the office to hide while I tried to ground myself on planet Earth again. This morning's revelations left me stunned, and probably too incoherent to discuss them with Kate.

About an hour later, I felt up to apologising to Kate for abandoning her. She was preparing lunch. "Your timing is excellent. I was about to call you to come and eat. You saved me the walk. I assume we'll eat out on the deck?" Lost for words, all I managed was a nod in response. "Okay; here, you carry this lot. I'll bring the rest."

Kate looked normal and relaxed, while I felt shattered and confused. As I searched for the words to apologise, Kate opened a more relaxed conversation. "I'm still trying to come to terms with Inspector Taylor's visit. In spite of our best efforts, neither he nor I dug up anything to help you better understand Tremayne. I've been derogatory about him in the past – and, no, I didn't like him much – but it now seems Tremayne was even more of an enigma than I imagined. I hoped to pull together something to help you understand more about his life. I'm sorry, Lisa, but both the inspector and I were dismal failures."

"No need to apologise. Although I'm struggling to come to terms with everything I heard this morning, it was the session I needed to have. It was a kick in the backside to make me realise how little I knew about my husband, and how much I wanted to know about him. For me, the most significant outcome of this morning is that I am determined to find out all there is to know about Tremayne Bancroft. Now, if I could just work out where to start… Perhaps I was right when I mentioned going to see Justin Farley. That probably is the right place to start. There is bound to be information only he can access on my behalf."

"Maybe… but there has to be some preliminary work we can do here before you go to see Justin. I've been thinking about it. There must be some clues somewhere amongst Tremayne's belongings. It's possible he had a safe deposit box at the bank in which he kept significant personal items, like important documents. It's possible we might also find clues, however tenuous, in paperwork he held here. Did he have much paper work here?"

"There was a box of bits and pieces. I assumed it was personal and never touched it. He kept the box on a shelf in the storeroom. If it's not still there, it's with his things over in the cottage now."

"I don't have a busy afternoon planned. Do you think we might go and find out?"

The contents of the downstairs storeroom hadn't been disturbed for some time, not by me anyway. Once I turned on the light, gaps on the shelves were obvious and surprising. "I knew Tremayne's box was in here, but I wasn't aware he kept anything else in this room. The gaps on the shelves suggest there was more than one box." I told Kate.

"I don't think I can be much help to you. Over the years, I've been in this room only a couple of times. See your mother's or grandmother's two old hatboxes on the top shelf… they are only things I remember being here. Remember, many years ago, curiosity got the better of us and we looked in those?"

"Oh yes, I do remember the hats in them. If I'm honest, I don't remember what was stored in here either. It's a bit like the proverbial attic: somewhere to store things you really should throw out but can't bear to part with. In recent years, I only visited this room to store boxes of aged financial records removed from the filing cabinets in the office upstairs."

We both stood, hands on hips, and surveyed the dusty storeroom. "How do you want to tackle this?' Kate asked.

"I don't have any bright ideas. The gap on the shelf over there is where I believe Tremayne's box was stored. As it's not there now, I assume he planned to take it with him when he left. In view of what happened, logic says the box should be with his other belongings in the cottage. Maybe, instead of searching the storeroom, we would be better occupied searching the cottage."

Moments later, Kate led the way into my former home. An uneasy feeling flooded through me as I forced myself to cross the threshold. What is this nonsense, I asked myself? Am I afraid to find out about my husband? Don't be such a wimp. There is nothing in there to hurt you … Surprise you perhaps, shock you even, but not hurt you. A couple of deep breaths, and I strode in to stand beside Kate in the cottage's lounge room.

In her usual business-like manner, Kate demanded, "Right, let's get on with it. Where do we start, and what am I looking for?" I described the box I believed might hold Tremayne's private papers, and suggested she start her search in the spare bedroom, while I went through everything in the main bedroom.

Kate finished her allocated room before I had made much impression on the main bedroom, not surprising I suppose given the spare room didn't contain much. She came and flopped down on the bed. After watching me going through the pockets of clothing hanging in the cupboard for a few moments, she stood up and asked, "Lisa, exactly what are we looking for?"

"Tremayne's box of papers…"

"Yes, but what's likely to be in the box if we find it? …And are you likely to find it in one of those pockets?"

"Point taken; I'm hoping we find anything that provides a clue about Tremayne or his life; something mentioning names or places, or membership of a club or organisation. I suppose the most we can hope for is anything suggesting where we might go to start asking questions."

"Let's step back and think about it for a moment. If Tremayne was so cagey about keeping everything about his life from you, was he likely to leave papers providing such information lying around where you could find them?"

"I wouldn't find them, because I wouldn't go looking for them. We respected each other's privacy. What Tremayne kept in that box was his business, and would remain so unless he showed it to me. He knew that, and trusted me not to go poking about in his things."

"Is his wallet still here?" She asked. I pointed to the wallet lying on top of the chest of drawers, along with a couple of pens and a pocket notebook. "Okay, is there anything different about it; anything missing or anything new added?"

"How would I know? I never looked in his wallet."

"Okay, maybe you never looked deliberately but, on some occasions, you must have seen what was in it."

"No … But then, I'm sure he didn't know what was in my purse either. We didn't spend our lives checking up on one another."

"Are you sure about that? Somehow, I'm not so sure about Tremayne not knowing what was in your purse."

"Kate, what's this conversation about? Is it going somewhere?"

"Dunno … It occurs to me Tremayne wouldn't keep anything he didn't want you to see here at the farm, even if he trusted you enough to believe you wouldn't go digging through his things. Do you have a copy of your marriage certificate? The official certificate I mean, not the thing they give you at the church after the wedding."

"Ye-es, I think so. I remember ordering a copy because Tremayne needed it for something or other. It's probably in our personal papers filed in the office. What about it?"

"You have to provide certain information when you apply for a marriage licence. That information goes on the marriage certificate. It's worth having a look at the details on yours."

On our way back to the house, I asked myself several times why I hadn't thought of checking the marriage certificate. No answers were forthcoming. Perhaps I was trying to ignore the logical one: maybe I didn't want to know what it might tell me. I still didn't have any answers when we reached the office, but I had thought of an argument. "Kate, you suggested Tremayne would make sure there was nothing here to expose the background he was hell-bent on keeping a secret. If that were the case, wouldn't he provide the barest information on our application for a licence?"

"And, would the information be true? I know this is a long shot, but let's have a look anyway." Searching for Tremayne's box might have been quicker and easier than trying to find my marriage certificate.

When our search of the office failed to locate the certificate, the logical conclusion was that Tremayne had kept the certificate, and it might be in his elusive box of private papers. "Shall we return to the cottage and resume our search?" I asked as we accepted our defeat in the office.

We indulged in a coffee first. As I sat sipping it, I let my mind run free. "I wish I could remember why he wanted the certificate in the first place. I remember the reason seemed odd at the time. Now I think about it, I remember he said something about 'proof of identity'. Why, or in what context, wasn't explained."

"You're spot-on about it being a little odd. Blokes rarely have to prove their identity. On the other hand, women, especially if they change their name on marrying, are constantly being required to prove who they are."

Kate was right. Women often find it difficult if they change their surname. I suppose, if a man changed his name for some reason, there might be occasions when he would have to prove his identity. But, if Tremayne changed his name for some reason, a marriage certificate wouldn't help prove who he was.

While still mulling over the question of why Tremayne needed a copy of our marriage certificate, I thought I heard a car arrive. "Kate, did a car drive up?" Before she could answer, we heard the loud 'thunk' of a car door being slammed.

"It's probably Connor. I'll check if he wants to join us for coffee."

"No, it's unlikely to be Connor at this time of day. I'll come with you. Once we deal with whoever it is, we'll go back to searching the cottage."

The vehicle was unfamiliar and the woman scrambling out of it was not Connor. I needed only a glance to know she was a stranger. Short, and what might be described as comfortably rounded, our visitor had stiffly coiffed, yellow-blonde hair. Although time, perhaps, had softened the shape of her face somewhat, the set of her jaw matched the severe cut of her navy blue business suit. By the way she strode towards my front door, I guessed she was no stranger to being in command. And, the set of that jaw suggested she was not a happy woman. Kate noticed it too and whispered, "She's probably lost and fed up with trying to find her way around out in this area."

Whoever she was, she wasn't about to waste time on niceties. "I've come for my husband's things. Show me where they are so I can collect them and be on my way."

Dumbstruck, I stood blinking at the woman as I tried processing her request. Although it took her a couple of moments, Kate recovered from the shock before I did. "Are you sure you have come to the right address? I don't know who you are, but neither your husband, nor anyone else's husband, lives here."

"No, not anymore he doesn't, not since his death. Now, whatever your game is, stop wasting my time and show me where my husband's belongings are. I don't know what's going on, but I don't intend spending any more time here than is necessary to collect his things."

At last, my brain and vocal cords synced. "Excuse me, Madam, but who the hell are you? Not that it matters who you are, your husband does not, and never did, live here. There's nothing here for you to collect. I would point out that you have come onto my property uninvited and made unpleasant demands. Please go back to your car and get off my property."

"So, that's how you going to play it, eh? Well, we'll see how high and mighty you are when I return with the police."

"It's a pity you didn't arrive this morning," Kate growled. "The police were here then, and it would have saved you the trouble." Kate took a couple of steps towards the woman. Kate is what might be described as 'statuesque': tall, well-muscled, but with not an ounce of fat. She now glared down at the woman she towered over.

"This is ridiculous. Go to the police, it's only your time and effort you will be wasting. On the other hand, if we had a name, we might be able to save you the trouble. In a community like ours, just about everybody knows everybody. Perhaps we've come across to your husband at some time. So, can we at least start with your name?"

"Don't try sweet talking me out of this. I am going to the police. But, yes, you should make a note of my name. I am Roslyn Williams, of the Williams Enterprises family. So, perhaps now you realise I mean business, and that I have the means and the connections to make your life miserable if you try steamrolling me. Is that clear enough?"

Kate and I exchanged looks and slight shrugs when the woman announced who she was. I had never heard of her, or her family's business. Judging by Kate's reaction, the information didn't do anything for her either. Still, now we had her information, it would be easier to make the situation clearer for her. "Mrs Williams, I'm sorry our meeting has been less than pleasant, and your long drive out here was for nothing. But, I can only reiterate what I said earlier: Mr Williams has never lived here, and I can't say I've heard of his being anywhere out in this area. I'm sorry, but we can't help you."

"It's Miss Williams. I retained my maiden name."

"Right… Well, thank you for that, but I'm afraid it puts us right back where we started. We still don't know who your husband is, but we can tell you he didn't live here."

"Stop wasting my time. I know he lived here. What was your relationship to him? Were you his landlady, or was there something more involved? Don't worry. I'll get to the bottom of whatever was going on here. You might be a bigshot landowner out here in the sticks, but I have the means…"

"That sounds very much like a threat." Kate's growl had moderated a little and was now a quiet snarl. "I think the police will be happy to have you land on their doorstep to save them the trouble of looking for you after we report your threat. Perhaps you should give us your husband's name so we can add it to the information we give to the police when we talk to them. After all, it sounds like they have a missing person situation to look into."

My admiration of Kate went up a few notches. Apart from the snarl in her voice, her demeanour as she spoke to the woman was relaxed, and maybe even a little offhand. And, Kate's delivery hit its mark. I saw the woman blanch as Kate mentioned reporting her threat to the police. A simple case of incorrect information had turned ugly. Maybe the situation was beyond redemption, but I felt obliged to reinject some stability into the meeting. After all, it seems she and I have something in common. Both of us lost our husbands recently. Our shared recent widowhood status was enough to oblige me to try smoothing things over before she left.

"Miss Williams, my colleague has a point. If we knew your husband's name, we might have heard of him, or we could ask around our friends and neighbours to see if they have come across him around here."

Hmm … Perhaps you have a point. His name was Trevor; Trevor Cross. I have it on good authority he died here."

"My condolences; this meeting must be rough so soon after losing your husband. Although I would love to help you, knowing his name doesn't change anything. I've never come across a Trevor in this area, and I'm sure no Trevor has lived on this property during my lifetime. May I ask how long you were married?"

"Not that it's any of your business, but our twentieth wedding anniversary was a couple of months ago."

"That is sad. If your whole family managed to get together for the occasion, at least you'll have one last happy memory of being together. You mentioned Williams Enterprises. I'm not aware of a business by that name anywhere in this area. Were you and your husband from up here in North Queensland?"

"For someone holding my husband's belongings illegally, you ask a lot of questions. They don't make any difference though. If I don't leave here with his possessions today, I will go to the police. So while you consider that, I will answer your questions. We had no children. Oh, don't go getting all sympathetic for me. There were various reasons, none of them cause for regret. We lived in Sydney, in a harbour-side mansion, but my husband's work brought him up this way for a week or more every so often. If someone who knew of him hadn't told a friend of mine about his death, and that friend hadn't told me, I'd still be sitting at home waiting for him to return from his current business trip."

The situation was getting the better of Kate. Nothing was being resolved regardless of how much we talked about it. I felt we shared the same feelings about the situation, but Kate was the one who was sufficiently in command to bring it to an end. While her tone returned to normal, her statement left little room to manoeuvre.

"Miss Williams, it appears everyone at this meeting has shared all we know. It may not have helped your quest in any way, but the bottom line is, we cannot help you. That was the situation when you arrived, and nothing has changed as a result of our conversation. Please leave the property now. What you do after that is entirely up to you, but this has gone on long enough. There is nothing more to say. You came here uninvited, and we have asked you to leave more than once. If you don't leave now, we will be forced to call the police to report a hostile trespass."

It was obvious Miss Williams was about to unleash a renewed verbal attack. I felt compelled to intervene. "I'm sorry your trip was a wasted journey. Do you plan on staying long in the area?" The look in her eyes as they slid up and down me was enough to warn me of a forthcoming vitriolic response. I rushed on to prevent it. "I was going to ask if there were somewhere we could contact you should we hear anything of your husband, Trevor Cross. If that's not possible, or you would prefer we didn't, please say so." She didn't say not to contact her and, with some reluctance, gave me her contact details. While it didn't eliminate the tirade she was going to deliver, I think I did soften it a bit.

After that, and with her feathers still well and truly ruffled, Miss Williams stalked off to her car and slammed the door before driving off. As we turned to go inside, I noticed Kate was deep in thought. It wasn't until we were about halfway up the stairs, she elected to share those thoughts with me. "Lisa, it's up to you because this is your property, but I recommend a phone call to Inspector Taylor. Who knows what that woman might do, but it is likely she will go to the police. It would be wise to tip them off in advance about what might happen, and explain why."

I agreed it was the right thing to do but, it was such an outlandish story, it was going to sound like we'd had a touch too much to drink. "Poor old Inspector Taylor probably won't thank me for adding to his workload. I don't think the woman is delusional, but I would like to know more about how she came to the conclusion her husband had lived here."

The soft late afternoon breeze had a cathartic effect as I flicked through my contacts for Inspector Taylor's number. He answered almost on the first ring. "Miss Soldarno, what has happened? It's unlike you to call me, especially when we only spoke this morning. Have you found something relevant to the case, or has something I should know about happened?"

"The latter, Inspector… I don't know whether it's relevant to your investigation or not, but I thought it wise to let you know. It might be a case of 'forewarned is forearmed', if you follow what I'm saying."

"I know it's late, but I happen to be out your way. Would it suit you if I called in on my way past, rather than trying to discuss it over the phone?"

It was better than I hoped for, or he could imagine, but I simply thanked him, and told him whatever time he arrived would be fine with us.

Chapter 10

After checking on the harvester's progress, Connor spotted me still out on the deck. He simply gave me a thumbs-up before continuing on his way home. I wouldn't have managed without the support of Kate and Connor. But, Connor has more to do than look after me. Both Rankin men are kept fully occupied on their own property. Tomorrow, I must pick up the reins again and get on with running this place. First thing tomorrow, I'll tell Connor I'm back in control. …And, I need to talk to Kate. She can't jeopardise her job by continuing as an unpaid housekeeper here.

Twilight had descended, and Kate and I were sipping our drinks in the soothing dark solitude on the deck when headlights appeared. Inspector Taylor had arrived. With an icy white wine in hand, Taylor made himself comfortable at the table. "It is glorious out here, especially at this time of day. But, it's late and you will want to get on with dinner. I'll stop prattling and let you tell me what happened."

Recounting details of Miss Williams' (aka Mrs Cross) visit took less time than I thought. The subsequent question and answer session took considerably longer. By the time Inspector Taylor finished going over everything I gave him, and asking questions I couldn't answer, I felt mentally exhausted. Perhaps it was due to the late hour, or because I was tired, but my dark side made an appearance in my next outburst.

"Inspector, there is nothing more I can tell you. Kate, have I left out anything, or maybe not explained something well enough? You were there. Feel free to give us your take on what happened."

"No, I don't have anything to add, but I believe there is more to the story than we were privy to today. We were on the defensive from the moment she started firing accusations. Maybe our reaction created an information barrier, which prevented her from being more forthcoming."

"Are you saying I didn't handle the situation well? I don't know what more you think she might have told us."

"Calm down… You asked for my take on the visit. As for what else she might have told us, the first thing to come to mind is who tipped her off about her husband living here and that he had died. She hinted at a convoluted information flow, but we didn't explore it … and she didn't volunteer an explanation."

"Oh…," was my inane response as I studied my empty glass. Kate was right – again. I was so busy being offended and defensive; I didn't try to extract the finer details. "I'm not so sure she would tell us more. Regardless, I realise we should have tried for more details. Perhaps, a bit more effort on our part might have helped her accept the reality of the situation here."

Taylor chuckled. "Well, I wasn't here but, from what you've said, it doesn't sound like she was ready to listen to reason, or anything else you had to say. By the way, do you think you two might call me Dan?"

"I think we could manage that." Kate nodded in agreement. "Inspector… sorry …. Dan, my reason for calling you was two-fold. While I was concerned about the woman's visit and, as she achieved no satisfaction today, I was worried about what else might follow? Neither Kate nor I need more tension or upset in our lives at the moment. The main reason I called you was to warn you she was threatening to go to the police with her accusations. While I'm sure your mob can deal with whatever happens, the way she referred to having 'the means' to make things difficult was concerning."

"Under different circumstances," Dan said, "I might be tempted to make contact with her to nip it in the bud, so to speak. In this case, I'm not sure that's the best approach. Did she give any indication of what her movements were likely to be over the next day or so? Having achieved no satisfaction today, I doubt she will pack up and leave quietly."

"At the end, when I was trying to calm her down and persuade her to leave, she did give me her contact details. Your assumption is correct. She is not planning to leave the area any time soon. So, who knows how much havoc she might create while here?"

"My advice: don't contact her unless you hear something about her husband. Sit tight and see what she does. I admit to being intrigued by her marriage. …Strange that it took an outsider to tell her about her husband's death and where he was. Still, the way people live their lives is their business. Who are we to judge?"

Taylor's phone played its tune and he moved away to answer it. During his brief call, Kate came and whispered while she refilled my glass, "It is dinnertime and we still haven't prepared anything. Should we just cook a couple of steaks and have a salad with them? …And, should we invite *Dan* to stay for dinner?"

"*Yes* to the steaks, and *no* to the invite. With any luck, his call will lure him away and off to a crime somewhere else." The gods were on my side. As soon as his call ended, he announced he was needed elsewhere. A few minutes later, Kate and I were alone in the kitchen preparing steaks and salad for dinner.

We elected to eat in the dining room instead of returning to the deck. It developed into a drawn-out session consisting of moments of spontaneous conversation interrupting long periods of silence. Today had delivered so much to process and comprehend. Over dinner, my mind exercised every skerrick of computational power it could muster in a bid to make sense of the strange visit by Miss Williams. It appears Kate was preoccupied in much the same way.

"There are so many questions we should have asked Miss Williams. As a journo, I can't believe I couldn't react quickly enough to come up with what we should have asked. I've conducted some difficult interviews but, on this occasion, it appears I wasn't up to the task."

"Don't beat yourself up. I didn't do any better. Today was a classic case of being wise after the event. Over dinner, I thought of so many things I should have said to her, and questions I should have asked. While I hope we don't encounter her again, a part of me wants another meeting with her."

"She was unhappy with the outcome of today's visit. She might return for 'Round 2' before the matter is over and done with."

"No one resolved anything today, and now I have so many questions I want to ask. I'm almost tempted to try setting up another meeting … but not out here this time."

"That seems a reasonable idea to me. A meeting in town at a coffee shop or restaurant should keep things civilised. While not polite, at least shouting would be avoided in such an environment. I think you should go ahead and try to set it up. Mind you, I'm not sure what *Dan* might have to say about it."

The thought of setting up a return bout with Miss Williams persisted for some time after lights-out. If I had decided whether to do it or not, it might have resulted a better night's sleep. While staring into the darkness in the wee hours of the morning, I knew I would be like death in tomorrow, and not at my sparkling best for making important decisions.

*****

My thoughts about being sub-par this morning proved correct. I had a thick head and felt grumpy. Nevertheless, I was awake early, and took myself off to check on the farm before dealing with Kate or breakfast. The harvesting contractor's gang finished my area yesterday and moved on to another farm today. A brand new calf was added to my herd since I last checked the cattle. But, there is only so much to be done on the farm today, and the lure of coffee was strong.

I followed the aroma of freshly brewed coffee up the stairs. Kate had the machine doing its thing and, several minutes later, we were in our usual positions on the deck with our breakfasts and steaming mugs of coffee. I had almost emptied my mug before I started to feel human again. Then, with a refill in front of me, I felt sufficiently revived to engage in conversation.

"Kate, do you have anything requiring your attention today? I don't have anything planned, but I should try to catch up with Connor sometime. Apart from that, I'm free if you have any bright ideas about what we might do."

"There might be a couple of work related phone calls I need to make, but first I'll check if the details I need were emailed. As soon as I have the information, I can start making arrangements for when and where I need to be for the work they want me to do." While Kate dealt with emails and phone calls, I spent the time in the office, and made my catch-up call to Connor.

By the time we both finished what we had to do, it was morning-coffee-on-the-deck time. Kate revisited the earlier question. "Right, Lisa, now our pressing business is dealt with, how do we fill in the rest of the day?" I didn't have an answer, but my phone chirped at just the right moment for me to avoid having to find one.

"Inspector Taylor… sorry … Dan, to what do I owe the honour of this call?" I switched it onto speaker so Kate could hear.

"I thought you might like an update on your Miss Roslyn Williams…"

"She's not 'my' Miss Williams, but do go on. I can't wait to hear what has occurred. By the way, Kate is hanging on your every word as well."

"Thanks to your heads-up last evening, the boys on the front counter were prepared for her when she arrived at the station this morning. I had clued them in, and told them to refer her to me if she came. They did. The episode didn't last more than about ten minutes before she was on her way out of the station again. She had nothing new to say: claimed you are illegally preventing her collecting her late husband's belongings, and wanted a police escort to accompany her and force you to hand them over."

"Wonderful…! And, what was the outcome of all that, pray tell?"

"As you would realise, when such a claim is made, I must ask a lot of questions. Well, not too many in this case – no more than one or two in fact. The important details I needed were: the name of her husband, and why she thought he had died leaving his belongings in this area?"

"And what did that get you?"

"Nothing really… no more than you gave me anyway. She told me her husband's name was Trevor Cross, and that a friend-of-a-friend is to be thanked for her finding out about his death. She refused to be drawn on who the initial informant was, but I gathered she did not know him personally."

"So what happens now – from your point of view, I mean? Should I be expecting her to arrive with an armed escort sometime soon?"

"Of course not... Nevertheless, as an officer of the law, I am obliged to investigate any such claims. If you do manage to shed any light on what this is all about, your input would be most welcome. Let me know if you hear from the woman again."

"Is that a possibility?" Kate asked as soon as the call ended.

"Anything is possible I suppose. I suspect, in this case, another visit is a probability. She seems determined to follow through on her claims and threats. All we can do is wait and see." We didn't have long to wait.

Lethargy and introspection ruled the day. Once morning tea was over, neither of us showed any sign of wanting to do something else. So, we relaxed in relative silence and ensconced in our own thoughts. It was almost lunchtime before either of us stirred. Kate climbed out of her chair, stood up and stretched several bits of her anatomy before coaxing her legs into motion. Stiffly, she strolled to the other end of the deck, and leant on the railing for a moment. I heard her catch her breath.

A second or so later, I thought I heard a vehicle close by – too close to be ignored. "What's happened, Kate? Is there a car coming?"

"The witch flew in and parked her broomstick outside the front door. I don't suppose we can pretend we're not here."

"Argh, I take it Miss Williams has arrived?" Kate's only response was a wry smile. "No, we are a tad too exposed out here to stand a chance of convincing her no one is home."

"How do you want to play it? We don't know any more about her missing husband than we did yesterday and, somehow, I don't think that's what she will want to hear."

"True; but we won't know for sure until we go and find out. Shall we make our way downstairs to welcome her?"

"If we must … should I take garlic, a wooden stake … or a crucifix perhaps – just in case?"

"Might not hurt to bring along whatever protection we have available." Kate didn't respond because she didn't hear me. My words were drowned out by the pounding on my front door. The viciousness of Miss Williams' attack on my door told me this was not a friendly visit, and definitely not one intended to make amends for yesterday's upsetting encounter.

Kate led the way down the stairs. "Stand behind me when I open the door. I might be able to protect you from evil spells – or worse," she quipped. Maybe protection of some sort was called for.

"Hang on, Kate. This is our opportunity to ask questions and – hopefully – receive answers that might help us better understand what this is all about. We owe it to Inspector Taylor, as well as ourselves, to find out whatever we can. If we play it well this morning, she might accept the truth of the situation and leave us alone. Let's at least try to make nice."

Miss Williams was pounding the door again as I swung it open. I hoped my smile looked at least vaguely genuine. "Miss Williams I wasn't expecting to see you so soon. We are about to make coffee." The lie rolled off my tongue like someone well practised in the art of deception. "Would you care to join us? It's quite pleasant out on the deck upstairs."

Wrong-footed, the woman stammered, but produced no answer other than a slight shake of her head. I rushed on before she had a chance to collect his senses. "Kate, perhaps you might go back up and make an extra cup for Miss Williams while I show her through to the deck."

As Kate scampered up the stairs two at a time (no doubt in a rush to give credence to my lie about being ready to sit down with coffee), Miss Williams hesitated on the doorstep. I invited her in with a sweeping gesture. My face muscles were beginning to complain about all the smiling. I hoped the subterfuge didn't have to last too much longer. Surely, once we sit down with coffee, normalcy will return.

By the time we sat down with coffee and slices of leftover cake, it was clear Ms Williams was working on regaining her previous objectionable demeanour … But perhaps that was normal for her. Her sour face and stony silence made continuing the pretence of welcoming friendship difficult. I struggled to hold the red mist at bay. So far, the woman hadn't uttered a word, but I knew that, if she resumed her vitriolic attack of yesterday, I would lose my battle and she would encounter my dark side.

I made one last bid to establish polite dialogue. "Apologies; I haven't asked what brings you all the way out here again today. You're going to be disappointed if you are hoping I have information for you. I haven't spoken to anyone from around here about your husband. What was his name…? Trevor, wasn't it?"

Her mug was halfway to her mouth when I asked my question. The mug returned to the table with more force than required. Kate's eyes darted to the mug's handle to check if it was still attached. All I could do was feign surprise at the woman's action, and try to rustle up another beaming smile. Maybe it was my lack of acting ability, but my ploy didn't work. All it did was unleash Miss Williams' pent-up tide of vitriol.

"You know damn well why I'm here. I've come for my husband's belongings … and I want some straight answers. Who the hell do you think you are to deny me my rights; to deny me what's rightfully mine? You should know, I have spoken to the police about what's happened here. You can expect them to come knocking on your door. They will investigate what you're up to. I thought I'd give you one last chance to do the right thing before the law descends upon you. Up to you now. I've given you that chance. What's it going to be?"

"I was pleased you came back today, but I…"

"There is nothing like the threat of a police investigation to make people see sense. So, what have you to say by way of apology? And could you make it brief please, so I can collect his things and be gone from here."

"I was about to say I was surprised I found no change in your attitude. All I can say is the same as I told you yesterday. I have never heard of a Trevor Cross, and no one by that name has ever lived here. Being recently widowed myself, I can sympathise with your situation."

"I'm not interested in that. After twenty years of marriage, I am determined to collect every last reminder of him. Maybe your marriage was more recent, and you are unable to understand the depth of my loss."

"Although I was only married for twelve years, I don't consider that 'recent'. I don't think the level of grief at the loss of a partner is governed by the length of the marriage. Nevertheless, the way you learned of your husband's death must've made the grief worse. You said you learned of it by some roundabout means."

"My husband loved chess; not just any game of chess, but competition level chess. Whenever he was in a city, he took every opportunity to visit its leading chess club. Whenever he was in Brisbane, he played as often as possible with the professional players there. When at home in Sydney, he did much the same thing. One of the men he often played with in Brisbane is a close friend of my father's and I've known him all my life. It was through my family, my husband met him in the first place. He was the one who broke the news to me. He is an old man now, so I don't have to tell you how difficult it was for him to do that … Or for me to find out like that."

"True… But, if your family's friend lives in Brisbane, how did he know your husband had died up here in North Queensland? Was he visiting here at the time?"

"No, someone who worked for my friend for many years contacted him with the news, and then my friend contacted me. The former employee took early retirement to embark on a working holiday around the country. He happened to be here when my husband died, or I might never have known he was dead."

"Yes, that was a lucky coincidence and something to be grateful for."

"Grateful…! You couldn't even get my husband's name right. The only luck was the man thought the body might bear a resemblance to someone he had seen at his employer's house on a couple of occasions. He wasn't even certain it was my husband."

"Is it possible it wasn't your husband? Was your husband supposed to be in this area at that time? …And what do you mean: *I couldn't even get your husband's name right?* What am I supposed to have had to do with it?"

"My friend tried to get more information but his informant had moved on from here. All he could tell my friend was the name of the person who arranged a funeral; you. The final insult was finding my husband was buried under the wrong name. You might have at least used his correct name: Trevor Maybanks Cross."

"Maybanks…? That's an unusual name. I've never heard it before."

"It's a family name, from his maternal line I believe."

"Ah, I see. I'm now convinced I didn't know your husband. Again, it looks like you've made a wasted trip. I can only make you the same promise as I did yesterday, if I hear anything, I'll pass it on to you."

Her tone had become aggressive again. I didn't like where this was heading. In a stream of abusive language, which accused me of just about everything imaginable, she assured me that, if she left empty-handed today, she would drive straight to the police station.

"Miss Williams, I tried to help you sort this matter out. On both visits, I tried being patient with you, but to no avail. I've had enough of this nonsense. Leave my property now, or I will be calling the police to have you removed." The red mist was well and truly down. I stood, grabbed the back of her chair and dragged it away from the table. Towering over her, I screamed, "Now, get out and don't come back here again."

Kate had remained silent throughout the interlude, but now came and stood at the end of the table. She gave the woman an emphatic gesture to get out. Looking somewhat taken aback by the current situation, Miss Williams rose unsteadily. With a nervous sidestep around Kate, she made her way off the deck and onto the stairs. Kate thundered down the stairs in Miss Williams' wake, while I trailed along behind them.

A few moments later, Miss Williams fired up her hire car and roared off my farm.

Chapter 11

Our footsteps sounded loud in the heavy silence. Neither of us spoke as we lumbered upstairs and out onto the deck. Incapable of doing anything more, I collapsed into one of the chairs and cradled my head in my hands. A few moments later, Kate broke the prevailing brooding silence. I looked up. She leant against the railing.

"Lunchtime has come and gone. Should I fix something for a late lunch, or would you prefer something else first?"

"I don't think I'm up to food. Perhaps something strong and liquid is required instead."

She plonked two glasses of scotch down on the table, collapsed into the opposite chair, and gave me a sarcastic sounding, "Cheers." We both took a couple of long sips of our drinks before Kate spoke again.

"So, do we call Inspector Dan to brief him on this morning's developments?"

"We should analyse everything we remember about this morning's event before we call the inspector. That might not be so easy. My head feels as though it's full of cotton wool. I'm not sure how much of this morning's conversation I retain, but it is important that whatever we pass on to Inspector Taylor is accurate, and not just our preferred interpretation. Perhaps we should make notes of the pertinent points and analyse them before we forget exactly what was said."

"Having to remember what was said isn't necessary. We can analyse the whole morning's session as we listen to it." Kate walked over to the main table and went to the chair next to where she sat while Miss Williams and I carried on our discussion. She reached down and picked her phone up off the chair.

"You recorded the whole session? Is it illegal to do that without telling the parties involved?"

"It depends on what you plan to do with the recording. I intended it just for us. Even if Inspector Taylor listened to it, he wouldn't be able to use it in evidence. Although, if you wanted to bring an action against Miss Williams for harassment or something, it might help inform Justin Farley's preparation of the necessary paperwork."

"Should anyone else know about it? It never crossed my mind to covertly record our discussions. Thank you. I will listen to it again before I talk to the inspector."

"Remember, I'm a journalist. We are good at recording things we shouldn't, without the other party knowing about it. Fetch a notebook. Are you sure you don't want a sandwich to chew on while we're about it?"

Contrary to my earlier thoughts, food now seemed a good idea. I produced sandwiches and coffee while Kate fetched a notebook and set up a workspace on the dining room table. "Oh, I didn't realise we were going to eat inside."

"It will be better to listen to the recording in here where there isn't so much extraneous noise. We sat at the table, ate our sandwiches, listened to the recording and discussed just about every point and comment made. As we did so, Kate scribbled notes of our deliberations.

"Kate, the first intriguing thing about all this is that 'an informant' knew about Tremayne's death in the first place ... That he saw the body and thought he recognised it as someone else. Outside a select handful of people, no one knew Tremayne was dead, let alone anyone knowing about the funeral arrangements."

"Yeah, I wondered about that too. But, it seems the person didn't know the whole story. She claimed her husband was *buried* under the wrong name. Perhaps the informant didn't know all the details, and could pass on only as much as he knew. The bit about a burial might be an assumption on Miss Williams' part."

Our examination of the section of the recording regarding burying her husband under the wrong name attracted the longest attention. Kate made an interesting observation. "Lisa, the husband's name she gave us – Trevor Maybanks Cross – has a certain ring to it. Might this be a case of inaccurate recall on the part of the informant? He recalled a man from somewhere in his past with a vaguely similar name to Tremayne's. It's a long shot, but is it a possibility worth considering?"

"This might be a case of *if I close my eyes and squint, I might see similarities.* If we ignore the husband's middle name, Trevor Cross doesn't sound much like Tremayne Bancroft." As I spoke, Kate was preoccupied with creating hieroglyphics on a new page in her notebook.

"Give me a moment…" After a frenzy of wild strokes and scribbles, she exclaimed, "Bloody Hell…! Can that be right?" She sat back and studied her handiwork.

"If I could see what you are talking about, I might be able to answer. What did you come up with, and why are you questioning whether it's possible or not?"

"Okay, but bear with me while I walk you through it. Here is a sheet of paper and my pen. Write across the top in big letters 'Trevor Maybanks Cross'." I did as I was told and Kate continued.

"Now it becomes difficult to explain what to do. That is an erasable pen. You use the rubber tip on the end to erase things. Here is what you are going to do: Go to the word 'Trevor' and erase the final three letters, 'vor'. That leaves you with only the first three letters of the name: Tre. Are you right with that?" I nodded. "Good; now move onto the middle name: Maybanks. This one is a bit tricky. First, separate 'May' and 'banks'."

"What…?"

"Do it. Now erase 'banks'. Move along a bit from 'May' and write 'banks' again." Kate supervised my efforts from over my shoulder. "Right, the rest of it is more cosmetics than anything else. Erase the 'ks' off the end of 'banks', and then erase the 'ss' from the end of 'Cross'. Can you see where this is going yet?"

This whole exercise had me feeling a tad irritated. Instead of this charade, why doesn't she just tell me what she wants me to know? Rather than admit I didn't have a clue, I just shot her a hard look. Kate interpreted it correctly and continued. "Okay. Now you should have the following left on your sheet: TRE .. MAY .. BAN .. CRO. All will be revealed when you add a few letters here and there. To the end of 'MAY', add 'NE'. Then, to the end of 'CRO' add 'FT'."

"No! This can't be right."

"Finish it, and then tell me whether it's right or not. Get rid of the space between TRE and MAYNE. Then, remove the space between BAN and CROFT. ... Any questions now?"

"It's unbelievable. I couldn't see the connection. Without you I might never have seen it. Just a little fiddling about made Trevor Maybanks Cross become TREMAYNE BANCROFT. Or, if you prefer, her husband became my husband. I can't take in what that means."

"I don't know what it means, but it suggests someone else thinks your husband was still her husband. One of any number of possible misunderstanding scenarios might apply, but the small matter involving his name tends to indicate intentional deceit. Nevertheless, we should keep an open mind until we investigate further. So, our first move should be the one we abandoned when our visitor arrived: finding your marriage certificate.... And... I don't think... you should dismiss the possibility ... he wasn't your husband... not legally anyway."

"Irrespective of what this means, I *know* *t*here was a marriage in the local church, and I *know* there was a marriage certificate. When our visitor arrived, we were about to head back to the cottage to continue searching for Tremayne's papers, including a copy of my marriage certificate. Shall we resume from where we left off?"

"Lead on. The cottage isn't huge but it took a while this morning to search only a part of it. The rest of the place is likely to take some time. It's possible we still won't have found anything by the end of the day." I pushed open the cottage's door as Kate finished speaking, and stepped inside.

"There are no preconceived ideas about what I might do after the sun goes down. One way or another, by tomorrow this place will be searched from top to bottom, even if I have to work all night. That is my mission. But I don't expect you to lose sleep over it. Feel free to pack it in whenever you've had enough. Anyway, I'm probably not going to be much company while I'm about it."

As dusk slid into twilight, I still had plenty to search. Kate announced she was going back to the house and would call me when dinner was ready. There was no argument. I needed time alone; time for my mind to absorb the implications of today's conversation with Miss Williams. Was it possible my husband's name was nothing more than an anagram of her husband's? … That my marriage was, simply put, a bigamous event?

It looked that way and, the more I thought about it, the more convinced I became. "Stop it," I counselled myself aloud. "Remember Kate's advice about keeping an open mind." So far, we had proved nothing, but the evidence gathered supported her claims rather than mine. When Kate called me for dinner, I had completed an unsuccessful search of the interior of the cottage. There remained only the garage and the vehicle in it still to search.

All through dinner I kept trying to think of places Tremayne might stash things he didn't want people to find; people such as me. It proved a futile exercise until later in bed when a couple of possibilities came to mind.

After dinner, Kate worked on persuading me to leave searching the cottage until tomorrow. I had other ideas, but she prevailed. By still being cranky about not continuing the search after dinner, I managed to keep me awake until after midnight.

*****

'Zombie-like' describes my presence at breakfast this morning. I had a thick head from lack of sleep, and my neck and shoulders were stiff after having spent much of yesterday taut with tension. Kate was her usual bright self. "I don't need to ask what you're going to do this morning," she chirped. "Can I help you search the rest of the cottage?"

"Feel free to join me. There isn't much to do, but I have farm work to do until about coffee time." By the time I returned a little later than expected for coffee, Kate was finishing the laundry after taking care of a number of other domestic chores. She had become my housekeeper, and it did not sit well with me that she had taken over all the domestic chores. Perhaps tonight will provide an opportunity to discuss the situation.

"Are we going to the cottage straight after coffee?" Kate asked as I helped myself to another brownie. I still had to sort out a few head of cattle to send to this week's sale, so going to the cottage was postponed until after lunch.

Over at the cottage after a quick lunch, I directed Kate to an area I overlooked yesterday, while I went to search the garage. The spacious storage cupboard occupying one wall of the garage was empty except for a large plastic storage box with a badly damaged lid. That left only the car to investigate. The little voice in my head asked me whether it was worth the effort. I doubted I'd find anything in the vehicle.

If the rest of Tremayne's belongings remained strewn throughout the cottage, why would there be anything in the car? I tried the tailgate. It was locked. Okay, that is odd. It was unusual for us to lock our vehicles when they were parked in a locked garage. There's probably some rule that says you should, but we don't. The question now is: where are the keys? I suspected it was a false hope, but I went to check the keys rack inside, on the wall beside the door to the garage.

"Finished already?" Kate asked as I came in. By the look on your face, I'm guessing you didn't find anything of interest in the garage."

"I haven't finished out there. The car is locked. I just came in to see if the key was on the rack. ... And, now I can see that it's not. Bugger... That's not helpful."

"Where else might it be? I haven't seen the key lying around anywhere."

"We are not going to waste time looking for it. I'll go back to the house to fetch the spare key." My stomach was tightening as I hurried for the key. While it was odd finding the car locked, finding the key missing did not bode well. A few minutes later, Kate accompanied me into the garage and watched me unlock the vehicle. Then I went to the tailgate again, while Kate walked along, peering in through the windows on the far side of the vehicle. "From what I can see, there doesn't appear to be much inside the car," she reported.

Disappointment flooded over me. There was nothing in the cargo area either. So, why had Tremayne locked the vehicle? The only is reason would be if there was something important in the car, something significant or sensitive, he wanted to keep safe. I reached up to pull down the hatch to close it. A stray thought drifted in from left field. The little voice was in my head again, reminding me I hadn't made a thorough search. "Okay, okay; I'll do it."

"You will do what?" Kate asked in surprise. "I didn't ask you to do anything. Who were you talking to?"

"Short answer: me… Complicated answer: my conscience. There was nothing in the cargo area, but my conscience reminded me I hadn't checked the well that holds the spare tyre. I think this car has a 'spacesaver' spare wheel, although the well is big enough to hold a full-sized wheel. Something could be stashed in the free space around it."

In spite of the sceptical look she gave me, Kate came to help me wrestle the flooring up out of position and manoeuvre it out of the vehicle. We both peered into the wheel well. At first glance, only the expected paraphernalia was obvious: spacesaver wheel, a hydraulic jack and its handle, a wheel brace, and a roll containing the necessary tools for changing a wheel. The wheel brace and tool roll were loose in the bottom of the well. Large clean rags had been rolled up and packed around those items to prevent them rattling around.

'Thorough' being the keyword, I pulled out one of the rolls of rags and unrolled it. A small hard covered notebook and a wallet fell out. "Curiouser and Curiouser…" Kate quipped as I picked them up. "What are they and why would he hide them in there?"

"Let's check the rest of the rags before looking for answers."

The moment we started unravelling the last of the rags, we knew we had hit the jackpot. The unimposing looking bundle disgorged a pile of papers, some of them crumpled and creased from being so tightly rolled. "Kate, in that storage cupboard, there is a plastic box. It will be useful for keeping all this stuff together." Moments later, everything we extracted from the rolls of rags was safely in the box.

"Are we going to examine all the stuff here, or should we take it back to the house to look at it there?" Kate asked.

I hadn't thought about it. Rational thought had shut down the moment we found the first object. I ignored the squirming mass in my stomach, now on its way to becoming a lead ball, and concentrated on rebooting my thinking. "Uhmm … I think … I want to take it all back to the house. Yes, let's lock up here, and take it back there to look at it."

"Lisa, are you okay? You seem a bit distracted. Is it just the shock of finding this stuff, or is there something else I should know?"

"From the moment I found the vehicle locked, I've had a bad feeling. My instinct has been right so far, and now it is telling me there is no good news amongst all this stuff we found. Come on, let's get on with it. Once we know what's in here, we can start coping with whatever it reveals."

We commandeered the dining room table for the next phase of our investigation. Kate covered it with an old tablecloth, and I tipped the contents of the plastic box onto it. Our first task was to unravel all the bits of paper, smooth them out, and stack them. In the process, several other interesting items came to light.

Kate stole yet another glance at her watch. "You keep checking the time. Are you waiting for something – or someone? If you are, don't let this stuff get in the way."

"No, it's not that. This morning, I threw together a pie for tonight's dinner. I do need to get it in the oven now, if we want to eat at a respectable hour tonight."

As Kate was speaking, the headlights of an approaching vehicle dancing across the dining room windows caught my attention. "Were you expecting anyone?" She shook her head. "I do hope it's not Miss Williams honouring us with yet another visit." Kate was already on her way out to the deck. I saw her lean over the railing to check on the visitor.

"O-o-h… Hell, yes … I was supposed to move a few head into the yard this afternoon ready for the truck to collect early tomorrow morning." My response was delivered on my way down the stairs. I met Connor at the front door.

"Sorry, Connor. I forget to put the cattle in the yard. I have eight head I want to send off. I'll do it now. Was there something else you wanted to see me about, or did you just come to check on me?"

"When you didn't let me know, I wasn't sure whether you had stock to send off or not. I'll give you a hand to yard them now."

"Thanks for coming over." With so many other things happening, it had slipped my mind. "And, thanks for the offer, but I can manage on my own. …And you probably should be home getting ready for dinner." He insisted on helping and, about half an hour later, we were back at the house. The least I could do was ask him to stay for dinner.

It turned into a pleasant and leisurely meal out on the deck. Good food, good wine, good company, and a cool night breeze wafting in the scent of the surrounding bush, all combined to make for a pleasant and relaxing evening. The only downside, if there was one, was that it was almost eleven o'clock when we said goodnight to Connor.

"I'm hoping you consider it too late to begin going through Tremayne's papers," Kate said.

Tempting though the pile of stuff on the dining room table was, Kate's hope was fulfilled. Tomorrow was another day, and a good night's sleep would clear my head of tonight's wine.

Chapter 12

First thing this morning, there was the cattle truck to load, and then irrigation to set up. By the time I returned to the house, I felt almost human, and the effects of last night's wine had all but disappeared. Kate straggled out to the kitchen as I brought the coffee machine to life for my first cup of the day.

"Yes, please…" she croaked in lieu of a 'good morning'.

Conversation was non-existent until we were both standing in front of the coffee machine waiting for our second cup to finish brewing. "Do you have anything to do today, or are you planning to make a start on those papers?" Kate asked.

"I thought the answer was obvious. Of course we are going to deal with those papers. I'm shocked at having resisted their siren call this long. A part of me still wants to leave it a while before starting on that material. Call it trepidation. I'm on edge about what we might discover amongst them."

"Finding divorce papers would ease the tension a bit around here."

"Agreed, Kate, but I'm certain that won't happen. If Miss Williams believes she was still married to Tremayne when he died, I think there is better than an even chance she still was. Why else would she go to all the fuss and bother of coming all this way to harass me about everything to do with his death?"

"Yeah, her actions tend to support her claims. There is another significant aspect to all this. For me, there is no doubt she doesn't know the nature of your relationship with Tremayne. She thought you were his landlady or something. I'm convinced she is unaware you were married to the man she claims as her husband. If those papers don't clarify the situation, we will need to sit down and discuss how to proceed with sorting out the mess. Regardless of how we go about that, it's likely to cause varying amounts of pain and suffering for all involved."

"Right, let's dive into it. There's nothing like encountering bad news early in the day. It allows the rest of the day to deal with it however you choose, so it's under control and you don't carry it forward into the next day."

We marched into the dining room. "How do you want to do this, and where do we start?" Kate asked.

"Let's leave the other bits and pieces to one side while we look at the documents. I'm curious about why those documents were so special they were kept secret and hidden until the end." We made a start on the stacks of flattened out paper we created last night. At first I was confused about what they were. The first few pages constituted three separate documents, which appeared to be of no consequence at all. After delving down deeper, I realised their significance.

While Kate did her best to help me, even recording what each of the documents we looked at was about. I knew this was something I should be doing on my own. To comprehend and come to terms with everything in them, I needed to read every page for myself. It was obvious from the outset, even if I did it myself, there was a fair chance I still wouldn't understand Tremayne's other life.

It took until lunchtime to complete an initial examination of the papers. I still had to go through those documents Kate had dealt with. Having resisted the temptation to look at the other material rolled up with the documents, that material would be our priority straight after lunch.

As we sat down for lunch, Kate asked, "How are you holding up? If you want to talk, I'm here for you. But, I'm fine with it if you would rather eat in silence."

"Truth is, I don't know what I feel at the moment, apart from confused. It has been like reading the story of a different life, of a different person from anyone I know. How could I have been so blind – so unaware – not to see what was going on, to not know something was not right?"

"Don't beat yourself up. It seems Tremayne – or whatever his name was – held a black belt in creating false identities. I'm concerned what we've found so far might be the tip of the iceberg. Before this morning, we believed the man guilty of leading two separate lives with two different wives. Now, I have a suspicion there might be other lives we are yet to discover."

"Are you suggesting there are more wives hidden in that pile of paper?"

"No-o-o; I'm suggesting it might be a possibility. Some of the documents I looked at don't seem related to either you or Roslyn Williams, but they are associated with a household somewhere ... somewhere we don't know about yet. Did the papers you looked at create similar impressions?"

"I can't say they did. Maybe I didn't sense anything along those lines because I wasn't *reading* them. I only checked what they were about. I didn't look at the *who, where,* or *why* referred to in the contents. All I did was check the subject matter of each document. Perhaps my built-in self-preservation set up a barrier to prevent me fully comprehending in the first instance what I looked at, and it's possible it might make me return to the documents several times. That way, I'd absorb their details in slow, small doses, rather than have it hit me as one massive shock."

"Okay; you make up your own mind about that. Do we carry on with the documents, or look at those other bits and pieces next?"

"Perhaps we should look at those other items. They might contain information to help us better understand some of the documents. Hand me that big envelope please. Let's have a look at its contents first." Kate gave the envelope a sound massaging before handing it to me.

"It feels like it contains small notebooks, probably the pocket notebooks all journalists tend to carry when they are on a job. They might provide an insight into the stories Tremayne worked on." I undid the flap and up-ended the envelope. Its contents fell out onto the table.

"What the…?" I gasped, before a cold wave of nausea engulfed me. My legs turned to jelly and wouldn't support me. I flopped down on the nearest chair and sat there staring at the envelope's contents splayed out on the table.

"Lisa…," Kate shrieked as my performance unfolded. "What is it?" Suddenly, I was aware Kate no longer was on the opposite side of the table. She was beside me, her arms wrapped tightly around my shoulders. "They … are … passports, not notebooks. Why did he need so many? Look, this one is a British passport. Was he British?"

"Will you be all right while I fetch you a glass of water?"

Still numb with shock, all I could do was nod. I couldn't drag my eyes away from what was on the table. After a couple of gulps of water, the power of speech returned. "We should… No… I should check these before jumping to conclusions about them. Here, Kate, please check if these two are still current." She checked a British and an Australian passport, while I checked the other two Australian passports.

When I looked up at her, she looked devastated. She nodded, and swallowed hard before saying "Sorry, Lisa; they both still are current."

"…And so are these two."

"Perhaps they are not all Tremayne's."

"Chance would be a fine thing. Okay, let's see who they supposedly belong to." I caught the sound of Kate's sharp intake of breath.

"Uhmm … this older-looking Australian one belongs to Trevor Maybanks Cross. That's not someone we haven't heard of before. What names are on the ones you have?"

"Perhaps I should be thankful for anything familiar." With my thumb holding it open at the picture and identity details page, I waved one at Kate. "This one belongs to none other than Tremayne Bancroft." I waved the one in my other hand at her. "But, this one belongs to someone called Travis Cridland. Pray tell, to whom does that British one belong?"

"No surprises; it *doesn't* belong to anyone called Tremayne. This one belongs to someone named Telford Maybanks Cresswell."

"God, where did that name come from? To summarise, we have four passports, all issued under different names. We were familiar with two of those names. Now, I'm almost not game to speculate on what the other two might mean."

"Is it possible Cresswell is Tremayne's real name? I never took him for a Pom, but I suppose he might have been here since he was a child and hadn't retained any of his original accent."

"Don't ask me. I don't know any of these people, and that also includes Tremayne. I can't believe I was married to the man for more than twelve years and had no clue about any of this. The question now is whether there is another wife somewhere."

"Lisa, while you go through the other bits and pieces, I'll examine the passports and make a list of where they've been in recent times I don't know if it will be useful, but it might help us develop more specific questions."

"It occurs to me, we probably owe Inspector Taylor a call. I'm sure the good Miss Williams has given him an earful regarding her last visit here. Kate, I have to admit I'm surprised he hasn't contacted us about it. Regardless, we have to share with him whatever we find out from all this stuff."

"Yeah, we do, and that might not be a bad thing. He might be our best bet of getting to the bottom of some of this stuff by asking questions of people in places where we can't."

I spent about half an hour looking at the other material. It told me nothing, but I could see how it might be useful if we knew more of Tremayne's activities. Some of the material related to Southeast Asia, possibly Thailand. It was enough to whet my curiosity. Might we be on the scent of at least one strand of this mystery? "Kate how are you going with listing the places recorded in those passports?"

"If I'm honest, I don't know what to make of it. Our man was a busy lad. All four passports have seen considerable use since they were issued, including right up to recent times.

Part of me thinks he might have been working as a journo, or perhaps some sort of operative for one of the agencies. Many of the entries could be attributed to such work. If he were working as an operative for one of the security agencies, it would help explain the different names involved."

"That doesn't explain his bigamous marriage to me… Or was I just part of his cover for whatever the work he was doing? Was he working at all? I paid money into his bank account every week, a percentage of the wage the farm paid me. It cost him nothing to live here; not even vehicle expenses. Yet, he never had any cash to spare. Every penny I gave him every month was gone by the next payment."

"Now that you've mentioned it, I wondered about his financial situation. I knew you were paying him, and wondered whether Miss Williams might be supporting him as well. According to the Internet, she is one well-heeled lady. Williams Enterprises is a major operation, and daddy is a multimillionaire. Roslyn Williams is his only child and heir. She is managing director of their Sydney operations, and is second in command of her father's total empire. Her wealth is estimated in the millionaire class. All that had me wondering about the financial arrangements in their marriage. If she were supporting him financially, where was the money going? You just said he spent everything you gave him. So, what would he do with any additional cash handouts?"

"We are supposed to be looking for answers not finding more questions … such as, does Travis Cridland have a wife hidden away somewhere as well?"

"… And are there offspring running around somewhere?" Kate quipped.

"That too … And, to add to my frustration, I don't know how to find out about any of those things."

"As I said earlier, this might be an instance where Inspector Taylor could prove useful. He might be able to ask questions of the right people to find out."

"Ye-es, and he could go back to his contacts in the world of spooks to ask about the other names we've encountered. They might never have heard of Tremayne Bancroft, but one or more of the other names might be familiar."

"Should I call him…?"

"No. We're not going to contact him until tomorrow morning or maybe later this evening, when it's safe to assume he won't jump in his car to come out here straightaway. We would do better to get our heads around all of this material before perhaps wasting Taylor's time on a wild goose chase."

"Right, so what do we do next?"

"We finish examining the other material from the bundle of rags. After that we can go back to scrutinising the documents. Perhaps what we learn from the odds and sods might help us better understand what the documents are about."

Another standard sized envelope remained amongst the 'odds and sods'. I picked it up. It wasn't big, but it was thick and heavy. I gestured to Kate with it. "Let's see what surprises we can shake out of this one."

My first half-hearted attempt to shake out the contents was a failure. The envelope was tightly packed. It took a few more determined shakes before the contents tumbled out onto the table. I looked down at the resultant heap in front of me and gasped. Kate's reaction was more vocal.

"Oh … photographs… Now, they could be interesting. They might tell us what he was up to, or even where they were taken. Did Tremayne have a camera he took with him whenever he went away?"

"He had several cameras. Well, more than one anyway. If he took one away with him on his trips, I imagine he took the small one he had."

"Let's clear a space so we can spread the photos out for a good look at them," Kate said as she started shoving things out of the way. "You might be able to identify some of what's in them."

The photos could have been snapshots from anyone's overseas holiday. They showed ordinary people doing ordinary things: walking along the street, buying food at a market, men launching a fishing boat. The interesting thing was those ordinary people were doing ordinary things in a foreign country.

It looked as though they were taken somewhere in Southeast Asia. The buildings and style of clothes worn by those captured in the images were the only clues to location but, the longer I looked at them, the more convinced I was of it's being a Southeast Asian location. And, there were quite a lot of photos of people.

People smiling for the camera… People posing for happy snaps… Again, a close look at the faces involved suggested Asian. That little voice in my head was trying to make itself heard, trying to ask a question. A question I didn't want to hear. A question I didn't want to have to answer. It persisted, and could only be held at bay for so long. When it broke through, it posed the question loud and strong: who are all these people, and why are so many of that one woman? Kate's mind must have been running along the same track.

"A lot are photos of women; quite a few of children too. Hmm… Do a lot them look as though they are of the same woman? Some are clearer than others but, these over here, are quite sharp. The woman's face is quite clear in them. She is an attractive looking lady whoever she is. Do any of the photos mean anything to you? Ring any bells?"

"Not a thing; it's a part of the world I've never visited. On face value, I might accept them as shots Tremayne took on one or more of his overseas assignments."

"And … if you don't take them on face value, but think about them in the light of what we've discovered amongst all this stuff today, what's your opinion?"

"I don't want to go there, Kate. The ones we're talking about now are of people close to the photographer. Dare I suggest they are of intimate moments shared between the subject and the photographer? It is possible to sense a close relationship – an intimacy of sorts – between the people involved."

"Yeah, I agree, but we need to remember we don't know who took these photos. There is nothing to suggest Tremayne was the photographer. If he were working as a spook, the shots might be of a contact or of the target. I've looked at the backs of some of them. There is nothing written on any of them. I suppose it's too much to hope to find something written on some of those more personal ones."

"Sorry, Kate, there's nothing on any of these either. If he took them while working as a spook, I expect he wouldn't write anything on them, especially anything that helped identify the people."

"While I don't want to add to your pain and suffering, you should have a look at the photos of the kids. See, these three kids feature time and time again. Now, look at this one over here. It's that same woman we looked at before. In this one, she is holding up a baby to be photographed. You mentioned the word 'intimate'. Perhaps there is more 'intimacy' involved in these shots than either of us want to acknowledge."

"Are you suggesting the children – that baby – are Tremayne's?"

"No, I didn't say they were his. I think the children have something to do with the photographer; a close relationship perhaps. But, we don't know the identity of the photographer, and have no reason to assume it was Tremayne."

"Okay, I hear what you're saying, Kate. But I know we both are thinking the photographer was Tremayne, and those children were special to him in some way. It would have been real handy if the photographer had asked a passer-by to take a snap of him and the woman together. The fact that there isn't such a photo just adds more fuel to our suspicions, and I'm not sure that's a good thing."

"Agreed; so let's move on to the other objects. Maybe we can come back to the documents after dinner. What you think?"

I eyed off the remaining bits and pieces. "Perhaps we should go with the flow rather than trying to make plans. Look how long it took us to examine just these two items. Who knows what we might find amongst what's left?" On opposite sides of the table, we both stood, hands on hips, looking down on the jumble of objects still to be examined.

"That's a cute little velvet pouch," Kate said, pointing to a royal blue velvet pouch with a fancy gold clasp on the flap. "If it had a strap of some sort, I'd say it was a ladies evening bag. Whatever is in it fills it up completely. But, even if it were empty, it's a pretty thing in its own right."

"It does look more like it belongs to a woman, rather than something Tremayne would own." I picked it up and popped the clip holding the flap closed. "It's quite heavy, and the thing in it feels hard." I eased out the contents. Both of us caught our breath as a shiny object slid out of the velvet pouch and into my hand. I gently laid it on the table. We both stared at it for a moment before Kate spoke.

"Well, maybe not a woman's after all, but it's beautiful enough to belong to one."

"…And I thought my husband had grown out of his teenager obsession with carrying a hip flask to make him look like a big man amongst his peers."

"Do I detect a hint of something in that comment? I remember back to when he first came on the scene, he always had a hip flask. I never found out what he had in it, but I saw him swigging on it often enough at various functions."

"Yes, and we had words about it on numerous occasions. I haven't seen it for a while. Looks like I had a win. It seems he stopped carrying it and relegated it to his collection of memorabilia."

"Lisa, take a close look at it. It's not the hip flask I remember. That one was old and had been subjected to a hard life somewhere along the way. This one looks hardly used. It's shiny and not marred in any way; almost new. A-n-d, that's not the same monogram as was on Tremayne's hip flask. The design is different, not as elaborate and 'olde worlde' as the one I remember."

"I see what you mean. The initials definitely are T C, and the monogram is minus all the twirls, curlicues and decorative embellishments that almost obscured the initials on the one I knew about. Do we assume that, because the initials are not correct, it belongs to someone other than Tremayne?"

"It seems to be a special object amongst his belongings. You could put it down to coincidence. While the initials don't align with the name Tremayne Bancroft, they do fit with Trevor Cross. It's a bit of a stretch, but it is difficult to accept them as coincidence."

"I'm not sure I even want to say this... Is it possible we are now looking for yet another persona whose name has the initials T C?"

"It might have been a gift from Roslyn Williams to her husband, but somehow I'm not comfortable with that explanation. Let's have a look through what's left in this pile before we take a break for dinner," Kate suggested.

Twenty minutes later, we finished going through the pile of bits and bobs that fell out of the bundle of papers, and adjourned to dinner. We remained no wiser about any of it. Nor were we sure who owned any, or all, of the stuff on the dining room table.

Chapter 13

Once we had eaten, I returned to the mess on the dining room table. Should I make a start on scrutinising each document for anything linking it to the other objects? If I started now, it was a fair bet I wouldn't be able to stop until I'd gone through every sheet of paper. There was a lot of paper. Kate noticed my hesitation and queried it.

"I don't want it to be a rushed job. It has to be done properly and thoroughly. The amount of paper here is likely to take me all night. Maybe it would be best to leave it until tomorrow to make a start."

"If you go with that idea, curiosity will gnaw at you all night. You wouldn't get any sleep anyway. Each pile is a particular type of document. Select one pile of paper – any pile – and work on just those documents tonight."

Why is she always right, and able to see things more clearly than I? "Good thinking; I'll try it your way." I closed my eyes, bent over the table, reached down and grabbed one of the stacks of paper. Disappointment hit when I glanced at what I selected. I was about to choose a different one when Kate chastised me.

"No you don't. We won't mention the method employed, but that's the stack you chose. Now, get on with it. What's wrong with it anyway?"

"It looks like ordinary utilities accounts or something similar. I didn't want to waste tonight on anything that wouldn't help solve the mysteries we've uncovered. You're right though. After today, I'm not at my sparkling best. It probably is wise to deal with some of the rubbish, and leave the important stuff until tomorrow when I'm fresh and a bit brighter."

Having finished in the kitchen, a few minutes later, Kate came and sat beside me. "As you finish each document, hand it to me to read too. As I do, I'll put them into separate sub-piles so it's easier to return to specific information later if we need to."

Over the next half hour, conversation was non-existent as I read each sheet of paper, scribbled relevant notes, and then passed it to Kate. After the first couple of documents, I announced, "This is boring – and a waste of time. I don't need to know any of this stuff. It's not telling me anything I want to know."

"Stop whining. It might not tell you what you *want* to know but, if you are patient and careful, it might tell you what *you need* to know."

Although sulking a bit after being chastised yet again, I did as I was told. While they didn't answer my questions, the documents made fascinating reading … and created more unanswered questions. With the last letter of the stack handed to Kate, I reached for another stack.

She slapped my hand away. "No… the agreement was to do only one pile tonight. It's now eleven o'clock, and we have finished that one stack. That's it. Now it's bedtime."

"Jesus, when did the Nazis recruit you? It won't hurt to do a few more."

"You said you weren't too bright tonight. Why risk overlooking some important clue by pushing on when you are too tired to see things clearly? Why work on, and risk being just as thick-headed tomorrow as you are now? Go to bed."

*****

Last night, my mind was processing information at a thousand kilometres per hour. While feeling a bit mentally exhausted, I expected to spend hours trying to fall asleep. Instead, sleep arrived minutes after I turned off the light. A restful night followed. Today's clear, bright morning brought the return of that heaving mass in my stomach.

There is something about early mornings out on the deck. In spite of the chatter of the birds in the trees and the rustle of the breeze through the cane, there is a quietness. A peacefulness that is almost serene. Neither of us spoke, content instead to just sit and soak up the ambience for a few minutes.

Kate seemed deep in thought; troubled even. In spite of not wanting to deal with anything too heavy so early, I felt compelled to ask. She looked up, a furrowed brow above her troubled eyes. "Do we think all those people – all those personas – we've discovered are one and the same person?"

"I'm trying not to."

"But, Lisa, the possibility of them all being Tremayne is beyond comprehension. Is there no alternative explanation?"

"Not unless you have one."

"I know I never made any secret the fact I didn't like Tremayne, and didn't think he was good enough for you, but this exceeds everything I thought and felt about the man. How do you explain such behaviour?"

"Before I answer that, there are a couple of other aspects to consider. We keep referring to him as 'my Tremayne'. That's fair enough for discussion purposes, but perhaps we shouldn't be calling him 'my' anything, when the bloke we're talking about appears to be Roslyn Williams' husband, Trevor Maybanks Cross."

"What…?"

"I'm suggesting we should be referring to him by his right name. If he were married to Miss Williams for twenty years, that gives her first dibs on the man. And, by virtue of their long marriage and no divorce, she rightly believed she still owned him at the time of his death."

"Okay, I hear you, but I don't agree. Stop and think about it. What gives Roslyn Williams the right to claim ownership? That sounds terrible, but it's what we're talking about. We know the man you married was capable of bigamy. What if his marriage to Roslyn Williams also was bigamous? What if one of those other names we found for him was married to someone else before he married Miss Williams? Can you see what I'm suggesting? We have no clear timeline for when this person existed, including when, and if, he married anyone."

"Yes, I accept there might have been marriages before the one to Roslyn Williams. I'm not arguing with that. My problem is how to establish whether there were previous marriages, or if the Williams one was the first. The first legal one, I mean."

"That's something we can think about after we determine if all those names belong to the same bloke. Lisa, I have to admit, a bloke marrying multiple women without the benefit of divorce anywhere along the line just doesn't compute for me."

"There is no denying it's difficult to comprehend."

"I suppose my real question is: why did he bother marrying you? Don't be offended. If being with you was what he wanted, why didn't he just live with you? Yeah, I know, you probably would have said no. If the bloke also married other women, were those women also of such high moral standards they wouldn't consider just shacking up, and would only settle for marriage?"

"All you have done this morning is pose another question to gnaw at me. For this discussion, let's assume each of those names did marry a woman somewhere. How long has each of them been married? So far, we only know how long two of those names were married: Trevor for twenty years to Roslyn, and Tremayne for twelve years to me. As I suggested, perhaps Roslyn wasn't the first wife and her marriage is no more legitimate than mine. Regardless, how often did each of those wives have contact with their respective husbands: frequently, occasionally, sporadically, or not at all? And, if there were contact, what was the nature of it? Was it by phone, email, letter, postcard, or in person?"

"Oh, I see. It's all right when you dredge up difficult questions. I assume you don't have any real answers to the questions you've just posed."

"Of course not; if I knew the answers, there wouldn't be any questions. Kate, I admit to being a bit overwhelmed by the complexity and impossibility associated with trying to make sense of this mess. I don't even have any bright ideas about where to start today."

"None required. We are returning to that mess on the dining room table to continue examining every document in those stacks of paper. Judging by past performance though, by the end of today, there is a strong likelihood we will have an even greater pile of questions … And, quite likely, no more answers than we have now. …Are we expecting visitors?"

"Visitors…? No. Oh God, please don't let it be Miss Williams again. Would you mind going to see who it is please?"

Kate clattered down the stairs and, soon after, I heard people coming back up. She bounced into the kitchen. "We do have a visitor, and he would love a cup of coffee – and I could go another one. If you take the visitor out onto the deck and talk to him, I'll talk to the coffee machine." Connor stepped out from behind a partial wall and waved at me.

"Connor, you heard the lady. I am to take you out onto the deck and entertain you while she makes coffee. What brings you here at this hour of the morning? If you've come to tell me about some new disaster, you're welcome to leave now. I assure you I don't need to know, regardless of what it is."

We made ourselves comfortable on the deck, and a few minutes later Kate arrived with the coffees. "I was joking before, Connor. Is this a social visit, or are you the bearer of bad news?"

"Neither of those, I came out of concern."

"Concern…? Concern about what…? What has happened?"

"You weren't at the cattle sales yesterday. You don't go to every one, but you do attend when you have stock in the sale. Is everything okay here on the property; okay with you?"

"Oh hell, I forgot about the sales. Don't look like that. There's nothing to worry about. I have a bit happening on the personal front, and it's grabbing all of my attention at the moment. Thanks for your concern. Now, tell me how the sales went."

"Geez, Lisa, we never even mentioned the sales. Did we miss out on a good day, Connor?" Kate asked

"Yeah, I reckon you did. There were more buyers than we've seen in a long time. The recent widespread rain and the

Bureau's positive outlook for the remainder of the year, created an interest in restocking after the drought. Most of the pens were sold and prices were good; very good. All of yours sold quickly. There should be a nice payment into your account in the next few days."

"Yay…; that's the first bit of good news for the week," Kate said, throwing her arms in the air in mock excitement.

Connor's eyes flicked between Kate and me a couple of times. "Ladies, if I've come at a bad time, I'll finished my coffee and be on my way. Apologies for intruding in what must be a difficult time for you, Lisa. I thought about your situation last night. Maybe a break away from the place, even just for a few days, might be a good thing. I'd keep an eye on everything here while you're gone. See if you can talk her into it, Kate."

"Thanks, Connor. I know you would look after the place if I needed you to, but I don't. I'm not going anywhere. Don't argue. I'm not going anywhere because I don't need to get away. I am fine. If I wasn't, there's plenty to do on the farm to keep my mind off other things."

"Do you need your mind kept off other things?" I shook my head but, before I could answer, he continued. "What other things? Don't tell me there aren't any. You two have faces screaming at me that something is going on here. I thought we were friends; good friends who can rely on each other. I know you are troubled so please, Lisa, tell me what it is. You know I will help if I can, and won't interfere if you don't want me to."

"There is nothing…"

Kate blurted out, "There's plenty going on here," and then continued quietly. "The problem is we don't know what is going on … Sorry… *that's been going on. Please note: that's past tense. What exacerbates the problem i*s only just finding out about it." Kate shot me a quick unfathomable look before returning to Connor. "Lisa's husband turns out not to have been Lisa's husband at all – not legally anyway."

"Ok-ay, I'll admit I'm not the sharpest cheese on the cracker, but … what … does … that … mean? Please take my lack of intelligence into consideration, and spell it out to me in words of no more than one syllable."

"That's it. There is no other way to say it. It appears Tremayne's marriage to Lisa was not legal. Apart from that, we now are trying to work out who the hell was the man who claimed to be Tremayne Bancroft. So far, there are only questions and no answers."

"I went to their wedding. I know they were married. What do you mean by 'it wasn't legal'? Does it mean he wasn't free to marry Lisa at the time?" Kate shrugged and nodded.

"Looks that way… His *other* wife is pretty sure the man we cremated was still married to her."

"Without a divorce somewhere in between…?"

"Not that we, or the other wife, are aware of and, before you ask, no, Lisa didn't ask him if he was divorced because she didn't know he was married."

"Doesn't that make it bigamy?" Kate and I nodded in unison.

"What man forgets to divorce his wife before marrying someone else?"

"Tremayne Bancroft does… or so it appears," Kate said.

"It was a rhetorical question. I wasn't expecting an answer. Am I permitted to know the whole story, especially how you discovered his complicated life?"

My turn to shrug before I responded. "Go ahead, Kate. You know the story and probably have your head on straighter than I do. You tell him."

She sucked in a long breath before beginning the story at the point of Miss Williams' first visit. Ever the journalist, Kate managed to incorporate all the information to date into a short, succinct presentation. "You'll appreciate how frustrating it is having found those other names and not being able to find out anything about the people they belong to." Having finished the story, she turned and raised eyebrows at me in question. "Did I miss anything? Anything you want to add?" I shook my head.

"I can't say I've taken it all in yet, and I admit to being a bit shell-shocked. What happens next? More importantly, what can I do to help?" Connor asked.

"Thanks, but there isn't anything you can do. I'm not sure what we can do. You're helping by running this place. Kate, we have the rest of those documents to look at today but, beyond that, I think your schedule is empty. Have you thought of any resources worth exploring, or had any ideas about what to do next?"

"There is something we were going to do first thing this morning." Kate's look suggested I should know what she was hinting at, but a search of my memory banks produced nothing. "We were going to share what we discovered with Inspector Taylor."

"Ah yes, but maybe we should leave that until later today. I want to finish all that stuff on the table first and have my head around it a bit better before we talk to Taylor about it."

"Well, it's your life, so it's up to you how and when we proceed. But, I would suggest not leaving it too long before you contact the inspector. We don't want him getting off side with us, do we?"

"Inspector Taylor's job is to investigate Tremayne's murder. There might not be anything in the stuff we found to help with his investigation. When we understand things better, and there are clues in what we've discovered, we will inform the inspector." The look Kate and Connor exchanged didn't go unnoticed. I chose to ignore it. "I could go another coffee. Anyone interested in a refill?" I pushed my chair back ready to stand up. Kate sprang up and grabbed the mugs.

"I'll make it. You stay and talk farming with Connor, or whatever it is you agricultural types talk about."

"Thanks, Kate," Connor said. "I do want to have a few words with Lisa." I felt a twinge.

Was there something ominous in Connor's words? Was this his opportunity to speak to me alone? And, was it something he and Kate engineered between them? God, I'm in danger of becoming paranoid about everything and everyone. I flashed Connor a wide smile as an invitation to get on with whatever he wanted to talk about. He did.

"Lisa, I run the risk of being way out of line, but I am concerned about you. Don't interrupt. Hear me out. You say you are fine. To anyone who didn't know about recent events here, you would appear to be okay. But, your behaviour says you are not. You haven't taken time to grieve; to come to terms with what happened. There's been no sign of grief, or loss, or anything else in response to your husband's death. Maybe, if you get away from the farm for a few days, reality might sink in. At some point in time, it has to happen. The longer you hold it at bay, the harder it will be when it hits you. Please think about what I'm saying. I'm not trying to interfere, just concerned for your well-being."

"Dear Connor, thank you for your concern. I know what you're talking about but, truth is, I don't feel any grief or loss, not really. The emotion is not there. Don't worry. I know Tremayne is dead. I arranged his cremation. My explanation won't make sense but, in spite of everything I know, it doesn't feel like he is dead. It's just like all those other times he was away, off on one of his jaunts to wherever.

When he went away, I never knew how long he'd be gone. Where he went and when he might return were things only Tremayne knew. That's just how this feels. Maybe, if he doesn't return after some extended period, the reality will hit me. Given all we've discovered over the last day or so, perhaps reality will be a cause for celebration. Perhaps uncovering the truth about the man – and our marriage – will make me happy I've escaped from an ugly situation. And, it's beginning to appear the same might be true for several other women as well."

"I'm trying to believe you, but convincing me will be difficult. There is one thing I can promise you, I will be keeping an eye on you. I don't know how long Kate will be staying here, but know this, when she leaves, I will still be here. You will not be alone. All the support you might need is right next door."

Kate's return with our fresh coffees brought a welcome end to Connor's heavy conversation about my well-being. "Did I miss anything I should know about?"

"No," Connor and I chorused in unison.

"Good; then, are we going to start work on that stuff on the dining room table sometime today? And, when are you going to call Inspector Taylor?"

"I'll go as soon as I finish my coffee. It's my fault you're not getting on with anything today. I didn't intend staying so long," Connor said

"No you won't," Kate retorted. I've made you two cups of coffee this morning. The least you can do is stay and pay me back. There's plenty of work to do in the dining room, so don't go thinking you're going to slope off and leave us with the lot to do ourselves."

"I'd be happy to help, but I won't be much use. I wouldn't know what to look for. All I know is what you've told me." Kate's demand had wrong-footed Connor.

"That won't be a problem. You won't be helping look for anything. You will be filing – in accordance with instructions I give you – the truckload of paper in there."

Should I interfere? Did we really need Connor's assistance? The answer to both of those was 'no'. But, the other two were enjoying their sparring match, and it had lightened the atmosphere around here no end.

"Right then you two, drain your mugs and let's get started. As Kate reminded me, sometime today, I need to call Inspector Taylor. Before I speak to him, I want to know everything there is to know from that stuff on the table."

Chapter 14

"Inspector Taylor… Sorry … *Dan,* I was about to ask you to call in when you had some spare time, before I realised how ridiculous that was. 'Spare time' probably is a foreign concept in your job. At the risk of interrupting your current investigation, we found material which might be of interest to you, but it might take you a while to look through all of it.

"I would like to see it today, but it would have to be late. If you think six o'clock is too late, perhaps we should leave it until first thing tomorrow morning, say, about eight o'clock."

Tomorrow morning suited me fine. It gave us time to get our heads around everything, and that was no short order. Apart from a quick break for lunch, we slogged through until three o'clock for a coffee break. Connor left then to catch up on his own work. By five o'clock, we had been through everything. On opposite sides of the table, Kate and I sat in stunned silence. I didn't know what Kate's thoughts were at the start of the day, but mine were quite clear.

My firm opinion was there could be little more to gain from the remaining documents. How wrong could I be? Maybe what we learned today shouldn't have made such an impact. In reality, it was just more of the same. More of Tremayne's life uncovered. Just confirmation of matters about which there might have been only vague suspicions yesterday. I wanted the little voice in my head to stop screaming: *How much more is there to find? How many more women were there? Don't stop now. Only the whole truth will do.*

The little voice's urging was unnecessary. I couldn't stop – wouldn't stop. I had to keep digging into the lie that was my life for more than twelve years; to keep peeling back the lies and subterfuge layer by layer. Perhaps there were names yet to be discovered – and more wives to go with them. Were there children? Those photos of the smiling Asian children gnawed at me. Tremayne wouldn't have those photos if he wasn't closely connected to the people in them. They appear to have the same level of importance as his many passports. Kate's voice cut through the tumultuous activity in my head.

"Lisa… Lisa, are you all right?"

"Of course I am; just deep in thought, that's all. Did you ask me something?"

"Are we agreed the Asian looking woman and children are associated with Travis Cridland?" I thought the answer was obvious, so I just nodded my agreement. "Okay, do we assume they were 'married' and she was yet another 'wife'?"

"Why would she be an exception? Argh, I'm sorry. I don't know. But, I suppose it might be safe to assume that to be the case."

"One last question, hopefully to clear away more fog from my mind: are we assuming Travis Cridland is the same man as Tremayne Bancroft?"

"Feel free to form your own opinion, but I don't harbour any doubts they were one and the same."

"I'm still struggling to take it all in."

"I empathise with that, but I am confident when we unravel everything there is to know about Tremayne Bancroft's life, all of those names we discovered will lead back to one solitary individual … whose name will probably turn out to be something like Fred Smith."

It was time to make a start on dinner, but we decided there were plenty of leftovers in the fridge and we could probably round up a meal out of those. I wasn't hungry; more interested in sitting on the deck with a drink. Trouble is, once I make myself comfortable out there, I might stay put for quite a while.

Without bothering to turn on the deck lights, we sat in silence with our long, cold drinks. The darkness' restorative quality was somehow calming. When we came out onto the deck, I knew I was tired, mentally rather than physically. I wasn't aware of being tense. After a minute or so on the cool, dark deck, I felt myself relax; feeling what could only be tension dropping away from me.

An involuntary sigh of pleasure escaped, and brought Kate up onto the edge of her chair. "Are you all right?"

"I'm fine; I realised everything we've discovered is irrelevant… No, not irrelevant… unimportant."

"What does that mean? How can your not knowing what was going on in your marriage – in Tremayne's 'other' life – be unimportant? And what happens now?"

"We keep going; keep digging until we know all there is to know. What makes it unimportant is more difficult to explain. I finally realised Tremayne is gone, and this time he won't be coming back. Having accepted that, the question is: how does that affect my life? …And, that's when the BIG revelation hit me. *It doesn't."*

"I don't believe that. Of course it will affect you and your life. Perhaps you haven't really accepted the situation; not deep down. Maybe a part of you still expects him to return one day as he always did in the past. Lisa, he is not coming back; not ever … Never again. That might be hard for you to believe, but you have to start accepting the truth."

"His permanent departure is unimportant. It took me a while to realise that, and to accept it. The way our marriage was for most of its twelve years, the time we spent together doesn't amount to much. Since we moved to live on the farm, we weren't particularly close. I don't mean we fought, or that things were unpleasant between us. We were living two separate lives, while sharing a house for short periods of time on odd occasions. The important thing is, I realised I didn't have feelings for him anymore. He contributed nothing to my life, or to this property. If I'm brutal about it, life now is easier somehow. I doubt I can explain what that means."

"Were you unhappy in the marriage? You don't suffer fools lightly, and are more inclined to take action rather than put up with conditions that don't suit you. But, you stayed married for more than twelve years. Was it so terrible that it's a relief now it's over?"

"No, I wouldn't describe it as terrible. It's more like there was nothing. There was nothing unpleasant about it, I was not unhappy … but I wasn't deliriously happy either. We weren't close. I would have to think long and hard to come up with happy memories of enjoyable times spent together. They just didn't happen. We weren't like that."

"Okay, I don't understand what you're telling me, and I'm not sure what you're saying is a true reflection of your feelings. If that is how things are for you, how do you go forward? What will your life be like from here on?"

"Only time will tell. I'm sure my life will be uncomplicated. Goodness, where did I dredge up that word? I never considered my life was complicated. There were times when I was aware of walking a fine line when it came to choosing between meeting the needs of my parents, or those of my husband. Once my parents were gone and I was responsible for the whole operation of the property, I knew it would be difficult to set aside time for just my husband. In fact, since then, his absences have been a blessing. My time has been my own, and that's how it will be from now on."

"Does that mean you've shut the door on any possible future romantic involvement? You're still a young woman, and I don't think a lonely old age is something to anticipate."

"Look at who is talking. I don't see too many romantic entanglements in your life at the moment, or in recent years for that matter. If the prospect of a lonely old age bothers you, you can come and live here and we can be two lonely old maids together."

"I don't know how I'm going to choose between the two options."

Kate's phone's tune saved me. She took a quick look at the caller ID before announcing she needed to take the call inside. I heard her clatter along the hallway to her room. For a moment, I wondered whether I was wrong. Perhaps there was a 'romantic entanglement' in her life after all. It was a long call.

Embroiled in my own thoughts, I lost track of time, but I think Kate was gone for at least forty minutes. When she finally returned, it took her a long time to settle down again, and there seemed to be something tentative about her. Whatever her call was about, it doesn't seem to have done her much good. Oh hell, what if there is a romance in progress? The other party might not be too pleased about her spending so much time up here with me. She seems reluctant to discuss with me what's going on in her life. How do I tackle the question of how long she plans to stay without ruffling her feathers in the process?

My concerns were short lived. Kate solved the mysteries of the phone call and a possible romantic relationship in two seconds flat. "Lisa, I'm not sure how you're going to react to something I did. I've done it anyway, so I'll tell you about it. I contacted a friend of mine in Sydney to ask her to do some research for me. She is a journalist and an author, and has written a swag of profile pieces on various well-known people. I suppose what I'm saying is, she knows how to delve into people's lives."

"She sounds like just the person we need if we wanted to do some research on our own into all these wonderful names we discovered. I know we can't hand everything over to Inspector Taylor for help. My gut feeling is that we should be researching as much as possible ourselves, and at least all the names that we think belong to one and the same man."

"That's a relief. I asked Sandy to find out what she could about Roslyn Williams' marriage to Trevor Cross… and to check if they were still married. My call was from Sandy. Should I go through it with you now, or would you prefer to leave the details until later?"

"To avoid the onset of starvation and the demise of both of us, perhaps we should leave it until after we've eaten – without wasting too much time on dispatching the food."

The food dealt with, we took our wines across to the squatters chairs at the end of the deck and settled in. "Right, please share what Sandy told you earlier this evening."

"I asked her to dig into the life and times of Miss Roslyn Williams. She confirmed all the stuff we already know about the woman, before adding some new stuff. Although these days, Roslyn Williams has a veneer of upper-crust respectability, that wasn't always the case. It seems she caused her father a few anxious years during her transition period from teenager to young adult. I'm not sure how daddy regarded her marriage to Trevor Cross, but it might have come as something of a relief. Prior to her marriage, she was the classic indulged wild child with a reputation as a party girl who enjoyed the attention of a procession of lovers. About twelve months before she was married, Roslyn made an abrupt exit from the party scene and was missing for a few months. The story doing the rounds at the time was that she was overseas somewhere taking the grand tour of Europe. Those less generous suggested she was pregnant and hiding low somewhere until after the birth."

"Sounds like just the fodder the gossip tabloids thrive on. The question is: was it real or just fake news? I can see how her father might've been relieved when she decided to settle down, even if her husband wasn't quite the man her father would have chosen. Without any information other than what you've shared so far, it sounds like the marriage must've come close on the heels of her return from 'hibernation'."

"Sandy is friendly with someone who was a member of that swinging set at the time. She confirmed for Sandy that Roslyn was only back home for three or four months before the big wedding happened. Prior the wedding, none of the group Roslyn hung out with knew her chosen husband. After the happy couple returned from an extended overseas honeymoon, it appears Roslyn dumped her old group of friends and embarked on creating a new 'high-powered businesswoman' persona. Within their first year of marriage, the couple moved to Sydney where Roslyn took over running the New South Wales part of the business."

"It could be nothing more than a case of the wild child seeing the light and settling down to become a responsible adult. Still,

I do have some difficulty reconciling Sandy's information with the woman who came to collect her husband's belongings. Did Sandy have anything more to share with you?"

"There is a bit more. No children from the marriage have been registered in any of the Australian states, and she considered it safe to assume there was no issue from the marriage. I also asked her to check on the current status of the marriage, that is, whether the couple were still married. She found no evidence of divorce proceedings ever having been initiated."

"So, it seems she was well within her rights to claim, after some twenty years of marriage, he was still her husband. Nevertheless, I still have trouble comprehending how she did not know he was living up here, and had been for all those years. It's not surprising it took such a long line of Chinese whispers for her to find out he was dead."

"I agree but, Lisa, you are overlooking a critical factor. We don't know that it was her husband you cremated. There is no hard evidence on that, only her claim and our speculation. So far, nothing Sandy told me confirmed our suspicions that Trevor Cross and Tremayne Bancroft were one and the same person. All we have gained is an abbreviated profile of Roslyn Williams. I can't see how that helps, or progresses our investigation in any way."

"Good point. It only proves Roslyn Williams told us the truth. We still don't know if the man she married was the one I cremated. Sandy gave us interesting information and, who knows, it might prove useful at some stage. At this point, it hasn't helped one bit. Where do we go next?"

"Tomorrow morning, you're going to be talking to Inspector Taylor. Maybe we need to pin our hopes on his investigative abilities."

"Sandy's information has me wondering about something. Did she happen to mention what Trevor Cross did for a living, either before, or after he and Miss Williams were married?"

"No I don't... Hang on. I think there was something in passing. I'll get my notebook to see if I made a note of it."

By the time she returned, I had poured us long glasses of mineral water and turned on the lights so we could read whatever she had written. "Now, let's see… Yeah, this is where she mentioned it. One of Roslyn's friends from her wild days mentioned in passing that she thought the new husband was brought into the fold soon after the marriage. She figured he must've been made a buyer for the company, as he travelled about a fair bit, including overseas sometimes. That's it I'm afraid. It's not much I know, but it seems like he wasn't a homebody, even in those days."

"I'd be interested to know what his cover was with Roslyn. Whether he had her convinced he was working for some intelligence agency as well. Or, I suppose he could have been telling her he was a foreign correspondent. I'm curious about what he supposedly was doing before they married. Whether he ever was a journo of any sort, or if he was a conman all his life."

"Roslyn Williams reputedly is rolling in cash. Was she paying him a nice little allowance as well? If she wasn't 'keeping' him, how did he afford his trips away, and whatever else he was getting up to?"

"We are back to that game again: finding more questions than answers. By the way, do you have any other friends, colleagues, or associates, digging around for information? I don't mind, but it would be handy if I knew what was happening."

"Er, well… I did speak to a couple of people I know. I considered them long shots, but worth a try. I had more confidence in what Sandy might come up with than anything the others might dig up. The bottom line might be, don't hold your breath waiting for something more exciting to turn up."

With nothing more to be said on the topic, I felt inclined to be alone rather than engaging in conversation with Kate. Perhaps she sensed it. After a few moments of sitting in silence with our thoughts, she announced she was off for an early night. As soon as she left, I turned off the lights and returned my chair.

The cool night air, the smell of the bush, and the sounds of the night birds, all combined to create something of a stupefying effect. I don't know how long I sat there. While I wasn't aware of any conscious thought processes, my mind seemed to roam freely and with no particular intent. Something kept trying to come through; trying to grab my attention. I couldn't focus on it, couldn't will it to come through to me. It remained lurking deep in the shadows in the back of my mind.

Elevated frustration levels are not good bed mates. They make sleep reluctant to visit, and end up resulting in a restless night. My last conscious thought at some tiny hour of the morning was about Inspector Taylor's arrival in a few hours' time. If he didn't already think me a ditsy woman in the process of losing her marbles, my sleep deprived brain in the morning would convince him of it. ...And, even if I was reasonably articulate, how was anything I might say or show him going to help discover the 'who' and the 'why' of Tremayne's murder?

*****

Accompanying me to breakfast this morning were last night's doubts about the likely waste of time this morning's meeting with Inspector Taylor might be. I was a seething mass of doubt and indecision. I shared with Kate my concern about what might result from this morning's meeting, and my regrets about setting it up in the first place. "Look at what we're going to be showing him. If we don't know whether it means anything or not, how is it going to benefit his investigation? I suspect I'm going to end up looking a right fool for having wasted his time, and brought him all the way out here for nothing."

"Jesus, Lisa, where is this coming from? What happened after I went to bed? Did you find something new? I don't understand why you now doubt the value and/or relevance of any of the material we found. Surely the passports, and the different names involved, have some relevance to Taylor's investigation. Smarten yourself up, Girl. Let him decide whether anything we found is important.

Now, how do you want to play this visit? If he arrives at eight o'clock, he'll still be here for morning tea, and probably at lunchtime too. How about I prepare accordingly and we see what happens?"

With a couple of cups of strong black coffee in me, I managed to feel relatively human when the inspector arrived. We wasted little time on discussing the background to the material we discovered and were about to show him. I felt obliged to warn him that, perhaps, much of the material might not be of interest. He laughed. I didn't know whether to feel embarrassed or reassured.

After taking him through to the dining room, I suggested it might be best if we left him to go through the material on his own. He didn't agree, and felt he would benefit from what we had already learned from our scrutiny of the stuff. Kate, citing her need to be in the kitchen with the baking she had in the oven, abandoned me.

I figured my best approach was to sit quietly until he sought input from me. I drew up a chair on the opposite side of the table and tried not to fidget too much as he pored over one item after another. I was thankful I directed him to the passports as his first port of call. After we discussed those at some length, he seemed content to go through the rest of the material without reference to me.

Chapter 15

The aroma wafting from Kate's baking commanded my total attention and had me yearning for coffee and some of whatever it was. A bit after nine o'clock, Kate came and whispered, "What time should we have coffee… go ahead as usual, or wait until he's finished in here?"

Before I could answer, the inspector looked up and was surprised to see the two of us on the opposite side of the table. "Don't let me hold you up. Feel free to get on with whatever you need to do. I'm okay on my own, but it will take me a while to look at all this."

In a bid to be helpful, I suggested, "When you start on the documents in the stack of files, only the top two folders contain anything worthwhile. They contain much of the same, but with different dates."

He said, if he was going to do the job properly, he had to go through everything, but reiterated there was no need for us to hang around. I wasn't sure if we were being dismissed, or if he was being polite and didn't want to impose.

Kate's response sounded as though she believed it was the former. "Fine, we won't hang around to watch how coppers examine evidence. Morning tea is at ten o'clock. I doubt you will be finished before then. If you can tear yourself away, you're welcome to join us for coffee.

Taylor picked up on Kate's tone. He shot me a surprised look before giving her a wide smile. "I look forward to that … and some of your baking. It smells so divine, it makes it hard to concentrate on the job in hand."

When we gathered on the deck for coffee, the inspector reported he still had 'a lot to go through'. That didn't stop him lingering over morning tea and being an active participant in the conversation. If he complimented Kate on her brownies once, he repeated it at least another three times before he returned to the dining room. I dissolved into a fit of the giggles.

"What?" Kate demanded.

"I think you have an admirer – maybe even won a heart."

"Who? The inspector…? More like my brownies scored a fan. Someone should tell him the local bakery sells a fair range of cakes and slices."

In spite of all her noise about my suggestion, I detected something else in her demeanour. Perhaps it's another case of *me thinks the lady doth protest too much.*

"All that aside, Kate, it looks like we will be three for lunch. I'll leave you to worry about lunch while I do some work in the paddock. Come up with something nice, and you could score a load more compliments from the inspector." The rest of the conversation is best not repeated.

On my return from tending the cattle, the aroma that greeted me as I climbed the stairs reminded me how hungry I was. "That smells marvellous. What are we having, and what can I do to help?" I asked as I strode into the kitchen.

"Spicy chicken legs; I don't know if they have a proper name. You could finish making the salad."

"I see the inspector remains welded to his chair in the dining room."

"Yeah, I think he started on the last folder a few moments ago. Lunch is okay to wait a few minutes until he finishes in there." Preparations for lunch were completed at about the same time as the inspector laid aside the last folder. I poured him a long glass of soda water, slipped in a slice of lime, and took it into the dining room. "You probably are in need of rehydration after your morning's marathon in here. I thought you might appreciate something long and cold. Lunch is ready when you are. There's a bathroom through there if you want to freshen up first."

His praise for Kate's lunch was effusive and more than a little embarrassing for her. "Lisa made the salad," she blurted out.

"And very nice it was too. Thanks, Lisa … but those chicken legs … Wow!"

I was in danger of exploding, not with pride but from trying to contain my laughter. I think Kate has won a heart – or is well on the way to doing so. Knowing her eyes would show absolute shock – or alarm, I carefully avoided them. With a skilful segue away from Kate's lunch and onto the material in the dining room, I asked my first question by uncomfortably addressing the inspector by his given name.

"Dan, has this morning proved a waste of time for you. Was any of the stuff in there useful in any way? I didn't get much out of it, other than a lot more questions."

"Oh yeah, it was helpful; not a waste of time at all. While it isn't a direct help in solving you husband's murder, it does provide an insight into what I might be dealing with in terms of your husband and potential motives for his death. What it didn't give me were any clues about what he was up to in this country to warrant killing him. It also didn't give me any clue as to what he might have been up to overseas. But, I am inclined to think it has something to do with overseas rather than here."

"Could it have something to do with his life in Sydney?"

He dismissed the suggestion with a shake of his head.

"I did wonder whether there might be a Sydney connection. After all, why go to all the trouble creating this second life and a new name so far from Sydney, if life was sweet in the southern city? Mind you, when that question first occurred to me, all I knew about was his apparent comfortable life with his first wife. I didn't know about his other lives until I went through the material in the dining room."

"The question is understandable. I assure you, we will examine every aspect of any other lives he established under whatever name. It will take time though. I don't anticipate any miraculous breakthroughs any time soon."

Kate chipped in to help me out. "It would be helpful if we could find out more about those other names. We need to confirm whether they are the same person by any other name, or not. The only way I know to do that is via official channels, like births, deaths and marriages records. It's unfortunate everything is so recent. Nothing will show up on any accessible index."

While I hoped he would take Kate's bait, I gave him a bit more to think about. "Would it be worthwhile going back to your contacts to determine if any of those other names we uncovered had anything to do with any of the security agencies?" If a man made frequent trips to Southeast Asia, might he have been intelligence gathering?"

"Way ahead of you, Lisa; I'll be making calls as soon as I'm back in my office. I understand how upsetting this journey of discovery is for you, particularly coming on top of your husband's murder."

After a barrage of questions about what I knew about those other names, the documents, objects and photos, he announced it was time to head back to his office. I walked him to his car. He opened the door and then paused. "As much as I hate to say this, the man you married is something of an enigma. Until we understand who he really was, both of us will struggle to move forward. It's imperative to the well-being of both of us to find out all we can by whatever means available."

Later, as we stacked the lunchtime stuff in the dishwasher, Kate seemed preoccupied. I wondered whether Inspector Taylor had triggered a line of thinking. "Kate, you appear to be dealing with heavy thoughts. Is there something you would care to share? Did I miss a crucial point in our discussions with Inspector Taylor?"

"If only… I was hoping for some clues we might follow up. Now, I'm wondering what we can do next. We have little to work with, and precious few avenues open to explore for answers to our questions. I can't accept the thought we might have to sit on our hands until Inspector Taylor comes up with something useful."

"You gave air to what's swirling around in my mind at the moment. I don't have any answers, other than I need to stir Justin Farley along. I don't know what I expect him to do. As executor of Tremayne's estate, there must be something he can dig up. I'm also thinking about the bank. There was nothing bank related, not even statements, in those documents we found. On what and where did he spend his money? The other thing niggling me is his Southeast Asian connection. Travis Cridland's passport records frequent trips to Vietnam. The three hundred dollars per week I paid over the last few years wasn't enough to finance those trips. How did he afford them? Talking to the bank might get me nowhere, but it's worth a try."

"Hmm… 'Confidential information' is likely to be the bank's response. Justin Farley might have to initiate any such enquiries. But, you're right. Tremayne's apparent lifestyle does suggest mysterious means of support." I could see she had more to say, but held back. It's unlike Kate, and not in keeping with the way things are between us.

"What are you not saying, Kate? Do you think it might upset me? If it is, you should know better than to hold back. Spit it out."

"All right… Something came to mind when I mentioned 'mysterious means of support'. What if he was financing his lifestyle through some sort of illegal activity?"

"What, drugs…?"

"I'm not sure, but maybe drugs are a part of it. I don't know much about Vietnam, or its reputation when it comes to illegal activity. But, I do know someone who is well-versed in everything Vietnamese. Maybe I have a phone call to make."

"Let me know what you find out. I'm off to be a farmer for the rest of the afternoon."

My work kept me in the paddocks until after five o'clock. As I drove the tractor back into the shed, Connor arrived. The three of us, accompanied by glasses of wine and a bowl of peanuts made ourselves comfortable on the deck. Connor explained, "I only came to let you know the harvesting contractor will be back tomorrow. I noticed the police inspector was here again today. Has his investigation progressed, or was it just a social call?"

Kate giggled and I shot her a look. I had no idea what she saw so funny in what Connor said. "No, I don't think his investigation has progressed at all, but it wasn't a social call. He came out to go through all the stuff in the dining room to see if there was anything that might help with his case. Apart from the possibility something amongst it might be useful to him, I'm hoping he uses his position to follow-up on the owners of those passports we found."

"What's your next move now you've finished all the stuff on the dining room table?"

"I think I'll see Justin Farley tomorrow to see how dealing with Tremayne's estate is going. But, I also want to try to inject some enthusiasm into him about digging into the backgrounds of some of those names we found. I'll probably visit the bank tomorrow as well. That material in the dining room raised a few questions about finance and its mysterious sources. I might not get too much traction with the bank on this one, so I may need to drag Justin along with me."

"What time is your appointment?"

"I don't have one. I only made the decision while I was in the paddock, and it was too late by then to make an appointment. In spite of what he wants people to believe, I don't think Justin Farley is all that busy. He seems to have plenty of time to play golf these days."

Connor took his leave. On the way back upstairs after we walked him to his truck, I nudged Kate in the ribs. "Right… Now, tell me what Connor said that was so funny you couldn't stop yourself giggling about it."

"Aw, come on; you are not that naïve. It wasn't so much what he said, as how he said it."

"How he said what?"

"How he asked if Taylor's trip out here was a *social visit*. It was fairly clear he has some concerns about the inspector's frequent visits to this farm."

"Oh, I see. He is becoming jealous about your spending so much time with Inspector Taylor. He might be justified after

Taylor's visit today. When you're around, Taylor carries on like a love struck teenager. So many compliments going your way, it's obvious he is interested." Her raucous laughter was confusing. This time, I couldn't see what I had said that was so funny.

"Lisa, wake up! Connor wasn't jealous of Dan Taylor spending time with ME. He was concerned about Taylor coming to visit YOU so often. Even the proverbial *blind man on a galloping horse* could see Connor is more than a little smitten with you."

Now that was something I did not see coming. How did Kate develop such an idea? I hadn't noticed any evidence of Connor's being smitten with me. Maybe I should pay more attention in future. The absurdity of such a situation never stuck with me until after I went to bed. Then, I lay in bed examining every aspect of recent encounters with Connor. By the time my eyes began to droop, I had reached the conclusion Kate was mistaken. There was nothing untoward or different in any recent encounters with my neighbour. He had always been a good friend. One who was always there to lend a hand if needed.

*****

Straight after her morning greeting, Kate asked, "Are you really going to try to see Justin Farley today without an appointment? He might be a small town's solicitor but, on principle, he probably will claim to be too busy to see you without one."

"Maybe, but, unless he has a genuine client appointment first thing this morning, I should be able to persuade him to afford me a bit of time."

My arrival at Justin Farley's office was timed to perfection. His receptionist was opening up as I climbed the three steps to his front door. "Is Mr Farley expecting you this morning?" She asked. She wasn't so much expressing confusion at my being there at that hour of the morning, as preparing me for the news that her boss couldn't possibly see me without an appointment. I scuttled the intention.

"He might not be expecting me, but he had better make himself available, unless he can prove without a shadow of doubt that he has another client booked in at this time. Don't let me interrupt your morning routine. I'll just go through to his office."

I tapped lightly on his door, and let myself in. The startled look on Justin's face was priceless. "Your receptionist was busy so I came on through. As a result of certain things that have come to light in the last couple of days, it's important I know what stage you are at with Tremayne's estate. Is there any definitive information regarding Miss Williams?" He shook his head. So far, my venerable solicitor hadn't uttered a word since I arrived. I continued. "Have you established the extent of his estate for probate purposes, and what's the situation with the bank now?"

Justin scrabbled through folders on his desk, finally selecting one that bore Tremayne's name. "Now, let me refresh my memory…" He made a great show of studying the contents of the folder, which didn't amount to more than half a dozen sheets of paper. Then he murmured, "Ah yes… Yes, now I recall. I'm not sure how familiar you are with the likely extent of your husband's estate but…"

"Before you embarrass yourself further, Justin, remember you're speaking to me, and not some other impressionable client. Cut the performance, and let's get to the report on where things are at."

"I don't … know … what you mean."

"Yes, you do, and I'm running out of patience. Perhaps this case is too complicated for a small-town solicitor. Maybe I should turn it over to my city-based legal representative. What are your thoughts on that, Justin?" Suddenly, Justin was back to being Justin.

"I found nothing to suggest Tremayne Bancroft was married to anyone other than you, and I have confirmed he died intestate. Advertisements placed in relevant newspapers, which called for outstanding claims by creditors, have produced no results. The documents have been prepared ready to be lodged for probate, but I probably will wait another couple of days, just in case a creditor does come forward."

While I doubted anyone would come forward, I agreed it was best to wait another couple of days before lodging the documents.

"Lisa, I don't know how to say this other than to be blunt. I don't know what you think your husband's estate amounts to, but I think you might be disappointed."

"Don't be silly, Justin. Tremayne had nothing much at all that was his, nothing of value that is. He didn't even own a vehicle. He used one of the company's cars. And, unless he had some secret bank account I didn't know about, I doubt there's any cash lying about waiting to be claimed. I'm not about to be disappointed by whatever you tell me. My interest in your progress in this matter is based on nothing more than a desire to see everything finalised and his estate wound up."

"If that's the case, you have no disappointments in store. There is no secret account. Cash in his bank accounts amounts to no more than a couple of hundred dollars. As you say, we discovered nothing else of any value owned by the deceased. On that basis, granting of probate will be a straightforward matter and unlikely to incur any delay. I have closed off his bank accounts, so no further transactions can occur. As soon as probate is granted, I will arrange for any cash holdings to be transferred to your account."

"So, possibly by the end of next week, probate should be through and the whole matter wrapped up." In spite of our shaky beginning, we parted on amicable terms. On my way out, I couldn't help but notice there was no line-up of clients waiting to access the inner sanctum. The reception area was starkly empty apart from the receptionist, who shot me a sour look as I strode out.

Although Justin said he found no secret bank accounts, being unaware of all those other names on those passports now residing on my dining room table, he was working at a disadvantage. A visit to the bank still seemed a sound proposition.

"Good morning, Nathan. Could you spare me a few minutes please, in your office if you don't mind?"

"What can I do for you this morning, Lisa? And, may I offer you my belated condolences on the loss of your husband. Here at the bank, we didn't know anything about it until Justin Farley came to deal with your husband's bank accounts – and that was after you closed your joint account."

"It's about accounts I've come to talk to you today. But, I do have to warn you, it's going to sound a strange tale. So, bear with me please. In going through my husband's things, I encountered several surprises that I don't yet understand." I explained about the passports we found and gave him a list of the names associated with them.

"You see why I felt it best to warn you my visit today was a little unusual. We haven't established whether all of those names, including Tremayne Bancroft, belong to one and the same person. I've come to establish whether any of those names, other than my husband's, have accounts at this branch – or perhaps at some other branch of this bank." He looked troubled, and studied the list of names for longer than I thought necessary before finally looking up to meet my eyes.

"Lisa, you know I would love to help you with your enquiry, but bank confidentiality prevents it, and I think you are aware of that. But, I'm prepared to go out on a bit of a limb today to share something with you. Let's just say the timing of your visit this morning is fortuitous. When you came in, did you notice the young woman sitting in the reception area?"

I hadn't, but then I wasn't interested in who else might be in the bank at the time. He gestured with his head for me to take a look at the person he referred to. I went to the small one-way glass panel in the front wall of his office and peered out.

A young, fair-haired, very pregnant woman sat uncomfortably in one of the overstuffed lounge chairs in the reception area. There were few people in the bank. The young woman was the only one in the reception area. Nevertheless, I asked the needless question. "Are you talking about the pregnant woman sitting by herself out there?" He nodded. I took one last quick look through the glass before returning to my chair. "Okay I observed the woman in question. So, what is it about her you think I might want to know?"

"She came in to make inquiries about an account at this branch. While different, her enquiry was much along the same lines as yours. While I don't know a whole lot more about her particular enquiry yet, I'm not in a position to share any details with you."

"Are you suggesting, if I want to know something, I have to go out there and interrogate the woman?"

"Of course I'm not suggesting anything like that."

"Well, what would it take for you to share such information as you might have? Or, perhaps that should be 'with whom would you share such information'?"

"Let me think. Perhaps, if a solicitor with a possible interest in a client's estate, or if a police officer investigating a serious crime that might have some connection to the account made enquiries, I could be obliged to be forthcoming with whatever information I have." He kept his eyes firmly on the papers on his desk as he explained his tenuous situation. When he finished speaking, he looked up at me with his eyebrows raised in question. I didn't need to be Einstein to understand his message.

"Right… Please bear with me for a moment. I have a couple of phone calls to make."

"While you make your phone calls, I'll go and see if I can rustle up some coffee. If I remember correctly, you take yours black?"

Chapter 16

In quick succession, I called Justin Farley and Inspector Taylor, and was surprised when both were available. My message to the two men was the same: Get yourself over to the bank now, if you can. You could learn something of mutual interest.

Inspector Taylor was followed a few moments later by Justin Farley. Nathan waited out front to escort the two men to his office where I waited. Not intended to hold more than three people at a time, the office felt cramped with the four of us in it. Nathan's quick phone call brought two extra cups of coffee.

Once everyone was equipped with coffee, the serious business of discussing the matter at hand began. In case anyone needed reminding, Nathan went through his spiel about the confidentiality of our discussions. When at last we got down to business, he led off.

"First thing this morning, a young woman enquired about an account at this branch. She had the name of the account and what she believed was the name of the account holder. She explained her visit was because regular transfers of money from that account to her account in Brisbane had ceased unexpectedly. It appears it is her husband's account. The nature of his work has him spending a lot of time away from home. In the past, payments into her account continued even while he was away. He has been away now for more than six weeks. During that time, she received no cash transfers."

We three on our side of the desk exchanged looks. Inspector Taylor expressed the thought running through my mind, and probably through Justin's as well. "This is beginning to have a familiar ring to it. What else can you tell us?"

"The woman, Mrs Bailey, claims the lack of cash flow has left her in an embarrassing position. She and her family live in a cottage on her parents' vast estate, but they are self-supporting. Now, she is without cash to support herself and her small child, and has been unable to contact her husband to establish what has gone wrong. She was concerned the money might have gone into the wrong account, and she is relying on her parents to keep her until things return to normal. She even had to borrow the money for the fare to come here to sort out the problem."

"We need to talk to this woman," Justin said. "Is there somewhere here we can do that in private?" Nathan checked the bank's small meeting room was available for the rest of the morning and showed us through to it. While we faffed about making ourselves comfortable, he went to fetch Mrs Bailey.

"Thanks, Nathan, we'll handle it from here, and won't take up any more of your time," Inspector Taylor said. Nathan, unsure what his position demanded in such circumstances, hesitated for a few heartbeats. It seems he concluded that, when the police suggest you go away, it's probably wise to do so.

Who was in command was obvious. Taylor made that clear from the outset when he introduced himself and explained to the woman how her visit had potential connections to a serious case he was investigating. Justin introduced himself as a local solicitor. I gave her only my name. I don't know what she thought about my presence. Perhaps she thought me a secretary there to take notes.

The introductions over, Taylor took command. "Mrs Bailey, please tell us what has occurred to make you come all this way to visit this bank."

Her response offered nothing more than Nathan had outlined previously. Taylor allowed a somewhat extended pause to occur, probably to allow her to think of anything else she might like to add. Nothing more was forthcoming. I was beginning to feel embarrassed for her, and chimed in. "In your condition, it must be uncomfortable travelling. How far along are you?"

"Almost eight months... Yeah, it was a bit rugged. I was tired by the time I arrived. And, I have the return journey to look forward to. I can't stay long. My little girl is fretting for me already, and giving my mother a hard time looking after her while I'm away." This might not be what the others wanted to hear, but I was interested. As our chat seemed to relax her, I soldiered on – and ignored Taylor's disapproving look.

"Your mother has my sympathies. Do you have any photos with you?"

"I carry two all the time. My husband knows about the one of me and our daughter, but not the other one. He won't let anyone take his photo. But, a few months ago, my mother sneaked a photo of the three of us together. It's the only photo of my husband I've ever seen." As she rummaged in her oversized tote bag, she continued, "Here it is. That's the three of us together picnicking on the lawn under a big tree just outside our cottage. My mother was trimming the hedge nearby, and just happened to have her camera handy."

Out of the corner of my eye, I saw the two men exchange looks as the woman handed me the photos. The top photo was of mother and daughter. I made what I hope were appropriate comments about her 'gorgeous little girl'. Then, I struggled to control my face. I did not want my emotions to show and ruin the opportunity. "What a lovely looking family group just enjoying time together. I don't know why your husband is concerned about having his photo taken. He is a very nice-looking man."

As I spoke, I handed the photo of mother and daughter to Justin. Then, willing my hand not to shake, I handed the snap of the family group to Inspector Taylor, who rose to the occasion.

"I agree. He looks alright. I don't know why he doesn't like having his photo taken. He hasn't got two heads or anything."

Mrs Bailey giggled. "Yes, he is quite good-looking isn't he? Although quite a bit older than me, and his work takes him away a lot, he is a good husband and father."

I was in danger of exploding as rage built up in me. *She was talking about my husband.* There could be no doubt. The man in the photo – the man Mrs Bailey claimed was her husband – was one and the same man as I knew as Tremayne Bancroft ... *my* husband. By then, both men had seen the photo and realised its implication. Probably for my sake, Taylor rushed to refocus discussions on the bank account.

"I assume the 'TB' in the account name refers to your husband's initials."

"Well, I assume that's what they stand for. My husband's name is Tristan Bailey."

While that's well and good, there are other details I want to know, and I doubt anyone else will ask the right questions. "You say you husband is away a lot. It must be hard for you, and for your daughter. She must miss him when he is away. What work does he do to take him away so much?"

"He is a journalist, and gets sent all over the place to write about whatever is happening there. Sometimes it's somewhere in Australia, but often he is sent overseas. He wants to stay at home more with us. That's why we are living on my parents' estate. We are trying to save enough money for him to change jobs and be able to stay home more."

It must be difficult for you now you are so close to giving birth. I hope you don't mind my asking, but how long have you been married?"

"Our fifth wedding anniversary was four months ago. Tristan managed to be home for that, and promised to be home for the birth of this one," she said stroking her swollen stomach. "He made the same promise three years ago for the birth of our first one – but didn't make it back in time."

Inspector Taylor decided to take back control. "So, have there been any cash transfers during the six weeks your husband has been away?"

"No, none at all… It used to come through every fortnight or three weeks but, sometimes when he was overseas, it only came through once a month. In the end, it was always the same amount; a total of nine hundred dollars every month. Before, when I was working part-time, it didn't matter if it was a bit late. Then, at seven months, I started having a few problems and the doctor told me to give up work to rest more. With no money coming through this time, I've run out of cash. We are eating at my parents' house because I don't even have money to buy food."

Damn Inspector Taylor for interrupting me. I still had questions needing answers, and jumped into the conversation again. "It's good you have your parents to fall back on at a time like this. How do they feel about what's happening?"

"Ah well, they're not too happy at all. They want me to move back into home with them, so they can look after me and my kids properly … and they want me to get rid of Tristan. Of course I'm not going to do that. Things will sort themselves out. We just have to be patient. My parents never liked Tristan, and I think they are just looking for something to use against him; to persuade me to leave him."

"To what sorts of overseas places does his work take him?"

"I don't know. He doesn't talk about his work. Once, when I asked a lot of questions about it, he hinted it was all hush-hush and he couldn't discuss it with anyone."

"Does he have a passport? Maybe, one day when he's not around, you might sneak a peek at it to ease your curiosity."

"If he goes overseas, I suppose he has to have one. I've never seen it, so I've never had the opportunity to look at it. Maybe he has to keep it with him all the time in case he is sent overseas at short notice."

At last, it was Justin's turn to contribute to the conversation. "All this must be quite distressing for you. Have the staff at the bank been able to sort things out for you?"

That hit a nerve. I saw tears well up. She sat wringing her hands for a few moments before answering. There was a catch in her voice when she did.

"Although they've been very nice and helpful, I still don't know what's going on. With no transfers made out of that account for at least six weeks, there should be well over a thousand dollars in it. They showed me the balance; only a hundred and seventy-three dollars. I don't know what to think. Maybe the company he works for hasn't paid him either."

"As a solicitor, I may be able to ask a few questions to help find out what's going on, and where he is at the moment. Who does he work for?"

"No, as I told you, I don't know anything about his work – or even how and when he is paid."

"Don't upset yourself," Taylor said. "Think of the baby. How long are you planning to be here, and have you organised somewhere to stay?"

"I'm due to leave again tomorrow afternoon. My mother booked a room at a local motel for me for last night and tonight."

"Okay, Mrs Bailey, here's what I'm going to do. I will check if your husband does have a passport, and if he has used it to leave the country at all in the last six weeks. Then I'm going to lean on the bank here, to see if we can find out more about who pays your husband. While I accept it is disappointing for you not to be able to sort everything out right now, I recommend you go back to your motel and rest. If you give me details of where you are staying, I'll contact you later this afternoon. Does it suit you to go along with that?"

She agreed. What else could she do? Inspector Taylor walked Mrs Bailey out of the meeting room and handed her over to Nathan who saw her to a taxi and on her way back to the motel. Our fact-finding mission was over. It was time to review what we learned from it. As soon as Taylor returned to the meeting room, Justin and I scampered back to our seats to allow the post-mortem to begin.

"Well, Justin, did you learn anything useful from our chat with Mrs Bailey?" Inspector Taylor asked without looking up from his scribbled notes.

"I'm not sure I'd use the word 'useful'. My search for family or relatives of Tremayne Bancroft came up empty. I was fine with that until Mrs Bailey produced a covert photo of the family picnic. There is no denying the man in that photo had more than a strong resemblance to Tremayne Bancroft. All the documents are ready to lodge for probate. In view of this morning's revelation, now I'm not sure how to proceed."

Although unaware of the legal implications, I chipped in with a suggestion I hoped would simplify matters. "The woman's situation is both embarrassing and difficult as a result of her husband's disappearance. The least we can do is to ignore that photo – and anything else we might think we know – to allow her to claim whatever remains in that account and any other cash he might have stashed away somewhere."

Taylor shot me a surprised look. "You don't mind, when the money is rightly yours?"

"No, not at all… She and her children need it, and probably have some entitlement to it. I don't need it, and I couldn't live with myself if I deprived her of it. It's such a paltry amount anyway. Let her have it."

"What if I find other accounts with more cash, will you still see it that way?" Taylor persisted.

"Yes… but, I would be interested in where the money came from."

He nodded, and appeared to consider my response for a few moments before turning his attention to Justin. "Let's bring Nathan back in here to ask him a few hard questions. I'll do all the talking this time because I will be treating it as questioning in relation to a police investigation." No argument from us, Justin went to find Nathan.

"Nathan, thanks for allowing us to use this room. Mrs Bailey provided information relevant to current investigations, some of it critical to an ongoing criminal case of mine. You probably are aware from talking to her earlier, she knows little about her husband's life or his work. She was no help to us in that regard. As a result of what she could tell us, information now is required on any other accounts held by Tristan Bailey. We also need to establish the sources of income flowing into those accounts to enable contact with its source." Taylor was exercising his authority again.

"I see, but I'm sure you understand such information is confidential and I am not at liberty to provide you with anything of that nature." Nathan was standing up well to Taylor.

"As acting manager of this branch, surely you can see your way clear to help the police with their investigation – and help ease Mrs Bailey's concerns."

"No, I'm afraid that's not possible. It's not possible to give even Mrs Bailey such information."

"Okay, if that's how you want to play the game, I'll be off to get a warrant, and also, to let it be known that the bank refused to assist in a murder investigation. I presume you realise the warrant will be sent to your head office, who in turn, will direct you to make the information available. They might not look favourably on this branch's involvement in potential illegal money laundering activities. As the acting manager, it might not reflect well on you. I thought you might want to avoid such a situation if possible, but I understand your difficulty in this matter. We will leave you to get on with your duties, but I'm sure I'll be back to see you quite soon."

"There is no need to go to all that fuss and bother."

"That's okay. I understand your position in regard to the confidentiality involved. I wouldn't want you to feel pressured to do the wrong thing. It occurs to me that, should we discover something 'not quite kosher' about this account, your alerting your head office about the matter might sit well for you at your next staff appraisal."

Blackmail works every time, or so it seems. At least Nathan appeared to understand that.

"Now you've made it clear why you need the information, I'm sure we can work around the rules. I must stress though that any information we make available to you is unofficial. Should you wish to use it in some official way later which requires acknowledgement of the source, I must insist you provide me with a court order or a document of some description to protect the bank."

...And your backside, I thought, but kept it to myself.

A mobile computer workstation was set up and the search began for any accounts which could have a connection to Tristan Bailey, regardless of how remote the possibility might be. As I deemed it likely a lengthy process, I opted for a walk along the street to stretch my legs. When I returned about twenty minutes later, I found the three men huddled over various printouts. "Does all this paper indicate your search met with some success?"

"You might say that," Taylor replied. "We found two other possible accounts. Well, one is a definite. It's in the name of Tristan Bailey, but the account is held at the Brisbane branch. The second one we found is not so obvious. He wasn't accommodating enough to use his name on this one, but the account does have 'TB' in its name."

"Does any of it provide useful information? I mean, is there any indication of where his money came from?"

Justin reached over and slapped a sheath of printouts down on the table in front of me. "Have a look and see what you think. We do need to talk after this little exercise is over."

My mind registered his words as having an ominous implication. "Okay, but I don't think I'm looking forward to it." A quick scan of the top page of the pile in front of me reinforced my feelings.

The account had a substantial balance, substantial when compared to amounts in the TB Household account over time. Subsequent pages of the printout showed consistent activity over a lengthy period. While vaguely aware of the other three's murmurings, I managed to shut out the conversation and devote my attention to the printout. Considerable money flowed into the account on a regular basis. The notation regarding its source was not helpful. Perhaps the men had worked out from whence the money was transferred.

"Mrs Bailey would be greatly relieved if she were aware of the amount in this account. Do we know where the funds come from?" I asked.

"We don't *know*, but we have a fair idea," Inspector Taylor said. "Nathan is working on it. It's a convoluted trail, but we think we know its origins. Until we connect all the 'dots', we won't know for sure."

"My question is: why was such 'convoluted trail' necessary? My mind jumped to the immediate conclusion that it was necessary because its source was related to some form of nefarious activity. Have you come across any such indications so far?"

Nathan looked up and cleared his throat. "What you're suggesting is a possibility, but it might be something more mundane. The way the transfers were set up makes the notation a bit obscure, but it should be possible… Wait! I think I found something. Give me a minute."

The only sound to intrude was the fevered clack of Nathan's keyboard as he interrogated the computer. His physical activity was accompanied by frequent emphatic nods of his head, as if acknowledging having discovered some vital nugget of information. Although I couldn't understand why it was happening, I felt the knot in my stomach tightening. The tension in the room was almost palpable. Then the typing stopped. Nathan peered at the screen, alternatively nodding and shaking his head.

After a couple of moments, he looked up and slid his gaze over us. While he hadn't said anything, the look on his face suggested success. Our sighs of relief were audible. Somehow, I managed not to cheer. After all, it might not be good news.

"Don't just sit there looking at it," Taylor demanded. "What have you found?"

"It looks like there are two sources of transfers. Both are from banks in the Sydney area, one of which is not a branch of this bank. From what I can make out, there is a large quarterly deposit into one of those accounts. Most of that deposit becomes an almost immediate transfer into a Brisbane branch of this bank. Into an account we identified as possibly belonging to Tristan Bailey."

"That's it then. We've discovered the source. Can you identify where it comes from?" Taylor was perched on the front edge of his chair. The excitement in his voice was reflected in his face.

"Hang on a minute. There is something strange going on with those transfers. O-o-h, I see…"

"You see what?" Taylor demanded.

"There definitely is something strange. I still need to verify what it is, but it looks as though the transfer from the Sydney account splits into two separate deposits, each one into a different account. That account (Nathan indicated printout on the table in front of me) only receives about three quarters of the transfer from Sydney. The remainder of the transfer goes into another Brisbane account with a different name. I'm trying to print out some stuff that will make sense to you."

We sat watching the printer spew out page after page. I realised lunchtime was fast approaching when my stomach started rumbling. There was no way I was going home for lunch. No way I was going anywhere until we sorted out those accounts. I tried convincing my stomach accordingly. It ignored me and growled loudly in retaliation. Its response didn't go unnoticed.

Justin checked his watch. "By the sound of that, I'm not the only one who is starving. How about I send out for lunch to be delivered. What does everyone want?"

Sorting out a lunch order took longer than expected. We were hungry, but no one wanted to waste time choosing what to eat. It resulted in each one of us telling Justin 'what everyone else wants will do'. For some reason Justin didn't find that helpful and continued badgering us for individual orders. In the end, we agreed on Chinese, and left Justin the unenviable task of choosing which dishes to order. That done, I took the opportunity to ask the question nagging at me since before any thought of lunch occurred. "Is there any chance we are talking about money laundering here?" I noticed Nathan becoming increasingly worried looking as he flicked through screen after screen.

"I haven't found anything to confirm it is," Nathan began. I gave him a hard look. "Okay, it could be. So far, there's nothing to confirm – or even to make me reasonably suspicious – that it's money laundering."

Justin announced lunch would be delivered in about twenty minutes. Nathan alerted his staff to the imminent arrival of food, and asked for coffee, water, crockery and other necessary hardware to be brought to the meeting room. While the three of us shared our speculations about what Mr Tristan Bailey was up to, Nathan continued searching his computer. There was an air of determination about him. The previous rhythmic clack of the keyboard had become frequent staccato passages of open warfare. Justin commented on it when he returned from ordering lunch.

"The thrill of the chase has him in its grip," I said. "I noticed a step up in pace after I mentioned money laundering." Justin's eyes opened to the size of saucers.

Inspector Taylor giggled. "Steady on, Justin, old boy. We don't know that it is. Lisa just raised the possibility. I don't know whether it was the fear of finding his branch mixed up in something illegal that sent him into such a frenzy, or if it was a sniff of a significant promotion for having discovered it."

Regardless of the cause, Nathan continued attacking his keyboard with some vigour until our lunch and all the other stuff arrived. While we all ate together, it was as if Nathan existed in a parallel universe. He contributed nothing to the conversation, and bolted down a minuscule amount of food before rushing back to the computer. On the other hand, we were in no rush to do anything. All we could do was pore over the earlier printouts. In an environment almost crackling with expectation, for the next twenty minutes, that's what we did.

A growl of frustration from Nathan made everyone stop and focus their attention on the man at the computer. "Sorry folks; didn't mean to get you excited. I haven't unravelled the mystery. All I've done is hit a brick wall on the money trail."

Chapter 17

The almost deafening sound of our deflating hopes was followed by a short period of silence during which each of us tried to regain our equilibrium. Then, chaos as everyone spoke at the same time. Questions were asked. Nathan tried explaining what happened. Nobody listened to anybody. Taylor exercised his self-appointed authority.

"Shut up! Nathan please explain where you found that brick wall. Was it in Sydney, Brisbane, here, or somewhere we haven't looked at before?"

"Ah yes, but it might be a bit hard to follow." We assured him we were up for the challenge, and to *please get on with it.* "Right … I found an account I think might be linked to the others. I'm not familiar with it, and I've never come across its strange name before."

"Is it just an interesting few dollars in a strange account?" Justin asked.

"If it contained only a few dollars, I wouldn't be interested in it. This one contains quite a lot of money. The trouble is, the account isn't with this bank, so..."

"How did you find it, if it's not held by your bank?" Justin persisted.

"On occasion, money from that strange account is transferred into an account with this bank. Our system allows me to see relevant details of those transfers, but it doesn't hold information about the originating account."

"Does your bank have a good relationship with the other bank in question? Are you able to make enquiries about the account you found?" Inspector Taylor asked.

"Not that I know of; it's a foreign bank. That shouldn't be an issue, but I think communicating with that other bank happens at head office level, and not at branch level. I'd be reluctant to talk to head office at this stage of our investigation, particularly due to the circumstances surrounding the search."

An idea battled its way through to the forefront of my thinking. It remained only half formed when I gave it air. "This will sound like a wild shot, but there was that British passport we found. It had an unusual name in it. Might there be some connection between the passport and the account Nathan found?"

"I hadn't forgotten about that passport," Taylor said, "but I didn't think it was relevant. I gave Nathan only the names from the Australian passports. It's worth a shot though." He scribbled the name of the British passport holder, Telford Maybanks Creswell, on a page from his notebook and handed it to Nathan, who shot a dismissive glance at it … and then did a double take.

"That's the name on the account. Tell me about this person. Who is he? Where is he?"

I left Inspector Taylor trying to explain Mr Creswell when, in reality, we didn't know anything about the man. Perhaps that's not quite true. Perhaps it might be more accurate to say, while we don't know who he is, we suspect he is the same person as Tremayne Bancroft, and all those other names given to Nathan earlier. And that's a fairly accurate summation of Taylor's response to Nathan's questions.

"So, it's a British passport. That fits with what I found. The account from which the money is transferred is held by a UK bank. Of course, the account could be held at an Australian branch of that bank. Nothing's changed. I still can't go to head office with this, but there might be a way around it. I need to think about it."

"Fair enough," I volunteered. "You've done well already. The information you found goes some way to explaining aspects of this mess. I am happy to leave you to carry on with it."

"Yeah, that's probably the best thing to do," Taylor conceded. "Before we leave you to work on in peace and quiet, may we recap everything we discovered today?"

Our review of today's efforts took no more than a few minutes. Then, we three were out on the street again. Justin bid us a hasty farewell, citing a client coming to see him in about twenty minutes as his reason for rushing away. Taylor and I watched him hurry across the street while we remained anchored to the pavement outside the bank. I knew I wanted to talk to Inspector Taylor, but I just didn't know why, or what about. Something about him suggested he might be dealing with the same quandary. He didn't seem anxious to return to his office, so I decided to risk it and see where it went.

"You probably are in a hurry to get back to your office, but would you have time for a coffee before you head off?"

The coffee shop was deserted except for the two elderly ladies settling their bill on their way out. Only a few minutes had passed since I posed the question, but it was long enough for me to get my head around at least some of what I wanted to ask the inspector. As soon as we ordered, I opened the discussion.

"Are we in any doubt all the names we found, including that of Travis Bailey, belong to one and the same person: the man I married, Tremayne Bancroft?"

"I don't think there can be any doubt. The best we can hope for is finding the evidence to confirm it, and uncovering what is behind it. This can't be easy for you. I admire the way you're handling it but, if I may suggest it, you need to stop and allow reality to sink in. If you don't, there could be unpleasant consequences at some point in the future."

"Your concern is appreciated, but I am okay. My interest now is in uncovering the real identity of the man I married, and discovering what this whole charade is about. Don't look so sceptical. I did care about my husband. But, unless you understand what our life – our marriage – was like, you haven't a chance of understanding how all this affects me. If you want to help, find out why he was murdered … and who the hell he really was."

Inspector Taylor was off to see Donna, aka Mrs Tristan Bailey, as I headed for my car. The impact of this morning didn't register until I was on my way home. Not only had we added another alias to the list, but another wife and two more children crowded into the picture of the life of the man I thought was my husband. As I drove up to the house, another thought slammed in from left field. Has anyone spoken to Roslyn Williams about our discoveries so far? Should I call her to talk about it?

The coward in me said it wasn't up to me to tell her about her husband. For once, I listened to my instinct, or whatever it was that said I should leave it alone. I decided not to call her. Nevertheless, it wasn't a comfortable decision. If I were Miss Williams, would I want to know? Of course I would. I do. The uncertainty is eating at me. Should I change my decision and call her after all? The coward in me surfaced again. I made a mental note to stick with my original decision.

Concern was etched deeply on Kate's face when she met me at the door. "Are you all right? I was worried when you didn't come home for lunch. It wasn't lunch I was worried about. My concern was whether something bad happened when you met with Justin Farley. You can tell me about it over coffee." Did I need another coffee? Probably not, but a glass of something cold might go down well. We took long glasses of iced tea out onto the deck.

Telling Kate about my morning took longer than expected. After all, what did I have to tell her? Met yet another of my husband's wives – pregnant … found a couple of interesting bank accounts with hefty balances … virtually confirmed all of the names, including Tremayne's, belong to one and the same man … still don't know the real identity of the man. In reality, I did have quite a bit to share, but almost none of it answered any of Kate's questions.

"So, what is your next move? Now you know a bit more, is any of the stuff on the dining room table likely to be of further help?"

"I doubt it. Nathan will try chasing up information on the foreign bank account, but it's likely Inspector Taylor will need to initiate something before there can be any progress in that direction. From my point of view, I guess it's a case of wait-and-see what the others dig up."

"Bloody frustrating…! I wonder how Miss Williams is coping with the situation."

"I'm not sure she knows about the stuff we've uncovered. Although, I think Nathan will find some of the cash he discovered in various accounts might have come from Roslyn Williams."

"Do you think she also was paying him an allowance of some sort?"

"Maybe that's something Nathan will discover. She did mention that, when they married, her husband, Trevor, was given a position on the board of Williams Enterprises. As a director, or whatever he was, he probably was paid some sort of fee. Hmm … Perhaps that's what those Sydney bank accounts are about. Maybe I should mention it to Nathan."

"Don't you have confidence in his ability to sort it out? I suppose it might be asking a bit much of him. He is only the acting manager, and probably has never had to do anything like this before."

"He has done all right so far. I think I might wait to see how he goes. If he looks stuck, I'll mention it then. I don't want him to think I don't have faith in him. He is a young bloke thrust in at the deep end and doing the best he can."

"Okay; but are we going to look through the stuff on the table again this afternoon?"

"Dunno; I'll think about it while I refill our glasses." That wasn't what I wanted to think about. A thought was struggling to come through to the forefront of my mind. I took my time refilling the glasses to give it opportunity to wriggle its way through.

After a couple of sips of her iced tea, Kate resumed question mode. "So, did you decide about the stuff on the table?"

"Ye-es, I think so. I don't know what I hope to achieve by looking through it all again. It's more a case of 'living in hope'. Perhaps we could go back to those passports. Don't ask me what we are looking for, but my gut keeps telling me that's where I should look."

"I'm surprised the inspector didn't take them with him. I didn't expect them to be still on the table after he left."

"I photocopied the person's details page from each of them for him. I think he intended going back to his contacts in the intelligence agencies to see if any of those names were familiar to them. He said he might come back for the passports. At the time, he couldn't be sure they were relevant to his investigation."

For a few moments, I sat looking at the passports fanned out on the table in front of me. It took that long for inspiration to dawn on me. "I don't know how useful this might be, but I think I would like to map where and when these passports have been over the last however many years. When I put the idea into words, it sounds like an impossible task. Nevertheless, I do want to try to map where the passport holders have been, when, and for how long. Does that make sense to you?"

"I'm way ahead of you," Kate said as she scurried out of the room. She returned a few moments later carrying a roll of paper. "I saw this flipchart in the office a couple of days ago. We can stick a sheet up on the wall for each of the passports. The information we enter onto each of them will provide a visual record of what was going on."

Setting up took no time at all. Trevor Cross' passport was the first one I selected. After a quick flick through all the stamped pages, I returned to the first page and began calling data to Kate, who had set herself up with a selection of markers ready to enter the information I gave her.

"Now that is interesting," I murmured, more to myself than to Kate.

"What is so interesting, and how do I enter it on Mr Cross' chart?"

"Trevor Cross' passport was in use prior to his marriage to Miss Williams. She said they were married for about twenty years. The first activity recorded in this passport goes back about twenty-three years. Still, I don't suppose that is of any consequence in the exercise we're about to carry out."

"Not at this stage anyway; let's get started shall we, or it'll be dinnertime and we won't have made a mark on any of these charts." She was right. Wondering about things beyond our ken was wasting time.

As I went through the passport, calling dates and places, Kate scribbled frantically to keep up with me. Having read out the last entry, I sat staring at it. "Lisa, what is it? What's wrong? You look stunned. What else is in there that's upset you?"

"Upset? No, I'm not upset; well, maybe a bit. I'm not sure what I feel. Look at that last entry. On his way back from overseas, Trevor Cross was in Sydney only a couple of months ago. If I think about those dates, he spent about three weeks in Sydney before coming back here."

"So, it seems his relationship… marriage to Miss Williams was still alive and flourishing. Although, the three-week gap between when he arrived in Sydney and his return here doesn't prove he was with her. I accept that, if he were in Sydney, he probably would have spent time with Miss Williams. …Or, he might only have overnighted with her before moving on to Brisbane to spend time with Mrs Bailey."

"Donna Bailey indicated she hadn't seen her husband for weeks before she came up here to try to sort out the money situation. I can't remember her exact words, but they registered with me as his having been away for at least a couple of months. She made some comment about it being a long assignment this time and she hoped he'd be home in time for the birth of their second child."

"Maybe we should wait until we have the information on the other charts before we start trying to put two and two together about his life."

Again, Kate was right. We were wasting time speculating about mysteries we had no way of unravelling. I picked up Tremayne Bancroft's passport, and again read out the details of his travels for Kate to enter on his chart. This time it was Kate who stood back and studied his chart for a few moments after we finished.

"I don't know whether you noticed or not, but we have a similar situation with this one."

"Eh…? What similar situation?"

"Well, you married Tremayne just over twelve years ago. This passport was first used four years before that. I know you knew Tremayne for a while before you were married, but was it as long as that?"

"Nothing like so long… I knew him for about maybe two years before we were married. At first, I saw him occasionally at social events, and then it developed into something else. By the end of the first year, we had a steady relationship going, and at the start of the second year, we moved in together for the best part of that year before we were married. So, it appears Tremayne's passport was in use for at least two years before I knew him."

"Lisa, I'm not sure this exercise is in your best interest. I have a feeling it's going to be one unpleasant revelation after another. Are you sure you want to continue? Are you sure you're up to handling whatever we discover?"

There was no doubt in my mind. We were going to continue. At last, I felt we were making some ground in solving the mystery of who this man was. I wasn't about to leave it hanging in mid-air. I needed to understand the last twelve, maybe fourteen, years of my life. The only way to do that seemed to depend on uncovering the man involved. Of course, we were going to carry on. I would worry about whatever the consequences were afterwards.

It took some time to work through all of the passports. We left the oldest one until last. The British passport of Telford Maybanks Cresswell appeared to have been in use for more than thirty years. It was considerate of the owner of all these passports to keep all the superseded versions together with the current ones. Without this, and with passports having a ten-year expiry period, we would never have been able to track their usage. In Telford Cresswell's case, the three expired passports and the current one were bound together with a grubby length of cotton tape.

With everything added to the charts, Kate stood back to admire her handiwork. She seemed to be wrestling with her thoughts. Eventually she shared them with me. "Our next task is to compile all this onto one composite chart, so we have a true picture of his life. There is one thing wrong with that though."

"What's wrong with it? I thought that was the objective of the exercise. Are you worried about how I might react to it?"

"Er, no… I hadn't thought about that. Are you likely to go all funny about it?"

"Of course not... If that is what's bothering you, rest assured it won't be a problem. Let's get on with it."

"Actually, that wasn't the problem. As I see it, the missing link is the problem."

"Missing link? I didn't think we were tracing this bloke's movements back as far as the Neanderthals."

"Not that sort of missing link. I'm talking about Tristan Bailey. We don't have a passport for him, so we can make only assumptions about what Mr Bailey was up to … Or, when our target was actually in Brisbane being Tristan Bailey. Once the man was back in Australia, he could go wherever he liked and whenever it suited him, without leaving a record for us to follow. Does the fact he doesn't appear to have a passport mean Tristan Bailey never ventured overseas under that name?"

"I see your point. All we can do is work with what we have. If what Mrs Bailey says is correct, Tristan Bailey should only impact the last five years of our composite chart."

"…Unless there is another Mrs Bailey somewhere else."

"No, I don't think that's likely. He seemed to adopt a different name to go with each 'wife'. So, while I'm not saying there is another woman involved, and whom we don't know about yet, she won't be 'Mrs Bailey'."

"Okay, point taken. That means there are a few entries towards the bottom of this chart I need to draw a line through now. They were assumptions on our part. I will, however, leave this entry. That's about when he was busy getting Mrs Bailey pregnant again. Sorry; maybe I should have put that a little more tactfully."

"No apology required. Damn! I know the chart is trying to tell me something, but I just can't quite grasp what it is."

"As you know, I've never made any secret of the fact I never liked Tremayne. But I have developed a new respect for the man. Such stamina…!"

"What's that supposed to mean?"

"With so many 'wives' the man must have been running himself ragged. As I said, *such stamina.*"

"*Stamina*…! That's rubbish. His sex life was no different from any other normal male's – at least, as I understand that to be. His 'marriage obligations' were scheduled so he was dealing with only one wife at a time. If he were attending to more than one wife at the same time, there might be reason to admire his prowess. In his case, it was more like having one wife who kept moving around in order to be in the right place to accommodate him when required."

Kate gave it a moment's thought. "Hmm… perhaps you're right. I wasn't thinking of just the physical demands. Most men seem to have trouble dealing with the complexities of life associated with having one wife, no matter how 'low maintenance' she may be. Maintaining matrimonial harmony with four wives was some feat. If for no other reason, you have to give him credit for such amazing ability. And, why do you keep frowning at my chart? Have you spotted an error somewhere?" she demanded

"Thank God for the change of topic. Yeah, something about the chart bothers me."

"Do you want me to cross out something else? Is there something on the chart that shouldn't be?"

"No-o… It's what's not on the chart that's bothering me. Look at where the chart starts; right up there at the top. This is going to sound ridiculous, but what do you see… More correctly, what don't you see?"

"It's too late in the day for me to play 'I Spy'. Tell me what you are on about." Kate was becoming defensive of her handiwork.

"The first part of the chart has a shortage of wives compared to the rest of it. Even the gap of about eight years between when he married Roslyn Williams and me is suspicious. With a gap of only three or four years after me before the next wife, and then a further gap of about three years to Donna Bailey, a gap of eight years without another wife seems unlikely."

"Oh, I see what you mean. I'll add 'margin notes' at the points on the timeline where he reputedly acquired a new wife. There is something else to think about. Now you've raised the question of those eight years between you and Roslyn Williams, were there wives before Miss Williams?"

"In Telford Cresswell's time…? Yeah, that's a good question. But, here's another good one: how the hell do we find out?"

Further speculation was cut short when my phone chirped. Inspector Taylor. The call was short. I relayed the gist of his call to Kate. "Taylor will be here first thing in the morning. He didn't say if he had any new information. His visit is to see if he can collect some samples for DNA testing."

"Well, that's a waste of his time. You already have Tremayne's DNA results."

"What…? Oh God, I had forgotten about those. I'm not sure what I did with them; where I put them. If you would like to make a start on dinner, I'll hunt them down."

Chapter 18

"Inspector Taylor is in for a surprise when he discovers you've already had Tremayne's DNA analysed. What happened? You had Tremayne's DNA mapped but, when the results arrived, you didn't even bother to open them. I'm obviously missing something. When and why did his DNA no longer become important? I thought it would be even more important after his death, but still you weren't interested in it."

"It's hard to explain. I'm not sure I understand it myself. In the back of my mind, there's always been a question about Tremayne's background; about his family. Somehow, I figured DNA might help answer the questions. By the time the results arrived, I realised it was a ridiculous idea. So, I had Tremayne's DNA results; then what? What was I going to do with them? They weren't going to tell me anything useful. The only way I could see of finding out anything, was to have it recorded on Ancestry, or a similar family history site. A place where people interested in tracking down family connections might have theirs recorded for possible connection with others with similar DNA."

"Ye-es, I've seen that sort of thing advertised. Am I to understand you decided not to make Tremayne's DNA available for possible matching?"

"That about sums it up. As I understand it, those sites do their own testing anyway. You provide a saliva sample. They test it, and then match it for commonalities with other DNA results in their databank. I don't think they accept DNA analyses done by other agencies. Apart from that, it all seemed a bit tawdry somehow. Both Tremayne and I were private people. Having his DNA recorded in some databank would not sit comfortably with Tremayne, and I didn't have the right to make it available.

Then, when he was murdered, I was more interested in possible DNA they might lift from the crime scene."

"It seems none was found at, or anywhere near the crime scene. I understand why Taylor now wants to go down the DNA track. It's not about finding Tremayne's secret family. It's about confirming whether all of the names we discovered belong to the same person – and, maybe, who that person was. Do you intend giving the inspector Tremayne's DNA results?"

"Of course, he can have a copy, or he can have the original, and I will keep a copy. I know that sounds ridiculous. What am I going to do with it? I suppose I see it as something personal that should be kept with the rest of Tremayne's things."

"Perhaps I do understand, and I don't think it's ridiculous to feel that way. Anyway, who knows, an outcome might be that you discover other members of his original family. It might be just my journalist instinct, but I smell a story buried deep in his background. I'm not suggesting finding out about his roots will be all good news. It's quite possible you know nothing of his background because he wanted to keep it that way; because of what lurked there."

"I've thought of all that, but I still want to know, regardless of what I might find."

"Taylor said he wouldn't be here until around nine o'clock. Is there anything you want to do before he arrives?"

"Kate, at the risk of sounding like I'm using you as a domestic servant, do you think you might produce something for morning tea. Even if it's a bit early, I'm sure Taylor will be angling for at least a cup of coffee. I'd rustle up something myself, but there is something else I want to do before he arrives."

"That's not a problem. Do you need a hand with whatever it is you want to do before Taylor comes?"

"Thanks, but no. It's just a wild idea I had. I need to follow it up for peace of mind, rather than with the expectation of finding anything important. In fact, I'll make a start now. I'll be in the downstairs storeroom if you need me for anything."

"This is ridiculous," I murmured as I stood in the middle of the storeroom. "What am I going to find down here?" It's a question I'd been asking myself ever since that wild idea occurred to me: what if there was something more to be found? What if Tremayne had secreted other information somewhere in the storeroom? The whole damned room should be cleaned out. Some of the stuff my mother kept down here is from when I was a baby. And, I don't know whose hats are in those hat boxes on the top shelf, but those boxes were there in my earliest memories of this room. No doubt, they were amongst the first things that could go out once I got into spring-cleaning-mode.

My search began at the right-hand corner of the bottom shelf. Nothing escaped my scrutiny. Everything was pulled out, opened, and its contents examined. By the time I had gone all round the bottom shelf, I was fast losing interest in the exercise. I was hot, covered in dust, and had broken a nail. And, only four more shelves to go! The temptation was to abandon the search, admit defeat, and take a shower. But the little voice in my head wouldn't hear of it, insisting I complete the task. I hope it knows something I don't. I will be cranky, if I spend so much time searching through everything, only to find nothing.

The second and third shelves produced nothing. Why wasn't I surprised? The fourth shelf looked as though it should be easier to search than the others. It was home to obsolete, redundant, and superseded bits of household equipment. There were a couple of old kerosene lamps, and old iron dating from the pre-steam iron days, an ancient pasta machine long since replaced by a newer model, and a whole host of 'good-idea-at the-time' kitchen appliances.

With only the top shelf left to search, I climbed onto the next rung of the ladder. This shelf had not suffered human interference in a l-o-n-g time. If it were at all possible, the dust and detritus was thicker up here than anywhere else. The built-in shelves ran around three sides of the storeroom, which was about the size of an average bathroom. It allowed plenty of scope for hoarding.

Being so high up, the top shelf was less tightly packed than those below. I ran my eyes around the objects on the shelf. A clean-out of the storeroom might well start up here. Apart from nothing on the shelf having been touched in years, I could see nothing anybody would ever want to see or use again. Still, if nothing else, this treasure hunt provided the opportunity to see what was in those ancient boxes.

After working my way a short distance along the shelf, I came to the first hatbox. With my backside firmly planted on the top of the ladder, I wrestled with the box's recalcitrant latches. I wasn't going to be defeated, but it looked as though I might need something to prise them open. "One last concerted effort," I told myself, "before I resort to drastic measures."

Another fingernail was sacrificed in the pursuit of victory, but the resounding clatter as the clips sprung open was the sweet sound of triumph. The force with which they sprung open shook the box a little, launching a cloud of dust off the lid. There still was plenty of dust to contend with as I applied brute strength to force open the lid. "Geez, how long have these been here?" I exclaimed as the contents revealed themselves.

Still in remarkably good condition, some of the hats looked as though they dated back to the thirties or earlier. Closer inspection showed a surprising number of hats stacked one inside the other; felt inside straw, and cloth sandwiched between others. Feathers of every hue, and faded and dejected artificial flowers were everywhere. What wasn't there, however, was anything Tremayne might have added in recent times. I made a mental note that this box and its contents could be disposed of with a clear conscience.

The second hatbox offered little resistance. Its clips sprung open with relative ease, and the lid's hinges offered almost no resistance. I raised the lid a couple of centimetres before lowering it again. There was no denying the box was covered in the crud of ages, but somehow it looked less so than the first box. My stomach tightened and I took a deep breath. Only then did I feel ready to open the box completely. Instinct told me this box had been opened in comparatively recent times … more recently than when Kate and I borrowed hats from it years ago.

I caught my breath. "Christ, how long has this stuff been here … and how much more can there be?"

Shoved roughly down one side of the box was a bundle wrapped in a grubby-looking rag, which I later discovered was an ancient heavyweight calico pillowcase. With extreme caution, I lifted the bundle from the box. A scrabble through and under the now crushed hats produced nothing more. I gingerly carried the bundle down the ladder and up the stairs. An onlooker might be forgiven for thinking I carried a nuclear warhead.

At the top of the stairs, Kate looked up from the brownies she was cutting up on the bench. Her eyes met mine. "What's happened? What's that you're carrying? Is it safe?"

"I don't know what it is, but it is safe. That is, in as much as it is unlikely to explode. Beyond that, I don't know what it is. Help me move the stuff to one end of the dining room table to give me room spread out this lot."

A space created, I put the bundle on the table and started unrolling its wrapping. "Oh, it's a pillowcase," Kate said, "Do you think it's safe to just tip everything out onto the table, or should we remove it carefully bit by bit?" I was feeling around in the contents of the bag as she spoke.

"It feels like a lot of paper, with just a few lumpy things in amongst it. I think it's safe enough to tip it all out in one go." And, that's what I did.

A mass of paper, some of it quite yellowed with age, tumbled out and landed in an untidy heap. The few small heavier objects which fell out first became buried under the paper. The look of disbelief on Kate's face was priceless. She stood, eyes wide and shaking her head, as she stared at the new pile on the table. "This is more of Tremayne's stuff isn't it?" I shrugged. How did I know? I hadn't looked at any of it yet. But Kate continued as if there could be no question about ownership. "How much more is there to uncover about the man? What other secrets can there be?"

Almost afraid to delve into whatever this new material might reveal, up until then, I hadn't been able to bring myself to touch any of it. After telling myself I was being ridiculous and to get on with it, I took a deep breath, squared my shoulders, and said, "Right, there's only one way to find out what else there is to learn. So, let's make a start on it."

Working as a team, we each took sheets of paper, smoothed and flattened them, and then stacked them in piles. At the end of that first stage, we had two neat piles of paper, including yet another passport, and a small collection of objects still in the centre of the cleared space. I cast my eyes over the objects. Immediately identifiable were a pairs of cuff links and a fob watch. While the objects might prove interesting later, my priority was the documents.

Kate reminded me Inspector Taylor was now running later than expected and would most likely arrive at any moment. "Are we going to show him this new stuff?"

I had forgotten about him but, when reminded about his visit, a decision was easy. "No. He doesn't see this until we have been through it. It will need to be out of sight before he arrives."

"That tea trolley thing might be useful."

Our minds seem to function in similar ways. I already was on my way to fetch the trolley as Kate mentioned it. The pillowcase and the two stacks of documents went onto it before I gathered up the objects and threw them on as well. As I checked we had left nothing behind, Kate said, "Just in time; I hear a car coming up the drive. I'll be surprised if it isn't Dan Taylor."

While I rushed the trolley into the office and shut the door, Kate went to meet the inspector at the front door. When they reached the top of the stairs, he was still apologising for arriving so much later than he had said. There was a good thing about his late arrival. It was just the right time for morning coffee. Kate bustled about making coffees while I quizzed the inspector about his progress on the case. It took until he was halfway through his coffee to stop asking me to call him Dan, and for me to reassure him his tardiness hadn't caused any problems. My only problem was, Kate seemed perfectly comfortable calling him Dan, whereas I just felt just plain awkward. Perhaps, if we continued meeting like this, it might become easier.

"Inspector … *Dan,* I don't understand how collecting DNA samples will assist with your investigation."

"The hope is that, if we analyse DNA from people connected to all those passports, we might end up closer to understanding who our murder victim was. Once we have that information, perhaps the WHY might become evident. I've taken a sample from Mrs Bailey and arranged for a sample from her daughter to be collected. Mrs Bailey's sample will establish the child's mitochondrial DNA, while the rest of the sample will be that of the child's father. Mrs Bailey has returned to Brisbane and will look for items belonging to her husband from which we also might be able to extract a clear sample."

"If you do collect a sample from his belongings, and/or you isolate his part of the child's DNA, you should end up with good DNA results for Tristan Bailey. Do you anticipate undertaking a similar exercise in relation to the other names we have?"

"Officers visited the home of Mrs Cross – or Miss Williams if you prefer – and collected samples from items in her husband's bathroom there. We have contacted the Vietnamese authorities to ask for their assistance in carrying out similar procedures with the wife and a child of Mr Travis Cridland."

"So, that leaves you to collect samples from Telford Cresswell and my husband. I might be able to help simplify that a bit." Inspector Taylor sat upright and slid forward on his chair.

"Anything to help speed up the process would be most welcome. Have you identified potential sources of samples for us?"

"Better than that… I can give you a copy of his DNA. Perhaps it will mean more to your boffins than it does to me." His curiosity about how I came to have Tremayne's DNA analyses was not unexpected. I gave him a somewhat abridged version of the story. He accepted it without question.

After a second coffee and yet another couple of brownies, Inspector Taylor was on his way back to his office … and I was on my way to my office to retrieve the trolley and our latest collection of material.

"I thought he was never going to leave," Kate said as I parked the trolley next to the table. "Curiosity about what's in this lot is killing me. I thought I saw a passport in one of the stacks of documents. Are we about to make the acquaintance of yet another alias? May we please look at the passport first?"

"That was my intention. I saved it until now so we had plenty of time to deal with whatever surprises it has to offer." I riffled through the papers stacked earlier and pulled out the passport with a flourish. "Right, now let's see who this belongs to." My light-hearted performance stalled at the page with the photograph and personal details.

"Are you all right, Lisa? What did you find?"

"…not sure really; the passport belongs to a young bloke called Thomas Maycross, whose details are accompanied by a photo of a quite young-looking Tremayne Bancroft."

"Well, at least this one doesn't leave much chance for confusion or doubt to occur. Do we add Thomas' details to our charts?"

"Oh, I would think so." Kate already had ripped off another sheet. While she stuck it up on the wall, I flicked through the passport's pages. "This one had a relatively short life. Okay, when you are ready, let's enter his travel details on Thomas' sheet, and then see how and where they slot into our composite chart."

After applying the same routine as with the others, it took no time to complete Thomas Maycross' chart. A long pause followed while Kate and I gazed at the chart in a bid to make sense of it. For me, the best way to achieve that was to think aloud.

"Right; I need to sort out the sequence of events. We know Telford Cresswell's passport was issued and became active about thirty-four years ago. Five years – almost six years – later,

Thomas Maycross' passport was issued and became active soon after. After that, both passports were in use for about six years. Then, for reasons unknown, Thomas Maycross' passport has no further entries." As I finished speaking, I raised my eyebrows at Kate.

"Yep, that about sums it up. I suppose it is possible Thomas died, or maybe he decided to settle down in one place."

"Kate, you are forgetting what we already know – or think we know – about all these passport holders: they are one and the same person as Tremayne Bancroft. And, if the photo in Thomas' passport is a genuine likeness of Thomas Maycross, he was alive and kicking until recently … until he was found dead in my cane paddock."

"That's true. I am having trouble keeping everything straight in my head. Okay … for this part of the exercise, let's assume Thomas is a young Tremayne. Does Thomas have a wife and family? For that matter, does Telford Cresswell have a wife and family?"

"Judging by this bloke's track record, I'd be prepared to bet both Thomas and Telford were married. Whether they had kids or not is another matter. What would interest me, even more than finding out about their wives, is what precipitated the long list of name changes in the first place."

"Both of those early passports are British. That might be where we need to start searching for information about those men. I have a colleague in London I worked with for a while when I was posted over there. I could call in a couple of favours. She was into the whole family history thing, so she probably knows where to look for the details we want."

"Sounds like a great idea. Send her an email to see if she is interested."

"No, I'll skype her. It would require an email about a mile long to have her even begin to understand what this is about. Much better to do it face-to-face first; then follow-up with the details in an email later." There was no question about it. Kate's approach made more sense.

"Now I think about it, one thing does occur to me. What if Thomas Maycross' wife wasn't British? Most of his travel was to the Middle East. What if he married someone over there somewhere?"

"You know, Lisa, it would be much simpler if you didn't keep coming up with interesting questions … to which we have no answers. On that note, I'm going to give my brain a rest while I deal with tonight's dinner." We agreed on steak and salad; quick and easy with both of us preparing it.

We didn't linger long over dinner. At eight o'clock, having worked out it was about 10.00AM in London, Kate went off to skype her friend. The call was something of a marathon. It was almost fifty minutes later before Kate joined me again on the deck. She looked pleased with herself. "Gabby is fired up and rearing to go," she told me. "She mentioned a few places she would check first, and she probably will make a start this afternoon her time, after she finishes something she has to do this morning. In the meantime, I need to email her the details. I might scan the details pages from both those passports and include them in the email."

"Okay; use the equipment in the office."

Kate disappeared into the office, leaving me alone on the deck. It was another glorious night. I left the deck lights turned off. Full moon was only a day or so away. The moonlight, coupled with the cool light breeze and the clear starry sky, created the perfect ambiance in which to sit and reflect. And, I was doing just that when Kate joined me again sometime later. "Is everything all right, Lisa?" she asked as she drew up a chair. "You seem preoccupied, but I can't tell whether it's with good thoughts or bad ones."

"Neither really… I was letting my mind roam free, but it became fixated on the question of who the hell I married. The real question is: how can you be married to someone for so long and not know anything about them? That probably highlights something about the quality of the marriage. We weren't close – not really – not in the sense of a close, loving relationship.

Don't get me wrong, we were okay together. There were no squabbles or blazing rows, but there wasn't much else either. I suppose spending so much time apart had something to do with it. Maybe we didn't spend enough time together to annoy one another and generate rows. The fact that the separations didn't bother me should have told me something. If I'm honest, I never thought about them. It was a case of accepting the fact that his work took him away, while mine kept me in the one place, at first when I was teaching and then later here on the farm."

"Am I hearing self-recriminations and regrets?"

"No, just a statement of facts. Whether we had a good or bad marriage wasn't the issue. What I now realise is, the way it was – the way we were together – probably explains why I don't feel any great sense of loss over Tremayne's death. There are all sorts of emotions involved: anger that someone would come onto my property and commit murder; resentment that Tremayne kept his life so secret; confusion about the multiple identities. But, there is no grief or sense of loss. Just a determination to unravel the mystery and know all there is to know about the man I married."

"In that case, I'm relieved. The fact that you are showing no signs of grief was concerning me. The last thing I wanted was for you to go down in a great heap at some time in the near future because you hadn't allowed yourself to grieve properly. After what you've said, it now appears it's full steam ahead with getting to know who this bloke really was. Let's hope Gabby comes up with something interesting."

Although I knew there was nothing else we could do for the moment, playing the waiting game is not something I do well. I am not comfortable with, or good at having to rely on other people to do things. I knew impatience would be my constant companion for the next few days.

Chapter 19

My agony eased a little when Inspector Taylor dropped by a couple of days later. "I was heading back to my office from a job out this way and decided to drop in to update you. Can you spare me some time?" If he was going to update me on the case, I could spare all the time he needed.

"The first thing is, the big boys upstairs contacted Scotland Yard. I don't know much about what happened, except that whoever the appointed person over there is, he will contact me directly in future. As I don't know what they've asked the Poms to do on our behalf, I don't know how soon to expect to hear from them. All I understand is that, because two of the passports were British, they asked Scotland Yard to find out what they can about the men in whose names they were issued."

"It would be difficult, if at all possible, for you to do much from here. As neither of the men seemed to spend much time in the UK in the last few years, I don't imagine it will be easy for your colleagues to make much headway in a hurry either. I'm trying to resign myself to the fact that 'patience' is the operative word, closely followed by the notion of letting people get on with what they need to do without harassing them."

"That is so-o right. I wanted to tell you the DNA sample gathering exercise is complete. We await the results from a full workup of all of the samples collected. After discussion with people in the know, my boss decided to take a punt on the analysis results you gave us. They forwarded a copy of the results to the Ancestry mob to see if their database produces any matches with those of their ardent family historians. I don't know how long that will take either, but I'll keep you informed."

After a couple of moment's hesitation, I decided to share my latest information as well. "I also have something to share with you. I managed to find another bundle of stuff secreted in the storeroom downstairs. There hasn't been time to go through it yet, but we found another passport. Again, it's under a different name, but this time it's a bit more accommodating. Come through to the dining room and I'll show you."

"Forgive me if I'm wrong, but that photo looks very much like your deceased husband. He was a young man when it was taken. Nevertheless, there can't be any doubt about the identity of the person in the photo."

"His likeness didn't escape my attention either. If the photograph wasn't enough, the similarity of the name tends to confirm it is simply another name for the same person we've been investigating all along. As it's another British passport, you might want to add this bloke's name to your British counterpart's woes."

Handing over a copy of the passport created a further delay in Inspector Taylor's departure. Kate demanded to know if he were staying for lunch.

"…Only if there's an invitation. It wasn't my intention to be here so long."

Kate gave a derisive snort. "Some might believe that. If this continues, I will recommend we start charging you board." Kate's forthrightness had me hold my breath for a moment, but the inspector's chuckle told me all was well, and his reply confirmed it.

"It's when the situation warrants charging me for lodgings as well that you will need to worry."

Hmm, was that a touch of pink I saw rise up Kate's neck to invade her cheeks? I wonder if the victims of other crimes the inspector is investigating receive the same degree of attention as we do. Somehow, I doubted that was the case.

A phone call sent Taylor scurrying back to his office. As Kate and I sat down for lunch, I commented, "The poor man ends up with more work every time he visits this place. Anyone with any brains would give us a wide berth, and avoid coming out here only to end up having that happen." That hint of pink slid up from below her collar again.

The next two days brought only silence from Inspector Taylor and everyone else. I thought it might be worth calling on Justin Farley. My frustration felt like it needed company. Adding a touch of frustration to Justin's day might be just what's required to quieten it down. He was with a client when I arrived, but a sneaked peek at his appointments confirmed he had nothing else booked for the rest of the day.

Not wasting time on the usual niceties, I went directly to the purpose of my visit. "I haven't heard from you for a few days and wondered where probate of my husband's Will is at. I appreciate it probably became complicated after our meeting at the bank the other day, but I hoped you were moving towards finalising Tremayne's estate."

"Information acquired at that meeting tended to complicate matters somewhat. I felt compelled to seek legal counsel on the matter."

"You spoke to your father about it?"

"Okay, so I spoke to my father about it. After so many years in practice, I felt sure he had experienced a similar situation at some time. It seemed pertinent to confer with him before progressing further."

"This is me you are talking to, Justin. So, cut the BS. Get to the point and tell me what you propose to do … or not do."

"Lisa, you are a classic example of why one shouldn't have former classmates as clients." I sat forward in my chair and glowered at him. "Okay. Okay … I followed my father's advice. As I already had lodged the application and all the preliminary paperwork, there was only the inventory to finalise and submit. It was held back until I completed my search for bank accounts and any existent Wills."

"Got that; so, when you didn't find any other bank accounts or Wills in Tremayne Bancroft's name, what did you do?"

"I finalised the inventory and submitted it. It's likely the application will be processed and probate granted in the next couple of days. With so little involved, there shouldn't be any delays."

"Thank you. That's all I needed to know."

"I have to admit to being a bit uncomfortable about this whole situation. While Dad's advice made sense, all those other names still bother me."

"It's unlikely you have any cause for concern in relation to my husband's estate. Those other personas probably each have their own bank accounts, and possibly other assets, which will be dealt with by the executors of their Wills when the time comes. Please thank your father for me for his input."

I wandered out to my car in a world of my own. Justin's information was satisfying, but thoughts of those other names and the people attached to them swirled around in my mind. It was like peering into some cauldron of roiling murky soup. In reality, it was the wives who concerned me most. Argh, not Roslyn Williams. She was financially well-off, and there were no children. Her loss would be negligible compared to Travis Cridland's and Tristan Bailey's wives, who now were left with families to support and bring up singlehandedly. What about the names in those two British passports? Did they have wives – and maybe families? One thing was clear. There would be a whole world of pain before this mess was sorted out and settled.

With no one else I needed to annoy in town, the temptation was to go for coffee. I was halfway across the street on my way to the coffee shop that has those chocolate-filled croissants that I love, when conscience got the better of me. There was a huge property I was supposed to be running, but had neglected for days. Thank God for Connor Rankin…! And, thank God, for Kate, who had shouldered the rest of my responsibilities since Tremayne's death. It's not good enough. I've been treating her as a live-in domestic help. It's way past time I got my act together. Forget the coffee and croissants. Go home and pick up your responsibilities, I chastised myself.

A suitably chastised version of me arrived home to be greeted by an excited Kate. "Have you had coffee? No…? Good, let's have it now. I have news for you." Two mugs of coffee were produced without the usual faffing about. Then Kate almost rushed me out onto the deck.

"Judging by all the rush, whatever you have to tell me must be important. Why don't you put us both out of our misery and share it?"

"Remember, I contacted my friend Gabby in London and asked her to see what she could dig up on Telford Maybanks Cresswell?" How could I forget something we hoped might result in a breakthrough of sorts? I motioned for her to continue. "Well, thanks to his fancy middle name, it wasn't too hard to find him in official records and to be sure she had the right bloke."

"Has she traced him back to his roots, and found Telford Cresswell is his legal name?"

"I was convinced he would turn out to be a 'nobody'; an illegitimate child of some poor young woman supporting herself as best she could. Turns out he is a blue blood; some sort of member of the English aristocracy."

"You have my undivided attention. Please start at the beginning and take me through what Gabby had to say."

"Your Telford was the second son of Lord someone-or-other. Gabby did tell me the father's title. It was a strange name and I didn't quite catch it. It seems the eldest child was the family's son and heir. Then there were four daughters, each of them married off to someone with a title and bags of money. Then, last of the litter after a bit of a gap, came Telford. It seems tradition dictates the eldest son inherits everything. The daughters all made 'good' marriages and were taken care of. That left the youngest child, Telford, with no prospects at all."

"Yeah, the aristocracy was a world of harsh realities. A 'lesser' son often was found a 'suitable position for someone of breeding' within the Civil Service. Their only chance of making good was to marry a woman, not necessarily from the upper class, but who had money by some means or other."

"It's likely that was Telford's intended future. His life had a rocky start. It seems the parents' marriage soured after the birth of the last daughter but, as was the 'done thing', they stayed together. Then, when Telford arrived after a gap of some years, rumours ran rife. For some time, consensus had Telford as the illegitimate outcome of one of his father's many extramarital affairs."

"Oh dear… With everyone who was anyone knowing about the state of the parent's marriage, convincing the population Telford was legitimate would be nigh on impossible."

"You would expect so, but apparently not… Another daughter arrived a couple of years after Telford's birth, but she survived only a few hours. That birth helped convince at least some people they had misjudged the state of the marriage, and that Telford might have some claim to being legitimate. Regardless, none of that improved his standing in the inheritance stakes. He still stood to inherit nothing. But, life was not all bad news for the young Telford. His grandmother left him a considerable sum of money. It was untouchable until he turned twenty-one, after which he was paid an annuity from the bequest, but still couldn't actually draw on the money or access it in any way."

"So, he didn't come out of it too badly after all. He wasn't left destitute, and wasn't penniless while married to me. It would be interesting to know details of his annuity. I suspect it went some way towards supporting his many wives and children."

"…Maybe it wasn't enough. Perhaps the annuity helped support his Vietnamese family, and maybe even his Brisbane lot, but wasn't quite enough to cover the costs. Adding two well-off independent females to his stable of wives might have been one way of 'making ends meet'. After all, you paid him an allowance, and we know he received income from his Sydney connection with the Williams family's business empire."

"I wonder how Nathan is progressing with tracing transactions on those bank accounts. Maybe I should have annoyed him as well while I was in town today."

"No, I think it's better if you leave Nathan alone to work on what he has to do. I'm sure Inspector Taylor is keeping a close eye on how he's going. If you are looking for someone else to annoy, maybe Taylor would be a good candidate."

"And then he would have an excuse to come for coffee or lunch again. The name 'Thomas Maycross' gnaws at me. He was still a young man when he adopted that name. Why? What caused it? By the way, did your friend, Gabby, say whether Telford was married or not?"

"Not yet; she's been on assignments and hasn't had a chance to go through those records yet. Don't panic. She knows we want everything there is on the man. We have to be patient and let her do what she can when she can."

"Mention of Thomas Maycross has me wondering whether he also had a wife and children. It might be worth asking Gabby to check on Thomas while she is checking the births, deaths, and marriage records."

"An email to that effect has been sent. I wish I was in London right now. Gabby knows so much more about which records to search and where to find them than I do, but research is part of being an investigative journalist. It's a big part of what I do, and I'm feeling frustrated by not being able to do any of this research."

"Are you sure that is the case?" Kate shot me an angry look and was about to argue. I rushed on. "There is so much stuff online these days. I'd be surprised if it wasn't possible to undertake at least some of that research from here."

"Geez, I'm losing my touch. I haven't even looked at what records are available online. Well, now I know what I'll be doing for the rest of the day. What are your plans?"

While I didn't have any plans as such, I did have a much-neglected farm begging for attention. I haven't lost interest in the place and I'm not blind. I've noticed things are being taken care of despite my not spending time in the paddocks over the last few days. I don't know how I'm going to thank Connor for everything he's doing for me. He and his father must be so busy with their place, but he still finds time to come and attend to things here.

As planned, Kate spent the afternoon in the office interrogating various online resources, while I attended to various tasks around the farm. I was heading back to the house just before six o'clock when I met Connor on the headland along the creek bank. He was on his way to check on my cattle. After thanking him for all the work he's done while I've been otherwise engaged, I assured him I would be back to normal from tomorrow. I offered a small token of my appreciation. "It's a bit short notice for dinner tonight, but check with your father to see if you're both available tomorrow night."

"He won't be. He's at a cattleman's conference, and likely to be missing for at least the next two days. As I don't need to confer with anyone, does your invite cover tonight as well is tomorrow night?"

"It covers every night your father is away, and lunch too if that doesn't disrupt your day too much. Shall we say seven o'clock for dinner? That should give us both time to get cleaned up and have a drink before we eat."

My priority was to be home in time to alert Kate to the news 'we would be three for dinner'. I needn't have worried. The moment I opened the front door, I smelled the roast she was cooking. Regardless, I called her name as I galloped up the stairs.

"What? Lisa, what happened?"

"Nothing… Nothing serious that is. I've asked Connor to join us for dinner. So, we will need to do a few extra vegetables, and think about something for dessert. You haven't made a desert, have you?"

"Because we never bother with dessert, I never gave it a thought. Any ideas about what you'd like?"

"I thought about it on the way home. After I wash up a bit, I'll make it." About half an hour later, individual panna cottas were in the top section of the fridge. Then I loaded the tea trolley with wine glasses, ice bucket and bottle of wine, and a bowl of nibbles. As I wheeled the trolley out onto the deck, Connor arrived.

Our pleasant evening stretched on longer than I expected. Delicious meal, good wine, and lively conversation; what more could you ask for at the end of the day? Connor confirmed his father was away for the next two nights, and only he would be coming to dinner. I assured him the invitation didn't have a defined end, but covered the whole period, however long his father was away.

Later, when I crawled into bed with a book, somehow I knew sleep would be a long while coming. Maybe something to do with the warm, fuzzy feelings I was experiencing. They weren't a concern, quite the contrary, and were probably linked to another phenomenon: I didn't seem able to stop smiling tonight. This was something new to me. I felt a bit like a giddy-headed teenager. …Must have something to do with the wine we were drinking.

*****

I had a few minutes alone out on the deck this morning, before a bleary-eyed Kate joined me. "I thought I would have trouble falling asleep last night after spending all afternoon looking at a computer screen, but it was the opposite. I died the moment my head hit the pillow. You seem all right this morning, so I don't suppose I can blame it on the wine."

"Talking about computer screens, Kate, did your afternoon's research turn up anything interesting?"

"Depends on your definition of 'interesting'. I discovered Telford – or Tremayne if you prefer – was older than I thought. While I knew he was a bit older than us, I figured he was coming up to his fiftieth birthday. Turns out, he was fifty-five last birthday. Did you know he was so much older than you?"

"Fifty-five…! Are you sure? Was it the right person? It is a bit embarrassing admitting I'm not sure of his age, but I thought he was in his late-forties. Is nothing about this man as it seemed? That aside, was there anything special about his birth?"

"No, nothing new. I confirmed Gabby's information about Telford and his siblings. Then I looked for any marriages for Telford Maybanks Cresswell."

194

"And, you found one… Based on his past record, we can't have a name for this bloke without a wife attached to it. Go on, enlighten me."

"You nailed it. There was a marriage. Telford was young, only about twenty-one or twenty-two at the time. Lady Annabelle was upper class; a blue blood – and about five years older than Telford. Her father was an Earl. She was her parents' sole remaining child, her two older brothers having died as young children. It stood to reason that, as the only offspring, she would inherit substantial property and cash."

"You established all that from searching the births, deaths and marriages records?"

"Nah, all that is too recent for those records. Church baptism and marriage registers were useful, as were the newspapers of the day. Being of the upper echelons of society, they received frequent mention in the social and other pages."

"Thank God for that then. At least we now know that much about him."

"… But, wait, there's more. While I was digging around in those records, I discovered Annabelle's father died just over a year after Annabelle and Telford married. I found his Will in the indexes and requested a copy. It probably came through overnight. I'll check after breakfast."

"It could prove an interesting document."

"After ordering a copy of the Will, I returned to the church registers. The aristocracy usually wasted no time in producing an heir. And, her father's death so soon after their marriage, suggested the young couple might have 'got on with it' in the hope of producing an heir before her father dropped off the twig."

"Oh good…! You're going to tell me there are more offspring involved in this mess."

"There's no getting away from it is there? He always was a 'busy' bloke. A son was born about eleven months after the marriage… and before Annabelle's father died. I kept searching and found a daughter born about eighteen months later."

"Okay, how many more were there?"

"That's the interesting thing. Everything screeched to a halt after their daughter was born. I thought maybe Annabelle died in childbirth, or soon after. I checked the death records for a period of twenty years after the birth of the last child. There wasn't an entry for Annabelle."

"Did they move from the UK, and subsequent births or deaths were recorded in another country, and not the UK?"

"It's possible, but it doesn't match up with entries in his passport. He made a few trips abroad after his son's birth, but always returned to the UK after only short absences. It seems he obtained his passport just before making his first trip."

"So, he obtained a passport in order to travel outside the UK. I agree, that he always returned, suggests his wife and kids were still at home in the UK. I can't help wonder what his excuse was in those days for his frequent trips away from home. It would be interesting to know where they lived. Was it up to Telford to put a roof over his family, or did they move in with her parents … either before or after her father died?"

"Although I don't know much about researching family history, I do know all this is too recent to access via the census records. Maybe the equivalent of our electoral rolls might shed some light on their address during the period in question, but I think finding out where they resided is best left to Gabby."

"So, it appears there is nothing more we can do from here. When do you expect to hear from Gabby again?"

"The next time I hear from her will be when, and if, she finds something more for us. In the meantime, I thought I might try searching *The Times* online index. I don't know how detailed it is in more recent times, or if it is likely to produce any more useful information, but it's worth a try."

"Good luck with that. I'll be spending most of the day out in the paddocks. Judging by the humidity level already today, the build up to the wet season has begun. I need to make sure everything on the farm is ready in case the rains come earlier than expected."

"I hope they do. I'm not keen on this weather. At least the office is airconditioned. It might take me a while to search those indexes."

"Enjoy! I'll be back around morning coffee time … and I'll expect a progress report."

Chapter 20

Today was another occasion when I applauded the foresight of engineers in developing airconditioned cabins for tractors. Not only do they allow operation in a relatively dust-free environment, but they make life bearable on days like today. After an early start, by mid-morning, I was ready for a coffee.

The aroma of fresh baking greeted me as I made my way up the stairs. For a brief moment, I wondered whether the baking was in honour of another impending visit by Inspector Taylor. I was sure Kate would have called me on my mobile if that were the case. Two questions arrived in quick succession: on such a muggy, hot day, did I really want something warm with my coffee? And, why was Kate wasting time baking when she should be searching for clues about Telford Cresswell's life?

Muffins were cooling on the rack in the kitchen, but Kate was nowhere to be seen. I brought the coffee machine to life before calling her. "I'm in the office. I'll be out when I finish skimming this last little bit."

A mental apology is required; it seems she can bake and research at the same time. She appeared as I finished making the second mug of coffee. By then, I was sure a warm muffin was exactly what I needed. While there was no breeze out on the deck, it was cooler than inside. Somehow, I restrained myself until I had consumed half my muffin, before asking the question gnawing at me. "How has your morning been? Did you manage any research in between baking and whatever else you've done this morning?"

"Yes – and no. The copy of the Will I asked for was in my inbox this morning. I expected it to be three or four pages at most. Turns out, the Earl was an aspiring novelist, or an ardent short story writer. The document is twenty-plus pages! While some of it is legal-speak type rubbish, there is quite a story involved. Fascinating … absolutely fascinating."

"Am I to be allowed to read this fascinating document, or is it for your eyes only?"

"What…? Of course you can read the damn thing. I've left a copy on your desk for you."

"Should we peruse it together over coffee? I do want another muffin, so I am going to be here a bit longer. We could use the time to start dissecting the contents of the Will."

Kate was right about the size of the document. Maybe the aristocracy produced weighty tomes, rather than basic serviceable documents as the rest of we mere mortals do. It led off with the usual bit about being of sound mind and the other routine legal ramblings, before finally coming to the bequests. Even that part wasn't straight forward.

It seems every issue mentioned was accompanied by a story – explanation in some cases – before stating the deceased's intention in relation to the matter being discussed. With only a wife and daughter to survive him, I expected the Earl's Will to be short and to the point. I was wrong.

The first bequest was to his wife. He extolled her virtues as loyal and steadfast in her role as wife and mother, and lauded her for supporting him so wholeheartedly in his many ventures over their married life together. "How sweet!" I murmured after reading the sickly rhetoric. "They probably fought the whole time, mainly about his philandering I don't doubt."

"Why say that? There's nothing to suggest they were anything other than a devoted couple."

"Watch out for low-flying pigs. From what I've read about the upper classes, he would have been odd-man-out if he weren't spreading it about a bit."

"You sceptic; you're basing your opinion on a total lack of evidence. Still, I agree his comments about his wife do lay it on a bit too thickly to be swallowed easily. Nevertheless, he did the 'right' thing by her. He left her some cash and a small annuity, and she could continue to live in the family mansion. Well, she could continue to live there and receive the annuity as long as she didn't remarry. Both arrangements ended the moment she became someone else's responsibility."

"There was nothing unique about such a situation. I think you might find the same stipulations even in more recent local Wills. What about his daughter, Annabelle, and our mysterious friend, Telford? No doubt they got a mention and scored okay from the Earl's death?"

"Yeah, they received several pages worth. Most of it was to do with Telford. …Not one of the Earl's favourites judging by the tone of it. Apart from anything else, it provides a glimpse into how the rich and titled do things."

"Don't keep me in suspense. I'll read it later, but can I have the executive summary now please?"

"Here's the gist of it. While Telford, as a second son, was well below Annabelle's station, so to speak, it appears he was all that was on offer at the time. Anabelle was getting on a bit. For her still to be unmarried was unheard of in their circles. Besides, the Earl was keen to have succession planning under control before he departed this mortal coil. With only one child himself, and no marriage on the horizon, no possibility of a legitimate heir to carry on the line was a concern. Then Telford appeared on the scene. Although not deemed a suitable match, under the circumstances, he would do as a husband for Annabelle."

"What a charming situation. How kind of the Earl to record it all so succinctly. Right, this wasn't a marriage made in heaven, but anything goes when you're desperate... poor Annabelle! By the way, does it mention if she had any physical deformities – like two heads or something – which might account for her remaining unmarried for so long?"

"No … and there was no hint of her being ugly in any other way either. Shall I continue with the story?"

"Please do."

"There is nothing to suggest Annabelle was bulldozed into the marriage. In fact, it appears to be her idea, and not her father's. An interesting aspect of the Will is that it was updated after Annabelle's son was born. Much of the Will reads as though written before the arrival of a grandson, but bits of it appear to be added after the line of succession was secured."

"Does it cater for changes that might occur in the future regarding Annabelle and grandchildren?"

"Yep. Annabelle, as his sole heir, gets the title, the manor house, the properties and the cash ... until such time as her oldest living son reaches adulthood. In the case of no surviving son, a daughter would inherit on attaining adulthood."

"Good to see at least token acceptance that succession might be down the female line in the future."

"There is acknowledgement such a situation might occur, but he included provisos to ensure his intentions carried on long after his death. There are a couple of interesting aspects that might help explain some of the existing confusion. In his lengthy epistle about Annabelle and Telford's marital situation, he states that, in order for him to approve the marriage, the couple had to agree that Annabelle would never take the Cresswell surname, and no children resulting from the union would carry the Cresswell name. The Will goes on to state that any attempt to change that arrangement, by any party, subsequent to the Earl's death would result in relevant inheritance being voided, and the line and its title being deemed extinct."

"Now that is interesting. Although Annabelle was well over the age of twenty-one, they still needed her father's approval to marry and, as a result of the conditions attaching to his approval, Annabelle and her children retained the Reymeston surname. That could be important when Annabelle's son succeeded to the title. It must have been galling for Telford to agree to the arrangement."

"By now, Annabelle's children are adults and, presumably, the title has passed to her son – if he is alive. That then begs the next question: if that is the case, what happened to Annabelle when her son became the new Earl?" I pondered aloud and Kate continued with the story.

"Annabelle could live in a lodge on the manorial estate for the duration of her life. There also would be a small annuity. The amount of the annuity indicates her father intended Telford should be responsible for keeping his wife and family. The annuity was to ensure she 'was comfortable' for the rest of her life. My interpretation of some of the comments is, although Telford had done his duty and provided an heir, his standing in the eyes of the Earl didn't improve much, if at all."

"If my maths is right and the children are now adults, and the new Earl is in his manor house, Annabelle has been relegated to a lodge in the grounds of the manor. Entries in Telford's passport suggest he hasn't been home to Annabelle in a long time."

"It's interesting that, in spite of her father's requirement for Annabelle and her children not to take the Cresswell name, the births of the two children we read about were mentioned as having the Telford surname. As Annabelle's father was still alive when her son was born, it seems they kept his registered surname secret from his grandfather."

"That's not necessarily so," I reminded Kate. "The kids could have been registered according to her father's requirement – and the surname changed after his death – or, there is a more likely story. Perhaps they were registered as Reymeston, but authors of the articles in the newspaper assumed their surname to be Cresswell."

True… that's possible. Now we're more aware of what went on within the family, I will search the records again to see if there is more to be found."

"It shouldn't be hard to discover the new Earl's name. *Burke's Peerage* should enlighten us."

As it was close to lunchtime, we opted for an early lunch before resuming our planned activities for the remainder of the day. My day's work finished with a last check on the cattle before arriving back at the house at about five o'clock. I was showered and sitting on the deck with a long glass of iced tea when Connor arrived. He and Kate came out together to join me. "We are having fish and salad for dinner tonight," Kate announced. "I baked that whole fish we had in the freezer and, as it has been such a stinking hot day, I thought salad would go down better than vegetables."

I hadn't asked Kate about her research this afternoon. Although Connor wasn't aware of what we were doing and I wanted it to remain that way, I couldn't resist asking her for an update. "While there's no need to bore Connor with the details, did you meet with any success this afternoon?" She picked up on my intent to keep Connor in the dark.

"Yes and no. It seems every discovery only brings more questions. My friend, Gabby, should be home by now, so I'm hoping for something more from her soon."

In spite of our efforts not to arouse Connor's interest, he picked up on it and started asking questions. A complex, but not too lengthy question-and-answer session followed before Connor lapsed into something akin to stunned silence. Dealing with his own thoughts, he remained remote for a minute or so. Kate and I were quiet while he worked his way through whatever he struggled with until he rejoined us in the here and now.

"Lisa, it's none of my business, but I can't help thinking you and Kate would accomplish a lot more if you were in the UK, instead of trying to do it all from here. You don't need to worry about this place. I'll take care of everything while you are away. Why don't you think about it?"

"Thanks, Connor. The idea crossed my mind, but I'm not convinced a trip to the UK is necessary. Inspector Taylor and Scotland Yard are working on sorting it out, and Kate's friend, Gabby, is doing a bit as well. What are your thoughts, Kate?"

"No-o, it's not necessary yet. There's still research to do before we are in a position to make such a decision. We haven't even looked at Thomas Maycross yet. After a bit of digging on him, we might be better placed to decide. And, we haven't searched for further Reymeston mentions. Maybe, after Annabelle inherited, they complied with her father's wishes – at least for the sake of their son's future inheritance. I imagine

Annabelle would be keen the next Earl to carry the title should also carry the family name."

"Possibly… but I'm not sure about that, Kate. I'm inclined to think Telford moved on to greener pastures – perhaps in a part-time fashion – soon after his father-in-law's death."

"The evidence doesn't agree with you, Lisa. Thomas Maycross didn't obtain a passport until about five or six years after Telford Cresswell had his. If what you are suggesting were true, wouldn't Thomas have obtained a passport much sooner?"

In spite of his recent and sketchy knowledge of the situation, Connor decided to add his voice of reason to the conversation. "While I'm having trouble keeping tabs on who was doing what with whom and when, is when passports were obtained so critical? Isn't what prompted the men to obtain the passports more important than when they did it?"

"Good point, Connor," Kate exclaimed.

"That's right. Tremayne's passport was necessary because of his supposed work as a foreign correspondent, and then as a spook on overseas assignments. Trevor Cross gave Roslyn Williams a similar intimation about his employment and, hence, he also needed a passport. Donna Bailey's husband's work also involved frequent and sometimes lengthy travel – but was it overseas?"

Connor laughed and shook his head as I finished speaking. "You know what you just did? You just posed the age-old question: what came first? In this case it's got nothing to do with the proverbial chicken and egg situation. It's about what came first, the job or the passport."

"I'm not sure I follow what you're suggesting," Kate said.

"Did they obtain their passports as a requirement of the work they were doing, and that then opened the door for other liaisons to occur? Or, were the relationships already in place, and obtaining a passport merely facilitated their progression in a bigger and better way?"

"Bloody hell, Connor, I can come up with my own questions without you adding to the list," I told him. "Now you've opened that can of worms, how are we ever going to find the answers? Information from the more recent relationships might not be too hard to track down, but that information about Telford and Thomas won't be easy to come by. At least, I imagine the facts will be difficult to establish."

Kate heaved a sigh. "My friend, Gabby, is about to be asked to do more work. She doesn't seem to mind, and is keen to do research for us, but I am starting to feel guilty about asking her to do so much. Added to that, I'm starting to feel a bit jealous about it. There's a damn good story in this messy situation, and I want it to be my story; my book. Of course, there are a couple of hurdles to overcome before that could happen. To start with, I need the approval of all the 'wives' to document the incredible stories of their husbands' lives."

"You have my permission to go ahead with it. I suspect Roslyn Williams won't be hard to persuade once she knows the story."

Connor cleared his throat, a sure sign he was about to say something sensitive and/or provocative. "Lisa, I might be out of line, but there is something I need to say."

Yep, I was right. I smiled and nodded for him to continue.

"Okay … I am amazed at how you've handled Tremayne's death. If you're putting on a brave face for the rest of the world, don't. That will only lead to your crashing and burning in a big way. From experience, I can recommend letting it all out now and having it over and done with, instead of bottling everything up."

"Thanks, Connor. That is sound advice, but it doesn't apply in my case. The way in which Tremayne died still haunts me a bit, but only because I don't know why or who was involved. I did try forcing myself to face the fact that Tremayne would not be coming back – not ever – this time. But, I couldn't shake the belief he just was away on another of his trips. After a while, reality happened. That delusion disappeared. Perhaps all the details we have discovered since then have helped. I don't feel any sense of loss or grief. I just want to know all there is to know about the man and why he died as he did." Connor and Kate exchanged a look. I ignored them.

Nevertheless, Connor wasn't done with handing out advice. "That's good, but I still think a trip to the UK might uncover more, and in less time, than trying to research from here. I believe it is important to your wellbeing to have answers to all your questions as soon as possible. You can go anytime. The farm will be fine. I will see to that. So, think about it, please."

Of course I would give it some thought, but I doubted I would change my mind about going to the UK right now. There wasn't much else to say, and farmers get up early. The night wound down rapidly and, about half an hour later, Kate and I were bidding Connor good night at the front door. On our way back upstairs, Kate proved the earlier conversation wasn't quite closed yet.

"I'm not arguing with you, but Connor's suggestion of a trip to the UK does have merit. It also gave me food for thought. Even if you don't take a trip any time soon, I'm thinking I might. The more I think about this enigma of a man, the more determined I am to write his life story. Don't worry. I'm not about to book a trip to England, but I will spend the next few days digging up as much as I can on the bloke before deciding about a trip."

"It's not that I don't want to go overseas, or that I'm concerned about what I might discover there. It's whether a trip is worthwhile or not. If we discover more about the man and his life in England, I might feel more inclined to go. If I know more about him, I'll know where to go, who to see, what to ask. At the moment, I don't know anything, and would be floundering around in the dark and wasting time. I haven't discounted the possibility of a trip to the UK. It's more a case of if and when it becomes necessary. If your inclination is to head overseas, please go. Don't hang around here because you feel you need to keep an eye on me. I don't know how often I have to tell people, but I am okay. It is safe to leave me on my own."

At last, the topic was done for the night. After she spent much of the day staring at a screen, I suggested Kate might appreciate an early night. Not so; it seems tonight's conversation only served to spur her on to do a bit more research before she turned in. It had me feeling guilty about her doing all the research … And I really wasn't feeling all that tired.

After booting up the other computer, which was much neglected since my father's death, I sat down to follow Kate's example. She allocated me information to search for, and told me where to look for it. Once I worked out how to use the index she mentioned, I was off and running. Success didn't come early, or easily – or by the bucket load. After about half an hour or so with no results, I was beginning to rue having embarked on such a frustrating venture. That was when I had my first breakthrough.

Thomas Maycross' name jumped off the screen at me. I let out a yelp. "I think I found him. He's not a figment of my imagination. He does exist."

"Does he exist in the context we think of him? Or, was some other man with the same name around at about the right time?"

"Well, now you being picky. Of course I don't know the answer to that. But I have found Thomas Maycross' name in this index. He is listed as the father of a child, a daughter, born to one Hilary Esdaile."

"When was this?"

"It was about two … no, three years after Thomas obtained his passport. I suppose I should look for a marriage now." Kate didn't answer, so I asked if she had a problem with the information.

"No. I was thinking about the timing. I'm betting there was a 'marriage' sometime during that three-year period. I use the word loosely, because I'd also be willing to bet there was no divorce from wife, Annabelle, beforehand."

"It might have been just a relationship. You know, just shacked up together without formalising the arrangement."

"Unlikely, I think. This man seemed to make a practice of marrying all his women without bothering to disengage from previous ones first. It seems he required the respectability of marriage – or, perhaps it was the women who demanded it."

I shrugged. I couldn't argue. But, she wasn't done with explaining her take on the situation. "Anyway, given the date of this birth, if the parents were not married, the child would have been registered as illegitimate – and with the reputed father's name not recorded."

"Okay, maybe Thomas and Hilary were married. The question remains: was this our man?"

This research lark isn't as straightforward as I thought. Kate was patient with me. Rather than undertake further research before we called it a night, she suggested drawing up a list of specific things to search for tomorrow. When finished, the list of events, and where to look for the information, was quite impressive. But, there was one last task before we left the office for the night: Kate allocated entries on the list to each of us to chase up tomorrow.

Chapter 21

"How are you going with your *real* work? You've spent a lot of time researching our mystery man. I hope it doesn't mean you're neglecting the project you are supposed to be working on for your employer," I asked Kate as she joined me. Alone out on the deck, as I dawdled over my breakfast, it occurred to me that, for quite a while now, I hadn't heard anything about the interviews and other work Kate, the journalist, was supposed to be doing.

"I have been working. I've done several of the interviews, so far without having to leave here. And, I have appointments for two more interviews this morning. I'll shoot some of the photos I need while I'm out and about. I'm actually ahead of where I planned to be by now. That's not a bad thing, as I want to have most of it done as soon as possible. I'm keeping an eye on the weather, and trying to prepare for the probability of the wet season setting in earlier than expected. Except for the writing, I'd like to have everything done by the time any serious rain starts. Then, I will be able to sit holed up here producing drafts and emailing them off to my boss as it buckets down outside."

Neither of us wasted time making a start on our day once breakfast was over. I had more tractor work to do and, when last seen, Kate was checking her camera and loading bits and pieces into the large bag she takes on assignments. The airconditioned cab of the tractor made it a pleasant place to be on a hot, humid day. My usual time for a coffee break flew past before I realised I'd missed it. For a moment or two, I dithered about whether to go back to the house or to keep working. The decision was made for me when I realised that, if I kept working, I could finish everything by lunchtime.

While I foraged for lunch in the fridge, Kate arrived home. Hot and bothered from a day 'out in the field', she went to freshen up. "Let's not eat out on the deck today," she suggested as she went past on her way to the bathroom. "There's not a breath of breeze out there. Please, may we turn on the airconditioner and sit at the breakfast bar instead?" I couldn't think of any reason not to.

We both headed for the office straight after lunch. I had accounts to deal with, and Kate wanted to check her emails again. She let out a squeak. "Oh good … Gabby sent us more stuff. Aaah, yes, this is good."

"Stop teasing and print out the stuff so we both can read it."

The printer sprang to life and spat out page after page before again falling silent many pages later. After a couple of minutes of sorting and stapling, silence descended on the office. Both of us settled in our chairs for a long, silent read. Impatient, I flipped through a few pages, scanned about half a page and then flicked on for a few more pages. "Argh, that's no good."

"What's wrong? Why is it no good? Are you missing some pages or something? What are you fussing about?" Kate demanded.

"No. I have all I need, thank you. I was in a hurry to get to the punch line, but all I did was confuse myself. I shall now read it slowly and properly, page by page."

About half an hour elapsed before either of us spoke again. It took me that long to read everything, and then flip back to reread several key sections of the printout. When I finally managed to convince myself I had read everything and there was nothing more to extract from Gabby's handiwork, I looked up to see Kate watching me intently. "Are you coping with all that?" she asked in not much above a whisper.

"I'm not sure. I don't know if everything – or any of it – has sunk in yet, but it gives us exactly the details we need to start piecing everything together."

"It is a start, but that's all it is; only the beginning of the story. We now need to know what happened afterwards to understand why and how the subsequent sequence of events occurred."

"You're right. Here we go again with the answer to one tiny part of it managing to create a whole truckload of new questions. Kate, maybe decorating the dining room walls with more charts might help make it easier to grasp all the facts in these pages."

"That's probably the way to go. In her email, Gabby says she has more stuff for us, but she probably won't have it ready to send until tomorrow." After the better part of an hour, another chart was ready to stick on the wall.

"Below Telford Cresswell's chart probably is the logical place to put it," Kate suggested as she held it in place for my opinion.

"There is nowhere better for it. Let's stick it up and then have a coffee while we consider this new chapter of the story."

We had just walked out onto the deck when Connor arrived and joined us. A light breeze had come up while we were ensconced in the office. With the sun starting its descent behind the distant hills to the west, the deck on the eastern side of the house now provided a pleasant respite from an afternoon spent indoors. After the usual niceties, Connor's simple question precipitated a long discussion.

"So, what have you ladies managed to achieve on this stinking hot day?"

Kate and I exchanged a look. Should we try explaining it to Connor, or not? Kate provided an answer which told him nothing – and triggered an avalanche of questions.

"Well, we're still not sure. We are waiting for the fog to lift so everything will become clear."

"What fog…? There was no fog this morning, and it certainly would have burnt off by now. Is this some mysterious language mere males like me don't understand? It must be, because I don't understand what you just said."

Poor Connor; I felt compelled to rescue him. "Today, Kate received an email from her friend, Gabby, in London, which documented the results of some research she did for us. All the stuff in today's email relates to Telford Cresswell, and we still are a bit stunned by it."

"Telford… Cresswell … His is the first name on the list isn't it? That sounds juicy. Tell me about it."

I exchanged a questioning look with Kate to determine who would brief Connor on the new details of our mystery man's life. Kate indicated I should do the honours.

"Your memory serves you well. We believe Telford Maybanks Cresswell was the name by which my husband was first known. Then, there followed a whole flock of names by which the same man was known until the list ended with the latest name, my husband's name, Tremayne Bancroft. At least, that's what we believe to be the case. So far, there has been nothing to disprove our assumption."

"Got it... I know which character in your saga you are going to tell me about. Now, what is the latest news about him?"

"As the second son, Telford stood to inherit nothing from his father and, as a consequence, had to find – or have found for him – suitable employment. From the information we received today, it appears that, at some point in his early adult life, he joined the Civil Service. In effect, he became a spook working for MI6. It's unclear whether he was engaged in that occupation prior to, or after, his marriage to Lady Annabelle, the daughter of an Earl."

"Would the Earl be happy about such a marriage? I thought the aristocracy always found someone of their own ilk for their daughters to marry, someone who would keep them in the style to which they were accustomed."

"Indications are the Earl disapproved, but the marriage went ahead anyway … Possibly because his daughter was getting on a bit and there were no other potential suitors in sight. The Earl needed her to produce an heir to continue the line of succession. She produced a son and was pregnant with her second child when her father died. No further children to the couple have been found."

"Ri-ight… Is that important somehow?"

"Yes and no. It's important to the overall story, but might not be important at this point in it. The information received today told us that the spook, Telford Cresswell, went rogue at some time around the birth of his second child. There was one brief mention of the fact in the newspaper of the day, but no further articles on the subject appeared during the following weeks. Gabby found a brief mention in another document which tends to confirm the situation. Again, it provided no details of the event, but mentioned a warrant being issued for Telford's arrest."

"Mention of a warrant for his arrest suggests he had gone missing. If he was where he was supposed to be at the time they wanted to arrest him, wouldn't they just march straight in and take him into custody?"

"Not necessarily; raising a warrant for someone's arrest is more or less standard procedure. In this instance, because a spook was involved, the security of the realm and all those other nervous twitches might eliminate any need to go through the process of raising a warrant."

"So, your assumption is Telford legged it to avoid arrest?" I nodded and Connor continued. "Is there anything in other information you have which supports that notion? And, do you have any clues about what he might have done to offend his handlers?"

"Still no clues about what he did to warrant his arrest. As for information to support the notion he legged it to avoid arrest, all we have are entries in Thomas Maycross' passport."

"Who is he, and where does he fit into the story?"

"Thomas Maycross appears to be the next iteration of Telford Cresswell. Again, this is an exercise in putting two and two together and hoping the answer we come up with is four. A passport was issued in Thomas' name around the time Telford appears to have gone missing. The first entry in the passport has Thomas travelling to the Middle East, which is somewhere Telford's passport shows he visited a few times before he dropped off the planet."

Kate chose to insert her two cents into the conversation. "Before you suggest we're making wild assumptions again, neither of us believe in coincidence. I don't know what Lisa's thoughts on the subject are, because I haven't discussed it with her. But, I believe whatever the nature of Telford's wrongdoing, it had something to do with what he was up to in that part of the world."

While I wasn't convinced, Connor seemed to almost agree. "Yeah, that sounds like a possibility. Although, if whatever he did related to the Middle East, would he choose to go back there once he established his new identity?"

Kate shot him a fierce look and slapped a hand down on the table. "No, no! That's not how you're allowed to play this game, Connor. You're supposed to help find answers, not come up with more questions." Kate's assumed air of annoyance was just what we needed. It had all of us chuckling.

Whether intentional or not, her response lightened the atmosphere. Tension had been building the whole time Connor and I discussed the latest news about Telford. It had reached the point where it was almost palpable. Kate's comment helped defuse it, and we all physically relaxed back into our chairs again.

"It's getting late. We should be thinking about what to have for dinner," Kate reminded us.

"I had a pasta dish of some sort in mind. How does everyone feel about that, and any preferences?" As expected, neither of them gave me any indication of what they would like. I was about to berate them for it, when Kate saved me the trouble.

"Remember those chicken and mushroom pies I made a little while ago? There was a heap of the filling left over and I froze it. That would work well as a pasta sauce. It might just need to be thinned out a little." Relieved of the tedium of having to make a decision, I wholeheartedly supported Kate's suggestion.

The night did not go late. Connor needed an early start in the morning, and I think Kate and I welcomed time alone to think more on our mysterious man and what he got up to all those years ago. After we cleaned up, I expected Kate to go to her room, but she had other ideas … ideas that didn't fit well with my intentions.

"I thought you were going to bed for an early night."

"No, I'm going to tidy up today's interviews and sort out the photos to go with them. That will give me a bit more done and out of the way. Aren't you off to bed either?" she asked as I followed her into the office.

"Not yet; it's still early, so I thought I might do a bit more in here before I turn in." For no particular reason, I hoped to have the office to myself, but Kate's presence wouldn't make any difference. I still could do what I intended. While my computer booted, I applied some thought to the sites I needed to access. After I scribbled a list, both the machine and I were ready to go.

I found the online newspaper archives I wanted and navigated to the approximate date where I might find what I was interested in. My thinking was that, at the time Telford supposedly went rogue, we still were fairly colonial in outlook. The major newspapers often carried regular sections of 'News from Home' *home* being the UK. Although I believed Telford was only 'small fry' in terms of the Civil Service, I figured his misbehaviour might have been sufficiently serious to warrant a mention in dispatches from the 'Old Country'.

It took me half an hour to find, but at last I was rewarded. There it was. The short article hinted at what I wanted to know:

A warrant is in place for the arrest of former Civil Servant, Telford Maybanks Cresswell, for his crimes against the Crown. Mr Cresswell's current whereabouts remain unknown, but it is feared he may have travelled to some overseas destination where he has gone into hiding to escape arrest. As his crimes amount to an act of treason, anyone having any knowledge of Mr Cresswell's current whereabouts is instructed to contact the Authorities immediately.

"Crikey, what did he do?" I thought aloud.

"What did who do?" Kate asked.

"Sorry, I didn't mean to interrupt you. Telford … I was talking about Telford Cresswell."

"Okay, I've got that. But, what did he do? Did you find something, or were you still asking the question? Come on. Don't keep me in suspense."

"Sort of; this whole thing is how I imagine unwinding a silkworms cocoon might be like; ever so carefully and little by little. All I discovered is that he was accused of treason."

"Treason…! Jesus, Lisa, who or what did you marry? Oh, this will give the book definite readability. Keep going. See if you can find details of what he did allegedly."

"I'm beginning to think there is no 'allegedly' involved in this. It's unlikely they would make so much noise so far and wide if there weren't substance to the claims. No, I'm sure he was guilty. I'm just not sure of what … or how bad it was." I saw Kate prepare to argue. No doubt she was preparing to go on about being innocent until proven guilty. I didn't feel inclined to suffer it. "Why else would his life have been the way it was? What if creating all the different aliases and living so many different lives was to bury his true identity – and keep it buried for all these years?"

She shook her head and gave me a look of surrender. "Think whatever you want, but keep digging for more details."

Trawling through subsequent weeks' editions of the major newspapers produced nothing but frustration. Surely, if the situation was serious enough, there would be more follow-up? Maybe London didn't want to make further comment, but what was wrong with the local journos of the day? Why hadn't any of them hunted down a story about it?

When I had progressed to a point I believed beyond the realms of possibility of further comment being found, I sat back to think on it for a moment. The old adage says, if you want to know something, you should ask. Maybe I should try that approach. I turned to Google for assistance, and typed in Cresswell's name, followed by 'guilty of treason'. It took a several moments to produce a meagre few hits.

After eliminating those which told me as much as I already knew, I was left with two possibilities to explore. The first one

I checked might have been the one Gabby found. It offered nothing new. Aware of my growing feelings of disappointment, I looked at Google's last offering in response to my enquiry. It appeared nothing more than a regurgitation of what had gone before. That is, until I reached the last couple of lines. There it was.

"Kate, I found it! I found what he is supposed to have done. Listen… I'll read you the whole article. It's not long." I read quickly through to the last significant part, then changed to slow and careful articulation. "There it is. He was producing fake intelligence which could have stirred the warmongers in Whitehall to action, and probably was enough to have him thrown in gaol. But, the worst aspect of the whole incident was that he was believed to be feeding highly classified information back to the other country involved in the situation."

"Sounds like treason to me … and a dangerous game to be playing. As we don't have any clues as to what motivated his actions, it's hard to comprehend what he hoped to achieve." Kate paused for a moment to ponder something before continuing. "If we knew what his role as a spook involved, we might be in a better position to understand what was driving him at the time."

"What do you mean by 'what his role was'? Aren't all spooks just spooks doing whatever spooks normally do?" I realised how ridiculous the question sounded as soon as I asked it.

Nevertheless, Kate was quick to set me straight. "No, there were different roles and functions within 'spookdom', and probably still are for all I know. Some led dangerous lives operating in the shadows in foreign countries to monitor activities of interest on the ground over there. Others sat in innocuous looking buildings at home monitoring airwaves traffic for anything which might constitute intelligence information. Telford would have been well-placed to create the havoc he was accused of, if he were operating in either one of those roles."

I had to accept she made sense. "I suppose it explains his need to create deep, deep cover for himself if he wanted to remain at large. Do you think, once he went underground, he might have continued to act in a way contrary to the UK's best interest?"

"Did he continue to commit treason… is that what you are asking me?" Kate asked. I shrugged.

"Well, I suppose that is possible, but my gut tells me that wasn't his game once he 'disappeared'. It was more about lying low, finding a means of surviving, and avoiding being found … rather than stirring up trouble."

"What are you suggesting, Kate? That he might have been forced to find some other way to support himself … forced into diversifying career-wise? Hmm… perhaps we should keep an open mind during our research; keep an eye out for him popping up in an alternative career. It is possible I suppose that, by going underground, his usefulness to any 'other country' would disappear. Along with that, any previous cash flow from his treason operations would also evaporate."

It was time to turn off the computer and go to bed, but I knew sleep would not come easily tonight. Yes, we had gained another brief glimpse into the man's life but, as with everything else we've discovered so far, it gave us more questions rather than answers.

*****

We both looked like death at breakfast this morning, and both admitted to feeling as though we had not slept much last night. Our appearance was accompanied by an all-pervading lethargy. Nevertheless, in spite of the way I felt, I risked asking Kate about her plans for the day.

"I think the short answer is, not much – if any plans at all. If you asked me last night, I would have rattled off several things I was going to do today. Overnight, that seems to have changed, and I now anticipate it developing into a generally unproductive day. What about you, what are you doing today?"

"My day threatens to mirror yours. At some time during the night, I did think of a couple more things I wanted to look up, but that is the extent of my plans for the day."

218

Seven o'clock had slid past, and eight o'clock was fast approaching when Connor drove up to the house. He couldn't mask his surprise at finding us still on the deck with our breakfast things in front of us. "What's happening here? Is everything all right? Are you both okay?"

I felt embarrassed but tried to be flippant. "Everything is fine. It's a case of nothing happening here. We are just off to a slow start this morning. But, what about you, what brings you here so early? If you've come to tell me about some impending disaster, perhaps you shouldn't. The way I feel this morning, just let it happen and I'll deal with it later."

"Er...no, that's not why I've come. As far as I know, everything is fine on the farm. I just wanted to let you know Dad is going to be away for an extra couple of days. I wondered whether my invitation to dinner would extend to cover the extra days as well."

"Really...? Connor, I thought I made it clear, you are welcome here anytime. In fact, now that you're here this morning, would you like coffee with us – since I'm about to make another cup?"

Of course he would like a coffee – and a slice of raisin toast if one was going, please. And, of course he wanted to know why this place looked like Zombie Central today. Kate volunteered to make the coffee and toast and left me to explain what was wrong with the pair of us.

"Sorry, but I can't help you with any of that stuff. I wouldn't even know where to start researching my family history. But, think about it, maybe a trip to the UK to undertake research first-hand might not be such a bad thing. Anyway, the weather bureau predicts the monsoons will be in place by the end of the week, so there won't be much to do around here."

Kate arrived with a tray loaded with coffees and toast just as Connor was suggesting the benefits of a trip to the UK. She looked pensive as she unloaded the tray. "Funny you should suggest that. The same thought occurred to me last night. I've given it more thought this morning. I'm thinking I might book myself a flight, if that's all right with you, Lisa."

"Why wouldn't it be all right with me? Your life is your own. You don't owe me anything, and I hope you know you are free to come and go as you please."

"Yes, I know all that and, under other circumstances, I wouldn't hesitate. But, at the moment, I feel I need to be here."

"Jesus, Kate, how often do I need to tell you I am fine and perfectly all right on my own. I do not need a babysitter or any other sort of minder. Go ahead and book your flight. Mind you, it means we are going to be busy in the interim sorting out what you're going to do and where you going to do it. There is no point in going all the way over there, and then running around like headless chook because nothing is planned."

"I agree," Connor added. "You should plan your trip before you leave so as to maximise what is achievable in the time available. What you shouldn't do, is worry about Lisa and this place. I will be keeping a close eye on her and everything else that happens here. I promise you, she will be fine. So, book your flight."

My protestations about being perfectly all right to be left on my own fell on deaf ears as Kate and Connor discussed how I could be monitored while she was away. It was all starting to grate, and I felt myself becoming more and more offside as the conversation progressed. "Stop it, you two. If I'm so fragile and can't be left alone, I must need monitoring twenty-four hours a day. Maybe the best thing I can do is get on the damned plane with Kate so she can keep an eye on me the whole time."

"That would be good," they chorused in unison.

What had I done? I suspected my throwaway line would come back to haunt me many times over the next few days. In fact, I was sure I'd be reminded of it until I booked a flight with Kate. For me, the question was: did I really want to go to the UK to undertake research, or for any other reason? If I had to question it, the answer probably was: no I didn't need or want to go.

"If I agree to think about it, will you both lay off me about going?" While they both promised not to continue hounding me about it, their assurances sounded a bit hollow. I didn't think either of them would follow through on their promise.

Chapter 22

It appears the weather bureau got it wrong. The weather remained oppressively hot and humid. The forecast start of the monsoon season still hadn't happened. And, the other thing that hadn't happened was no flights to the UK had been booked. I avoided asking Kate why that was so, as I feared she would start banging on again about not wanting to leave me alone. If I were less sceptical, I might accept that the urgency for such a trip had diminished over the last couple of days.

With the extra material Gabby sent through, combined with research we've done here, a vague picture of our mystery man's early adult life was starting to emerge. No sooner had we established what we believed was the reason for his subsequent life, than the next piece of information Gabby sent through launched us into another frenzied bout of research.

The day after we learned Telford Cresswell was accused of treason, we remained stunned by our discovery. Neither Kate nor I was feeling energetic. So, it wasn't until well after lunch, when we both ventured into the office to check our emails. Kate opened her inbox and let out a whoop. "Gabby has come through again. She has attached several documents, but the first one I opened is pure gold."

"You know the drill: print it out for me. Come on, don't keep me in suspense. What's it about?"

"There… grab one of those copies off the printer. She dug up something on Thomas Maycross, something that will help us do a bit more research." No longer listening, I was concentrating instead on reading the single page from the printer.

Gabby found a snippet in a newspaper's social columns. The first part of the article had me wondering why she bothered to send it. It was when I got to the last couple of sentences that I felt my pulse rate step up. According to the article, we now had the name of our mystery man's next 'wife':

Renowned British archaeologist, Hilary Esdaile, returned home last week from her dig in the Middle East to await the birth of her first child. She is currently staying in Dorset with her parents. Her husband, Thomas Maycross, remains on the dig site to keep an eye on work there. He plans to follow her home in time to be here for the birth.

After reading the document a second time, I looked over at Kate. Her excitement was evident on her face. "Shall we start digging too? Which do you want to search for, the marriage or the birth?" She asked.

I opted to look for the birth, thinking that might be easier to find than the marriage. After all, we had no idea where the marriage took place. It might have been somewhere near the dig site, wherever that was in the Middle East.

How hard can it be to find a birth entry in an archival newspaper when you know the parents' names and an approximate date of the event? It proved to be more time-consuming than I imagined. Granted, the article didn't say how long before the birth of the child Hilary had returned to the UK, but I guessed it would only be a few weeks – maybe six weeks at the most. After searching through eight weeks of entries after the date of the first article, I still hadn't found the birth. "I'm beginning to wonder whether this was a phantom pregnancy," I told Kate. "I've searched a period of at least eight weeks after her supposed arrival back in the UK and found nothing."

"I'm not an expert on such matters – in fact, I know nothing much at all. But, wasn't there some sort of rule in place back then about pregnant women not being allowed to fly? I sort of remember something about the airlines being nervous about a woman, if her pregnancy was well advanced, possibly giving birth on board a flight. It was the favoured topic of conversation for the female journos in the bureau at the time. Their view was that women were being discriminated against by the males who ran the airlines, and that, if a doctor said his patient was fit to fly, the woman should have the right to board a flight."

"Do you have any idea of the metrics associated with that rule? Like, at what point was the pregnancy considered too far along to be allowed to board a flight?"

Kate wrinkled her nose and shook her head. Okay, I could just keep ploughing through the newspapers for a few more weeks to see if anything turned up, or I could search for some information on that particular restriction. I settled for the latter.

As a secondary outcome of my research, I learned that, at that time, any woman more than six months pregnant wasn't allowed on board a plane. It was just a little more than three months after the date of the first article that the information I wanted almost jumped off the screen at me. "There it is," I yelped. "I found the birth of Jane."

"So, we have a wife and daughter to add to the second page of the Thomas Maycross' chart. I haven't found a marriage for the couple yet. Now that you've found the birth, it would be worth checking how that correlates with the dates of travel to the Middle East recorded in both Telford's and Thomas' passports."

Although unsure of my chances of success, I did as she suggested.

New as I was to this research lark, at first nothing made any sense. Not being brave enough to return to the office to tell Kate I didn't have a clue about the timings, I scribbled dates on a scrap of paper and tried linking them in a way I thought logical. About half an hour later, I tentatively returned to the office to report my 'findings'.

"From entries in Telford's passport, it appears he visited the Middle East on two and possible three occasions. On two occasions, he flew in and out of Jordan. On the potential third visit, he flew into Israel, but flew home to England from Jordan. Telford's trips were during the period 1986 to 1988/89. Thomas first went to Jordan in 1989 … which ties in nicely with when Telford was accused of treason. Thomas and Hilary's baby,

Jane, was born in 1992. There is an entry in Thomas' passport which ties in with his returning to England for the birth. Then, about three weeks later, Thomas flew back to the Middle East." I looked up at Kate as I finished reading from my notes. She looked confused.

"Kate, what's wrong? Did I stuff this up somehow?"

"No, not at all; you did great. It's my research that's not making sense. From your information, it's logical to assume Thomas and Hilary were married sometime between 1989, when Thomas appears to have fled England, and 1992 when their baby, Jane, was born. The only problem with all that is, I haven't found their marriage during the identified period."

"It's possible they weren't married in England and, therefore, there is no mention of a marriage. Perhaps it was more expeditious to marry somewhere close to where they were working, rather than dash back to England for the sake of a simple ceremony – maybe nothing more than a Registry Office type event. And, there was the risk of Thomas' being arrested if he returned. I wonder if Hilary had even an inkling of the precarious position he was in if he returned to England."

"I doubt it … and I doubt she had any idea about his existing wife. No, there was no point in changing his name and going to all the trouble to disappear, and then telling someone the whole sordid story," Kate suggested.

"True…," I conceded. "It would be difficult for him to tell her the rest of the story without mentioning the fact that he was already married. Although, I suppose he could always lie about his situation – tell Hilary he was divorced or widowed … or simply leave out that part of the story altogether. Let's face it. He was a master of misrepresenting truth and reality."

Kate gave a derisive snort. "What you meant to say is: the man of many names was a practised liar. In spite of my not finding a marriage for them, I have the feeling Hilary was not a woman who would be content to just 'shack up' with a bloke."

"What if they were married at the nearest town to the dig site where Hilary was working? I don't know what the procedure was in such cases. Would the British Embassy be notified of the marriage of two UK nationals, and then pass on the information to the appropriate body 'back home' for processing?" I asked.

"Good point; maybe they were married at the embassy. Perhaps our best option is to return to the newspapers in the hope the marriage merited a mention in the social jottings. What are you going to work on now?"

"Making coffee … it's past that time of the afternoon, and I think I need a caffeine hit before I tackle anything else." While I did need coffee, I was more interested in engaging in a spot of simple maths and logical deductions. After cranking up the coffee machine, I ducked into the dining room to copy a couple of dates from the wall charts onto a slip of paper.

Our coffee break was not an extended affair. Kate was keen to get back to her research, and I wanted to be alone to apply some thought to my project. We might not know when Thomas and Hilary were married, but we did know when their first child arrived. By some obscure means or other, I managed to convince myself it was safe to assume their marriage had occurred sometime in the preceding twelve months. So far, we know that five years after marrying Annabelle, Telford – now as Thomas – had a child with Hilary in 1992. If my assumption is correct, Thomas married Hilary in about 1991.

While I didn't think that man could surprise or shock me anymore, my reckoning that he married Hilary only about five years after marrying Annabelle did just that. From the dates in both Telford's and Thomas' passports, it appears likely Telford already had begun his wandering ways before his second child with Annabelle was born. As I noted all my assumptions on my slip of paper, another question occurred to me: when did Roslyn Williams enter the picture?

How long was Thomas with Hilary before his itchy feet moved him on to new pastures … and his marriage to Roslyn Williams? Another bit of simple maths told me it was no more than six or seven years after the birth of baby Jane when Thomas – then known as Trevor – married Miss Williams in Australia.

Such a substantial intervening period allowed plenty of time for Thomas and Hilary to produce more offspring.

While the man had proved a slick operator, he took his time in the way he went about things. Judging by his past performance, even at this early stage of his 'career', he would have spent time sussing out a suitable 'next mate' and getting to know her before waltzing her down the aisle. I needed to go back to the passports. Two questions now occupied by mind: did Thomas Maycross ever visit Australia? And, when was Trevor Cross' Australian passport issued?

After checking the two passports in question, I was fairly certain Thomas Maycross hadn't visited Australia. My other piece of evidence suggested Trevor Cross had an Australian passport for at least two years before he married Roslyn Williams. This rather shortened the time he spent with Hilary before moving on. While the temptation was to apply the same process to all the other 'wives' involved in this man's life, I was determined to take it step-by-step, and to know as much as possible about each phase of it before moving on to the next.

My efforts now led me to believe the man spent no more than four years with Hilary after the birth of their first child, Jane. My gut insisted it might be less time than that but, without evidence to support it, I chose to ignore my gut's message. Nevertheless, I was confident there was more than enough time involved for Thomas and Hilary to produce further offspring. Perhaps the only way to confirm that assumption was to return to searching the social notes in the leading UK newspapers. While the prospect didn't excite me, I returned to my computer and brought up an on-line edition of the same newspaper as in which I found mention of the first child.

We called it quits at around six o'clock. Kate and I worked in relays as a team taking showers and cooking dinner. By the time Connor arrived, Kate was in the shower, and tonight's dinner was at a point where it was okay to look after itself until we were ready for it. I poured us drinks and took Connor out onto the deck. A couple of minutes later Kate came out. After about twenty minutes, she disappeared into the kitchen and, a few minutes later, we were eating.

Conversation wasn't exactly stilted, but it wasn't free-flowing or light-hearted. Connor tried his best, but eventually gave up and demanded to know what was wrong. "Did you two have a falling out today, or has something major gone wrong?"

Kate and I exchanged looks before I responded. "Why do you ask that? Everything is fine. We haven't had a row or anything of that nature. We've been busy researching for most of the day."

"Well, trying to get a conversation going this evening is like clearing stumps: it doesn't matter how hard you work at it, sometimes nothing happens. And, that's about how much success I'm having here tonight. Maybe coming over for dinner was the wrong thing to do."

We both went to great pains to apologise and explain that, if there was a problem, it was because we both probably were brain-dead from staring at screens all day. It seemed to do the trick.

I liked the analogy. "You're right. It is a bit like clearing stumps I suppose. Sometimes you have to set it alight to achieve any result. It could become a late night if you set us alight by starting us discussing our research."

Connor chuckled. "So, how is your research progressing? There … did that light any fires?" Conversation flowed smoothly after Connor asked the fundamental question.

While the conversation was about to start flowing, I suddenly felt guilty. Kate had beavered away in silence for most of the day and I hadn't even asked about her research. "Maybe you should go first, Kate. You've been hard at it all day and hardly said a word. Even I don't have any idea about what you managed to dig up today."

"Argh, I'm not going to add much to the conversation. My findings today could be summed up in one, or maybe two sentences. All I did was check some of the information Gabby sent through to us. Sometimes, if you read a whole article, rather than just the relevant bit, you might find more information can be gained from it. That was the case with a couple of bits of things I checked. They don't change what we already know but, in terms of putting together the whole story, they help set other details in context. What about you, Lisa, did you find anything interesting today? I noticed you were missing for a while after coffee this afternoon."

"There isn't much I can add to the data we have." I took a few moments to talk through the timeline of events I'd created and explain my thinking behind some of the assumptions. It didn't sound like I'd contributed much at all and, when I added the solitary piece of information I dug up for the afternoon, it still didn't sound like much either.

"The only piece of information to come from my afternoon's research was the birth of Thomas and Hilary's second child, Donald, born in the first week of January 1995. From the piece in the social jottings section of the newspaper, it appears Hilary and her daughter came home to Dorset sometime late in1994, and spent Christmas and New Year with Hilary's parents before her son was born. This time, there was no mention of Thomas at all."

Connor looked shocked by the inference. "Are you suggesting he didn't go home for the birth at all? Surely he hadn't flown the coop again, leaving his pregnant wife to have the child alone. Isn't that what we think he did to Annabelle? What sort of man does that – or makes a habit of doing that?"

As his questions were directed at me, I felt obliged to answer. "It's not possible to answer any of those questions with any certainty at this point in time. The situation, as we know it in Annabelle's case, is quite clear. Telford absconded before the birth of the child. The fact that Thomas isn't mentioned in relation to the birth of his and Hilary's son is suggestive, but not indicative of a repeat performance. If, like me, you are sceptical and not particularly generous, you might consider Thomas took advantage of an opportunity. When Hilary went back to England to await the birth of their son, it might have provided Thomas with an opportunity to escape. It's unfortunate his passports don't indicate how or when he left the Middle East or arrived in Australia."

"But, we know when his Australian passport was issued," Kate said. "Doesn't that tell us something?"

"It might, if we knew where he was when he obtained that passport. The question to consider is: did he obtain a false Australian passport while somewhere outside Australia, or did he obtain it after his arrival here? To my way of thinking, the important issue is: how and when did he arrive here? Neither of those passports records his entry into Australia."

"Is there another passport you haven't found? Is that what you're suggesting?" Connor asked. "That, whoever this bloke was, he had yet another passport which he used to enter the country?"

Kate shook her head and went to say something but stopped, and shot me a horrified look instead. "Is that a possibility?"

"Why are you both looking at me? I don't know. I only found the questions. I didn't find the answers. Although, now that I think about it, was it possible for him to enter Australia in some way, which avoided all the usual immigration checks?" I looked up to see both Kate and Connor nodding sagely.

"It… might…. be possible I suppose," Connor said as he appeared to be giving the matter some thought. "If he worked as a spook before he went on the run, it's possible he made valuable connections, or knew someone, who knew of someone who would prove a valuable connection."

"Connor, you appear to be leaning towards illegal entry into Australia. How would you see that being a possibility?" Kate asked.

"I don't know… I don't know how any of this stuff works. But, it is possible, isn't it? You often hear of illegal immigrants being rounded up and deported."

While Kate and Connor debated the subject, my mind took me down unexpected avenues. "For a moment, stop and think about Thomas and his British passport," I suggested, "and the possibility of his having built up a network of useful contacts in and around the Middle East over the years he spent there. How hard would it be for him to travel through any of those Middle Eastern countries to reach one of the major shipping ports? He might have concocted some story to do with his work on the archaeology dig to use as a cover." I wasn't quite sure where my thinking was taking me yet but, as I gave it air, the bit I shared made sense to me so far. It seems it also struck a chord with Connor.

"Not hard at all, even without some fancy story to ease his way. It would be easy-going once he reached one of the ports. If he knew of a useful contact, and could pay the requisite price, I'm sure they could find him a merchant seaman's position on one of the bulk cargo ships heading for Australia. Then, as part of the prearranged deal, he could be put ashore at some isolated point along the coastline, and left to his own devices to make his way to his intended destination. Or, I suppose he could just jump ship when it reached port."

No, that wasn't the scenario I'd been developing in my mind, but Connor's version made a lot of sense. The more I thought about it over the next minute or so, the more convinced I became Connor had identified exactly how our man had arrived in this country. The question now is: how to prove it?

"That makes a lot of sense, Connor," Kate said. "It had to be some plan along those lines. At least, I hope it was. Otherwise, we'll be off on another wild goose chase looking for a missing passport that we aren't sure even exists. As for proving that's how he arrived here, does it matter at this point in time? Is there some reason why we can't just accept he arrived here by whatever means and, probably, wasted no time in obtaining an Australian passport? Perhaps, at some point down the track, by some stroke of luck, we might find out more about his arrival. But, for the moment, I'm happy to just accept that he arrived here by some unknown means."

Again, I found myself nodding. "I can go along with that. The only other thing we need to think about in relation to all this is whether we share our findings and thoughts with Inspector Taylor. My thinking is that it might prove beneficial in the long run."

"What's the time?" Kate asked. Both Connor and I checked our watches, but Connor was first to answer. "Okay, that's not so late, is it?"

"I might go and give Dan a call. You never know, he might just happen to be out this way on a job tomorrow and could call in." Kate bounced up off her chair and had her phone to her ear as she headed inside.

Connor chuckled. "Keen, isn't she?" he asked with a smirk spreading across his face. "Me thinks some chemistry is afoot there."

"Chemistry…? Do you mean between Kate and Inspector Taylor?"

"No, I mean between Kate and *Dan.* Haven't you noticed?"

"At the risk of appearing totally dense, no, I hadn't noticed. But now you've drawn my attention to it, I realise I must to be blind not to have noticed it." I wasn't going to admit I had been teasing Kate about exactly that. "Oh dear; and I thought it was her concern for me that was keeping her here…" We both dissolved into laughter, but for different reasons. It ended abruptly when we heard Kate returning.

"Dan says he'll be out here first thing in the morning. I suppose I'd better bake something for morning tea again." Neither Connor nor I trusted our self to comment.

Although it wasn't late, Connor made noises about the scourge of a farmer's life being constant early mornings. There was something I wanted to ask him, so I took the opportunity to walk him to his vehicle. Once we are safely outside the front door and I could hear Kate continuing to bang things about in the kitchen, I took a deep breath and launched into my question. "Connor, you don't have to answer this if you don't wish to, but is it proving difficult for you to witness what might be a relationship developing between Kate and Dan Taylor?"

"Why would it be difficult for me? I don't have a problem with it – or even an opinion about it. My only thought would be that, if it develops into something serious, I hope it works out for them. I don't understand your reason for asking the question."

"I'm sorry. I probably was out of line, but I thought I detected something between you and Kate, and seeing her attention going in another direction might have been hard for you." He laughed raucously for a few seconds before composing himself sufficiently to respond.

"Sorry … No, it is not difficult for me, because I have no interest in Kate apart from as a friend. My interest lies in another direction altogether." As he spoke, he strode around to the other side of the vehicle and climbed in. As he slammed the door, I didn't quite catch the last thing he said but, on my way back upstairs, I thought he had said something about 'being blind'. The recollection of those words was vaguely unsettling for some unknown reason, and it haunted me long after I went to bed.

Chapter 23

The already leaden sky darkened further as black clouds rolled in from the coast. There would be a storm before the morning was out. Maybe this was the anticipated start of the monsoon season. Heat and humidity were oppressive for days, but this morning, even at this early hour, it seemed worse, if that were possible. Kate came out to join me on the deck and collapsed onto a chair.

"We definitely have to clear off that dining room table today. If this weather is going to settle in for the duration, I for one will not be spending time out here on the deck. At least, if we clear the dining room table, we will be able to eat in airconditioned comfort. I don't know how people can survive up here without airconditioning, especially at this time of year." Her gripe over for the moment, she attacked her breakfast with a viciousness which suggested she thought it the root cause of her discomfort.

"A storm is coming. It will break sometime this morning. The lead up to the wet season is always like this but, once the rains come, it's much better. So, whatever you plan to do today, I'm guessing it will be done inside in airconditioned comfort?"

"Dead right… Oh … and I've made a decision," Kate announced.

I eased forward on my chair and tried to look excited about her forthcoming announcement.

"I'm going to book my overseas flight today. I'll head to the UK on the earliest flight with an available seat."

Her announcement was loaded with expectation. I'm not sure what she anticipated my reaction would be, but I don't think she thought that I would be happy or excited for her.

What did I feel? Nothing really, I concluded. Okay, so she was off to the UK. There was no surprise in that. For a few days now, she had been talking about booking a flight. My only thought on the matter was about what finally precipitated her decision. "Great … if you can get a booking in the next couple of weeks or so, it still will be low season and tickets will be cheaper. I'm assuming your motivation is the chance to undertake more in-depth research for the book about our mystery man."

"Yep, and I need to ask if you are still okay about the book."

"I've never had a problem with the idea. In light of our research so far, things have changed a bit. My caveat is that there are now a lot of other people involved, and whose approval you need to obtain as well, before the book can go ahead. The story is not just about me and my so-called husband. It's also about all those other people and the impact he had on their lives. If there is objection from any of those people, then the book can't happen."

"Yes, I am aware of all that … but I am determined to write the story. If objections were to prevent publication of the true story, I would produce a work of fiction instead. One that just happens to mirror the real story … where, as they say, *only the names were changed to protect the identities of the people involved.* So, you see, I will write this story. It cannot be let die without being documented. Sorry, Lisa, that's the investigative journalist in me talking."

There was no point in arguing with her. My philosophy was: let her go and do her research, and we will see what happens after that. Maybe that will be the time when the arguments occur, because they will occur, if needs be. The story is not just about me. I owe it to all the others involved to ensure their privacy and feelings are respected, and their lives do not suffer negative impact as a consequence of anything Kate might produce.

While I made no further negative comment, I suspect the negative vibes I gave off reflected my feelings anyway. It was time to change the subject before life became complicated. "Did Inspector Taylor say if he had anything new to tell us this morning? It's a while since we last heard from him. I hope he has good news to share about his investigation. Details of a breakthrough would be nice."

"No such luck I'm afraid. He didn't give any hints, and I didn't detect any trace of excitement in him. So, in terms of his investigation, it's probably going to be 'routine' rather than 'revelation' again – more about being seen to be keeping us informed, as opposed to actually telling us anything."

I was in the office when I heard Taylor arrive. Kate went down to meet him, and I heard them chatting as they came upstairs. They must have been near to top of the stairs when I heard Kate exclaim, "No! Really! How soon? When do you leave?" The excitement in her voice made me rush out to join them. I found the pair of them standing at the top of the stairs, and Kate looking flushed and a bit stunned.

"Good morning, Inspector. Is everything all right out here?"

Kate gave an embarrassed giggle. "Everything is fine. Lisa, why don't you take Dan out to the deck while I make coffee? … But, Dan, no discussing the case until I join you. Okay?"

He laughed and made Kate a light-hearted promise before following me out onto the deck. That's when I noticed he too looked a bit… A bit what… excited, embarrassed? Maybe all of that and more. Something definitely is going on between those two, I told myself. I also counselled myself to mind my own business and be patient. When – if –they want me to know about it, they will tell me.

As soon as Kate arrived with coffees and muffins, I initiated what I hoped would be an informative session. "So, Inspector, how is your investigation coming along? Do you have any good news for us?"

"We have had a bit of a breakthrough but I'm not sure you will call it 'good' news. Scotland Yard have reported matches with Tremayne's DNA. They point to close familial ties to your husband. I'm sorry, but some of this might be hard for you to hear."

"If you are going to tell me he had wives before me and there may be offspring roaming around out there, don't worry about it. I already know. At least, we think we have pinned down some chunks of his previous lives. But, don't let that put you off. Go ahead and tell me what Scotland Yard have discovered."

"Right… Well, they have discovered two separate lots of people who appear to share your husband's DNA; close enough to be his children. They found it confusing at first because the two groups of people come from two different mothers... as well as two fathers who went by different names. But, maybe I'm not telling you something you don't already know."

"Correct. You are not. We know there were British offspring from wives numbers one and two. How did Scotland Yard pick up on the matches?"

"It seems, when The Yard reported back to the families concerned, one of the offspring who was into family history admitted that, almost at the outset, he ran into a brick wall with his father's line. In desperation, he added his DNA to the Ancestry data base and got a match with a woman who had gone down a similar route some years ago. I'm told they are now trying to sort out their connection. They don't even share the same surname."

"I see, and I can imagine how confusing it must be for them. So, what happens now? I mean what happens from Scotland Yard's and your points of view?"

"That's what I was telling Kate earlier. I'm being sent to the UK to work with Scotland Yard on sorting out the mess. I leave next Sunday and won't be around for a while. If I do uncover anything interesting or earth-shattering, I promise I'll let you know, one way or another, straight away." I looked over at Kate. It was obvious she was bursting to say something.

"Kate, do you have anything you would like to add?"

"Well, Dan, I didn't have a chance to tell you before, but I am heading to the UK too. I told Lisa this morning I intended booking my flight today."

"Perhaps we could travel together. I'll give you my travel details. It would be good to have company on the flight." Dan's excitement was unmistakable.

God save us from lovesick forty-year-olds! They were positively beaming at each other. Best I interrupt I think, before the situation deteriorates any further.

"Inspector, we too have been busy researching over the last couple of days. News of the offspring doesn't surprise us, but we hadn't yet checked Ancestry for matches. Up to now, we concentrated on discovering who might be out there somewhere and how they connected with Tremayne. If Kate manages to book herself onto the right flight, she could fill you in on what we know on the way over. There are still a few days before you leave, so we will keep digging in the meantime."

"If you had checked Ancestry, you probably wouldn't have found anything. There is an embargo on any of it going up on the Ancestry site. And, the researchers who were DNA matches have not been informed of the connection yet. The intention was to tell them when we know more about the whole story."

With nothing much more to tell us, Inspector Taylor didn't hang around. When Kate came back upstairs after seeing him off, she looked pleased with herself. "Lisa, can you manage dinner with Connor on your own tonight? I'm having dinner in town with Dan."

"What sort of ridiculous question is that? You seem to forget I had a life before you came to stay. Of course I can manage on my own. Connor and I won't starve because you're not here. Go and enjoy yourself. We probably will spend the evening talking 'farm stuff' … and won't have to worry about boring you to death."

She seemed to spend an inordinate amount of the afternoon preening and fussing about what to wear, before heading off to town at about six o'clock for her dinner date with *Dan.*

It took Connor more than ten minutes to realise Kate wasn't around. "I don't think I've seen Kate since I arrived. Isn't she here tonight?"

I explained the 'dinner date with Dan' scenario.

"So, they are moving it onto the next stage, eh?"

"…But wait there's more. Kate booked her flight to the UK today, and guess who else will be on the same flight."

After bringing his laughter under control, Connor became serious and a bit hesitant when he asked his question. "What about you, are you going with them too?"

"What … and play gooseberry? I don't think so. Besides, I have this place to run, and goodness knows it hasn't had much attention lately. Although, if I'm honest, I would like to meet people and be a part of whatever happens over there. Oh, I know the others will tell me everything, but it's not the same as being a part of it and learning about it first-hand."

"Then go. As for looking after this place, you know as well as I do, now the rains have started, there's nothing to do except check on the stock occasionally. So now, what other excuse do you have? There are plenty of other flights you could go on – so you don't have to play gooseberry – and you could make your own accommodation arrangements if they are sharing somewhere."

"Yes, I know all that. But, then you would be looking after this place, and you have spent far too much of your time here already. I can't impose any further. Your father might soon become offside about your spending so much time here, and he would be justified in doing so."

"Lisa, let me tell you about my father … and maybe me as well."

"Good; we are changing the subject. What about your father? Don't tell he already is complaining about your absences from home."

"Don't be silly. He isn't particularly interested in what's happening here at the moment. Hadn't you noticed? The 'couple of days' he was going to be away has managed to become a week. He has another all-consuming interest at the moment. A lady he has known for years, and got to know even better while at the recent conference. He currently is settled in on her property up near the Gulf, and not quite sure when he will return … or whether he will be alone when he does."

"That's great news. He has been alone for so many years since your mother died. I know he has you for company now, but that is not quite the same. How do you feel about all this … and the possibility of a new step-mother?"

"I would be over the moon to see him settled down with someone, and there couldn't be anyone better than the woman in question. It would make things easier for me too. I want to leave home, but don't want to leave him alone again."

"Aw no; you're not serious about leaving again are you? What will I do if you leave? I'm sure Kate will move on soon. She has her own life and career to look after, regardless of whether this thing with Dan develops into something or not. It is time we returned to living our own lives again. If she and Dan make a go of it, maybe she will still be close by and we will still spend time together. But, if you go too… Connor, I would be lost without you. I don't mean by not having you to help me out on the farm. What I'm trying to say is, not having you around will leave a large hole in my life."

"That sounds serious."

"Sorry; I was being selfish. Of course you must do what's right for you. Life is too short not to do the things you want to do."

"My feelings exactly, and I'm pleased to hear you say it. I've held off doing what I wanted to do for far too long."

"Are you sure you're not running away because a woman who is not your mother will be taking over running the house? If you are looking to move out just to give them space to get on with their life together, without having you peering over their shoulders, you could move in over here."

"You would let me move in here? Are you sure about that … and on what conditions?"

"Of course you're welcome to move in over here. The cottage is empty, or it will be as soon as I clear the rest of Tremayne's stuff out of it." He appeared to deflate. A disappointed look spread across his face. "What's the matter? Is there some reason you would not want to move into the cottage?"

"Well, now that you're asking… no, I don't want to move into the cottage. I'd much rather be moving in here with you. If you weren't so blind, or at least took your blinkers off long enough to look around you, you would know why that is."

Blind…? A recollection flashed back across my mind. What did he say about someone being blind before he drove off the other night? A faint glimmer of understanding began to make its way through. I felt the heat rising up my neck and onto my cheeks. Is he saying what I think he is saying? "I am not sure I understand…"

"Jesus, Lisa, do I have to spell it out in words of one syllable. Why do you think I never married. There has only ever been one woman I wanted to be with, but she married someone else. And, I can't begin to tell you how hard it was to see how he treated her. Yes, I know it's wrong to speak ill of the dead, but I can't say I'm sorry he's gone. I know it's too soon by refined standards to be saying these things but, as you said, life's too short to waste it. You always have been the only woman for me, and I very much want to be with you, and to take care of you. There … now you know."

"Uhmm … Yes, and I don't know what to say. Connor, you are special and always have been. I did not see this coming. I need to think about it and what it means."

"Have I upset you? If I have, I didn't mean to. It was just a case of wanting to tell you for so long and, not knowing how you felt, was eating at me. Regardless of what your answer is, I hope it hasn't ruined something special between us."

"No, I'm not upset … Stunned, yes, but not upset. But, I need to think about it. There is so much to consider."

"While you are considering things, remember one thing, this is your place and it will remain so in every way. I am not trying to take over what is yours. In fact, I probably still would spend more time over on our place helping Dad than I would spend here annoying you. Take as much time as you need to think about it. I want you to be sure, whatever you decide. Book your flight to England. Go and do what you need to do over there

... And think about me while you're gone. Being away from this place – and me – might be the best opportunity for you to think about things with a clear head. I'll accept whatever your decision might be."

"You have a very persuasive line, Connor Rankin ... And I don't doubt you've been told that before today. I won't be sharing any of this with Kate just yet, but I think I might book myself a ticket tomorrow... On a different flight from the one Kate and Dan will be on."

We moved our conversation to safer ground, and spent a few minutes discussing Bob's lady friend, who might well become Connor's stepmother... A concept he wasn't too fond of. "I do wish you'd stop thinking of her as my future stepmother. A 'stepmother' for a man of my age almost sounds obscene. Nevertheless, I do hope it works out well for the pair of oldies."

With little else to talk about, and with both of us probably feeling a bit tentative after the territory covered tonight, Connor was gone by ten o'clock. He helped me with most of the clearing away of our dinner things before he left but, after I put the last few things in the dishwasher and started it, I retreated to the deck again. His revelation tonight completely bowled me over. But, it also had opened my eyes – or at least let me be honest with myself.

No, the feelings I had for Connor for the best part of the last couple of decades were not the feelings one has for a friend. They were more than that; deeper than that. But, was it merely a response to flattery that had me feeling the way I did now, or was it finally acknowledgement of long-held deeper feelings? One thing I did know. I would be awake for quite a while tonight, revisiting all that had been said. None of which had been unpleasant or unwelcome. And, I couldn't seem to wipe the smile off my face.

At some point during my reflections on the evening, I found my leg had gone to sleep. I scrambled out of my chair and hobbled around for a while to revive the circulation. When I checked the time, it was well past one o'clock. Where had the night gone?

The last thing I wanted was for Kate to come home and find me sitting out here on the deck. She'd think I'd been waiting up all night for her to come home, just as an anxious mother would wait up for errant teenager to come home after breaking her curfew. It would not be a good look, so I rushed off to bed. I needn't have worried. A couple of hours later when I again checked the time, Kate still hadn't returned. I didn't have to be too bright to work out I probably wouldn't see her until well after breakfast tomorrow.

*****

When there was still no sign of Kate this morning, and her bed hadn't been slept in, I set about making my day as normal as possible. Rain was bucketing down, so there was little I could do around the farm, except check on stock. That didn't take long, but I drove around to check on a few other things while I was out and about, before returning to the house.

As it had reached a civilised hour of the morning, I made coffee and took it and my phone out onto the deck. Minutes later, I was booked on a flight to London next Tuesday. It was an odd feeling not having someone there to tell about it. After a few moments' hesitation, I keyed Connor's number. "I'm booked on a flight to London next Tuesday. Would you be available to drive me to the airport?"

There was nothing forced or strained between us during our brief conversation. Of course he wanted to drive me to the airport, and see me off, and there was one other thing he needed to clarify, "Am I still invited to dinner every night until you leave?"

Not wanting to have to face Kate the moment she walked through the door after her night out, I took myself off to the shed. I'm not sure whether I didn't want to embarrass her when she came home, or if I might be embarrassed by the persistent smile on my face today. When I returned just before eleven o'clock for a late coffee, Kate was not long home.

She looked sheepish when I asked how dinner was. "I was surprised at how good the food was at the restaurant we went to. I don't know what I expected, but I was surprised by the standard we received."

She was awkward. I felt awkward.

What is wrong with us? Situations such as last night's had occurred many times over the years we had known each other and lived together. It never caused a raised eyebrow in the past. So, why were we being so coy about her not coming home last night?

In a bid to normalise the situation, I changed the topic and pressed on with what I hoped was safer ground. "Now the wet season has started and there is nothing much to do around here, I decided I would go to England. I booked my flight this morning." In spite of her best efforts, I saw her face drop for a brief moment before she recovered.

"Did you manage to book a seat on Sunday's flight as well? I thought it was fairly much fully-booked when I made my booking."

"No, I didn't plan to fly on Sunday. I'm flying on the following Tuesday. I haven't done anything about booking accommodation yet, but I thought I might do that this afternoon." Ah hah… that put the smile back on her face. So the prospect of my accompanying her *and Dan* to England didn't exactly excite her. A-n-d, I noticed my mention of accommodation didn't elicit any information about, or offers to share her accommodation. While I didn't know how long Inspector Taylor's stay in England was likely to be, I couldn't help wonder how much research Kate might fit in while he was there.

By the time Connor came to dinner, things had all but returned to normal. This was due in no small part to the fact Connor was unaware of how awkward Kate and I had been around each other all afternoon. His normal chatty self was infectious, and it seemed to make the world relax around us.

Perhaps tomorrow we would be able to discuss our plans for our time in England, and what each of us hoped to achieve from our trip. It also might be a good time for me to hint at the conversation Connor and I had while Kate was out dining with Dan. But, what was there to tell? So far, all that happened was Connor expressed his feelings towards me. Did Kate even need to know about it? If I was honest with myself, perhaps I had an inkling there was something more to tell. But first, I had to admit to myself what that 'something' was.

Chapter 24

The days until I drove Kate to the airport for her flight to London flew by in a research-induced blur as we slogged away at being as well-informed as possible before Kate departed. Inspector Taylor was already at the airport when we arrived, and rushed to help Kate with her luggage. I didn't wait to see her off, and drove away as they made their way into the terminal. It would have been a waste of time waiting to see her off when she and Inspector Taylor were so engrossed in one another

In the few days between booking our flights and taking Kate to the airport, we had discovered quite a bit more about our 'mystery man' – as we had taken to calling him. Gabby helped by sending through more information, which allowed us to expand our search parameters. It didn't matter how much more we discovered, our assessment of the man didn't improve.

We discovered a third child, James, born to Thomas Maycross and Hilary Esdaile in 1998. By then, Thomas, as Trevor Cross, had been in Australia for about two years. Around the time his third child to Hilary was born, he was 'marrying' Roslyn Williams in Brisbane, and preparing to set up residence in Sydney. It seems Hilary's marriage had not fared any better than Annabelle's, and they both ended up being single mothers bringing up their children.

From our earlier information, we already knew Trevor Cross and Roslyn Williams were 'married' in nineteen ninety-eight, and continued to be married seven years later when Trevor, having become Tremayne, married me in 2005. At least Roslyn and I fared a little better than his previous two wives. Neither of us had children, so we did not find ourselves bringing up our families singlehandedly. All that aside, it appears the man was incapable of changing his ways.

Inspector Taylor sent information via Kate after their arrival in London. It confirmed Tremayne, under his then name of Travis Cridland, married Mai Nguyen in Vietnam in 2012. Three children followed in fairly quick succession. The first was born late in 2012, followed by one in 2014, and a third one in 2017. So, unless there is yet another wife we remain unaware of, after marrying me, it was seven years before he took his next wife, Mai Nguyen.

From my discussions with Donna Bailey while she was here in town, I knew she and the then Tristan Bailey were married in Brisbane in 2014, and their first child arrived in 2016. The birth of her second child, if it hasn't already happened, should occur any day now. Again, this 'marriage' reflects the man's total disregard or concern for 'overlapping' marriages – or the legalities associated with marriage.

In a quiet moment, I found myself wondering about those other marriages. What were they like? What form did they take? Were they church weddings as mine was, or did they take place in a Registry Office or similar situation? Who were the witnesses at those other weddings? Surely, they weren't people who knew the man well, or they would know he already was married and that the impending marriage was illegal. Although, now I think on it, he was such a master of misrepresentation. Perhaps he had a plausible enough story to convince the witnesses he was free to proceed with marrying his new bride-to-be. Kate was a witness at our wedding, and Tremayne's friend – a work colleague – was the other.

So much thinking about brides and marriages in general brought Roslyn Williams to mind, and had me wondering about her wedding. The thought hit me like a thunderbolt. Never once had Kate or I thought to contact Roslyn about the research we were doing or the information we had discovered. She had the same right to know as I did. In hindsight, her position in this ongoing saga of marriages was no different from mine. When she visited me here, she might have adopted the high moral ground about being entitled to 'her husband's' belongings. In reality, she was no more entitled to them than I was.

Should I share what we now know with her? The question dogged me for most of the day before I finally came to a decision. Of course she should know, and it would continue to trouble me, if I didn't at least make an attempt to talk to the woman. Nevertheless, it took me until after dinner to find the courage to make the call. When it took her so long to answer, I thought she had elected not to answer. Then, just as I was expecting her voice message to cut in, she barked, "Hello, and why are you calling me?" Not quite the start I was hoping for but, having gone this far, I felt committed.

While it wasn't a pleasant conversation, some civility on her part did build as the call progressed. I don't think it was until she finally realised and accepted the true nature of her marriage that she conceded I hadn't called to create trouble. It would be an exaggeration to suggest our discussions ended on a friendly note, but her hostility had vanished. I would sleep better tonight for what my call had accomplished … and now, perhaps I was in a position to claim that higher moral ground.

The next couple of days before I flew to England were spent sorting out bits of paper and documents I needed to take with me. How much did the people I might be talking to in England know of this man's story? A large part of me hoped someone already had enlightened them before I arrived. Being the bearer of what might be devastating news for some was not a role I fancied.

*****

During my flight to England, my mind kept wandering back to the same big questions: is this trip really worthwhile? What did I hope to achieve? How would it help the people he left behind – people he discarded – if they knew what a rotten scoundrel their husband and father was? I convinced myself – almost – that their reaction to the information would depend on how much they already knew about the man, and to what extent his disappearance had impacted their lives. There was nothing for it other than to play it by ear when I arrived.

That then brought up the next question niggling away in the back of my mind for the last couple of days: was anybody going to meet me in London? I didn't know if Kate would be there to meet me or not. If she wasn't, I would simply go to my hotel and wait for her to contact me. There was one flaw in that thinking: what if no one contacted me? I didn't know how to contact any of our mystery man's family members. By the time I landed at Heathrow and boarded the train into the city, my stomach had almost tied itself in knots. Too many 'what ifs' with no answers had me nervous and questioning the wisdom of embarking on this trip.

I drew some comfort from the fact my booking at the hotel was okay. I was soon in my room and wondering what to do next. In the end, I did nothing apart from stretch out on the bed and doze off for a while. It was seven o'clock when my phone woke me.

"Where are you? Have you booked into your hotel?" Kate demanded.

"Arrived, and booked into the hotel early this afternoon." Kate said she would come straight up to my room. "I'm in room 3014." In the couple of minutes before she knocked on my door, I dashed to the bathroom and splashed water on my face in an attempt to look at least half human when she arrived.

There was time for a brief greeting before I had to get ready. Kate sat on the bed and watched TV while I showered and changed before we went down to the restaurant for dinner. I half expected to see Inspector Taylor waiting for us downstairs but, when he was nowhere in sight, I felt compelled to ask the question. "Isn't Inspector Taylor joining us this evening?"

"No, he's involved in something happening at Scotland Yard today, and said it would probably run late into the evening. When they finish for the night, he and the couple of the other officers probably will go to dinner somewhere close to where they've been working. Their investigation has made some progress.

Once we are seated at our table, I'll bring you up to speed on all I know so far. By the way, do you have anything planned for tomorrow?"

"There is nothing at all in my diary for the whole of the next week. I know what I'm hoping to do, but I've no idea how to do it, or if it will be possible for it to happen at all. My sole purpose for coming all this way was to meet with, and talk to, the other people whose lives were impacted by the man I married. I don't know how much they know about him, or what became of him, but I'm hoping we can share information so that, by the time I leave, we all will be a lot better informed."

"Okay, that's good. I'm staying with Gabby in her parents' unit here in the city. She has invited you to stay there too. The unit is her permanent home base now. She sold the place she used to own. Because she was away such a lot on assignments, her father convinced her to sell her place and move in with them. They spend more time overseas than they do at home anyway. So, having Gabby live there means that for much of the time at least, someone is there to keep an eye on the place. By the way, we both will be here to have breakfast with you in the morning, so you will be able to meet her then."

After giving the invitation a few moments thought, I agreed it made sense to accept Gabby's offer. But, I hadn't come all this way to socialise. "I was hoping to meet up with Tremayne's wives and children as soon as possible after I arrived here. While I have no idea how to organise that, I have to admit I'm also a bit nervous about how it might play out."

"Don't worry about it. A get-together is arranged for ten o'clock tomorrow morning. Dan, and one of the officers from Scotland Yard he's been working with, will collect us from here after breakfast – probably around 9:30 – to take us to meet everyone. There is no need to worry about how people are going to react to whatever we might have to say. Dan and his colleagues already have shared some of the story with them."

Kate had other news to share. Since arriving in London, Dan had worked with two Scotland Yard officers to identify and locate as many people as possible associated with our mystery man. As a result of their efforts, the Vietnamese wife of Travis Cridland, Mai Nguyen, arrived in London yesterday and would be a part of tomorrow's gathering. It seems she is the daughter of a well-to-do Vietnamese family, and she and her children continue to live a comfortable life on her parents' vast estate, and are supported by them.

I had an update for Kate as well. "In view of all our research findings, I felt it was only right I should talk to Roslyn Williams. Although a bit frosty to begin with, she thawed somewhat once she became aware of her role in this ongoing saga. In the end, the call proved worthwhile for both of us. I received a text from her just before I boarded my flight. She is due to arrive in London tonight and has booked into this hotel. It might be worth alerting Inspector Taylor he will have one more passenger to take to the get-together tomorrow."

She whipped out her phone and dashed off a quick text to Taylor. "It's as well he has plenty of warning. They might need to use a larger vehicle to accommodate all of us, or maybe need to take two vehicles."

There was little else from Inspector Taylor and his colleagues to add to our story, but Kate's research since her arrival had dug up quite a bit of background information useful for her book.

"I have a pile of release forms to take with me tomorrow. Provided the environment is okay, I will tell them of my intention to document our mystery man's story in a book. It's inevitable there will be some objections. If possible I'd like to address them while we are all together so that, if needs be, we can agree a workaround that will allow the book to go ahead."

"It would be great if there weren't too many objections, and if any that were forthcoming could be sorted out on the day. What about photos?"

"Of course, I'll be asking for photos and anything else worth an image in the book, but I don't expect to collect much on the day. But, that's why I have such a pile of release forms at the ready; just in case. There might be a chance to see what

Annabelle has. The meeting is at her ancestral pile. By the way, it seems she did whatever needed to be done to pass the title on to her son as soon as he reached his majority. So, although he now officially holds the title and owns all the property, everyone still defers to Annabelle as head of the house … and that includes her son. It seems she is one formidable woman. Well, according to Dan, she is. Did you bring any photos with you?"

"We both appear to have come prepared. Yes, I brought a couple of photos, but photos with Tremayne in them are rare. The other thing I managed to do was to put together a chart of sorts. I worked on the theory that a visual reference is much easier to understand than thousands of words. Working out how to do it was a bit tricky at first. After all, it's not your usual type of family tree chart. It's more like a number of family trees, which all have a 'common denominator'. How to show that graphically was a challenge. All those trees had to hang off the one common entry – Tremayne, the man they know by any other name.

After much trial and error, I think it worked out all right in the end. I brought two copies of the chart with me: one to leave here for the others to have copies made from if they want them, and one to take home again with me. I'm hoping, while I'm here, there might be opportunity to add further information by hand."

The rest of dinner was spent just catching up on Kate's activities since arriving in the UK … and, of course, what Dan had been up to. I discovered Kate and Dan had stayed together until the day before yesterday, when Kate moved in with Gabby after Gabby arrived home from being on an overseas assignment. It was good timing, as Dan had driven to Dorset the previous night and hadn't returned to London until this morning, and then went immediately to The Yard.

I noticed Kate seemed more relaxed talking about Dan now than she was before they left together for England.

After my long snooze this afternoon, I didn't think I would be able to sleep tonight. I was wrong. I went from not feeling sleepy at all, to being sound asleep five seconds after lights-out.

*****

As promised, Gabby and Kate joined me for breakfast. Before Gabby left for work, I agreed to move in with her and Kate – maybe today, but more probably tomorrow – depending on how today went. Then, it was time for Gabby to rush off to work. Roslyn Williams came down to join us in the reception area. We didn't have long to fill in with light conversation before Inspector Taylor arrived to drive us to the 'family' gathering at Annabelle's manor house.

I'm not sure what I expected, but I know it was something more low-key than the huge gathering of so many strangers. The event proper was launched by a few words from both the Scotland Yard Officer and Inspector Taylor to remind everyone about why we were there today. Then, in spite of being a former teacher who is not unfamiliar with public speaking, I was stunned to be called up to speak. I managed to pull myself together and deliver an overview of the story we had been working towards uncovering. Soon after I started my explanation, I asked if I might put up the chart I brought with me to help people follow what I was talking about. Kate clipped it to a whiteboard someone produced from somewhere in the building, and then stood by it to point to names on the chart as I mentioned them.

While my story rolled out, I kept an eye on my audience. From early in my presentation, my scan of faces detected anger and disgust in a large part of the assembly, but there were tears as well. As I approached the end of my delivery, I felt I had done a reasonable job and that the information I gave them was well received. I ended with a call for people to provide me with any missing information needed to update the chart, and explained I would be leaving the one on the board with Annabelle so anyone could obtain a copy if they wished.

Kate updated the second chart, my copy, with the new information – mainly dates and places – provided by those at the meeting, and which already had been added to the chart on the board. With the 'formal' part of the event over, attendees were free to mingle, meet and discuss. I was hesitant about the prospect of mingling with so many strangers whose lives I had just thrown into turmoil. My concerns were baseless. While I detected a whole gamut of emotional response running through the group, everyone was friendly, and quite a few welcomed me to their 'family'. Then it was time for the light buffet lunch laid on by Annabelle in the manicured grounds of the manor.

Once lunch was almost over, people clustered in small groups around the whiteboard to study and discuss my chart. I stood back some distance and off to one side. Hilary gravitated to my side. "You and Roslyn were the lucky ones," she began. "…Not having any kids to bring up, I mean."

"In my case, that situation was by mutual agreement. I can't speak for Roslyn, as she has never said anything specific. All she has ever said is that, in her case, there were 'various reasons' for it."

"So, in reality, you were his financier; a source of revenue to fund his lifestyle. Apologies … Please don't take any offence from that. I put it rather badly. What I really wanted to say was thank you. Thank you for helping out. For helping me make ends meet as I struggled to bring up my family."

I didn't take any offence from her words. In fact, what they did was cause me acute embarrassment; embarrassment that I had contributed so little to the funds he used to support his children.

When, the last contact details had been exchanged and the last update added to the charts, it was time to leave. I knew the morning had been unsettling in the extreme for many, and it would take them some time to adjust to their new-found knowledge of their family history. My own response to the morning was a mixture of emotions: anger at so many good people having been treated so badly; satisfaction at providing closure for some; sadness for the children who would never know their father.

Comments received some time after the event, confirmed my belief that many there would have preferred a different ending to the story. Belted into my seat for the trip back to the city, my mind was a churning mass as I dealt with my own emotions.

We three passengers were delivered to the door of the hotel where Roslyn and I were still registered as guests. As soon as we pulled up, Inspector Taylor jumped out and rushed to hotel's door to hold it open for us to enter. I caught Kate by the arm and held her back, so we lagged a little behind the inspector and Roslyn. "Kate, could you take Roslyn through to the lounge please? I'll join you there shortly." I expected a flurry of questions, but none was forthcoming. She simply stepped up her pace to catch up to the others, and shepherded Roslyn through the door and off in the direction of the lounge. Then I turned my attention to the inspector.

"Thank you and your colleagues for arranging today. It made it much easier to share the story we uncovered. Nevertheless, I don't see how any of this has helped your investigation into the death of my husband … Err, after today, maybe I should stop calling him that. That aside, the question is, are you any closer to discovering why he was killed?"

"I was going to talk to you about that, but I didn't want to do it before this morning's gathering. Could we meet somewhere this afternoon – say, five o'clock perhaps?"

"Is Kate invited to this meeting too?" He shrugged and said it was up to me whether she attended or not. "Right then, we both will be there. Where shall we meet?" He gave me the name of a bar further along the street from the hotel. Then, I was standing alone outside the hotel watching the police vehicle pulling away from the kerb… and the hotel's doorman was rushing to open the door for me.

Accompanied by coffees and a plate of scones with all the trimmings, Kate and Roslyn were settled in an alcove in the lounge. I opted not to mention our meeting later with the inspector until Kate and I were alone. It was a bit after three o'clock when Roslyn announced she was going to rest for a while before dinner. She asked if we would be eating in tonight.

Kate jumped in like a flash. "No, I'm sorry, but we already have other arrangements for this evening." Roslyn looked disappointed, but accepted it gracefully.

"What other arrangements?" I asked as soon as Roslyn was out of earshot.

"Dunno … but I'm sure we can come up with something. She is a different person from the one we met previously, but I felt we've both had enough of her for one day."

It seemed like the appropriate time to tell Kate about our meeting with Inspector Taylor. "Do you think he knows why it happened?" she asked, her face betraying the excitement behind her question.

It was my turn to say 'dunno', but I hoped that's what he wanted to talk about. Kate said she had something to do, which might take as much as an hour. When she returned, we could walk along to the bar together. It gave me time to freshen up and put my feet up for a while before going down to the lobby to wait for her. It also gave me time to get my head around what to ask the inspector this evening.

Chapter 25

The pub was one of those watering holes left over from long ago. Old-fashioned booths lined one wall, each booth resplendent in well-oiled leather and dark stained timber. Taylor had claimed the booth farthest from the bar area. Kate and I slid in opposite him and were soon sipping our first alcohol for the day. The Inspector opened our serious conversation with an apology.

"I'm sorry about the meeting place. While it's not the most private, it's the best I could come up with. I assumed you didn't want to meet at the hotel and run the risk of Miss Williams showing up uninvited."

We both nodded with a tad more enthusiasm than required. The pub did seem a strange place to be discussing the topic I had in mind. The smell of food, and raucous laughter from patrons playing darts at the other end of the room created a surreal environment in which to discuss murder. I commented accordingly.

"What better place than a dimly lit, smoky London pub?" Kate asked. "At the time, Jack the Ripper's murders probably were discussed by thousands in bars just like this across London." Her comment led us onto the topic we came to discuss.

Taylor again led the discussion. "While we haven't got anyone in our sights yet for the actual murder, we do have the background which led to Tremayne's death. As you established, he had spent many years on the run, marrying a number of 'wives' and fathering several children along the way. Such a lifestyle is expensive to maintain. Apart from having to support the families he established, he had considerable other expenses associated with facilitating and maintaining his changing persona for his life on the run."

"Yes, I appreciate that," I said, "and I believe his need for money was an ongoing concern. It was an attempt to screw big money out of me, which got him chucked out of the marriage, and brought anything he might have had from me in the past to an abrupt end."

"There are reasonable indications he was preparing to bolt again, to leave Australia and start another new life somewhere far away. It appears he began his 'other life' while an agent on assignment in the Middle East. Exactly how it started remains a mystery. Suffice to say, in its early days, the odd body or two were left strewn about that countryside. Then…"

"Are you saying he was an assassin? Was that a part of his role as an intelligence officer?"

Kate picked up on the horror in my voice, and reached over to grab my hand.

"No, it wasn't included in his official duties. We don't know yet whether it was a part of his rogue operation, or whether it happened after he was dismissed from the service. The other thing we don't know is whether this was something he undertook willingly or if he was coerced into it; if some form of pressure was brought to bear. Nevertheless, we do know that, after abandoning his life in the UK, he based himself in the Middle East. Sometime during his sojourn in that area, he became involved with drug running. In more recent years, his involvement in trafficking stepped up, and he became a big player in the Australian distribution network. Word on the street tells us something went wrong with a few deals. We haven't established whether it was a case of clients not paying up, or if he was skimming and running a rogue network on the side. The overlords – or whatever you want to call them – took offence and sent out an enforcer to bring him to heel."

"So, something went wrong with that negotiation, and he ended up dead in my cane paddock?"

"Not immediately … It appears the enforcer did try to discuss the matter with Tremayne on a couple of occasions but, when his attempts met with no success, the enforcer's instructions changed from negotiation to elimination.

As we all know, the enforcer was successful in carrying out his instructions. While we have yet to establish the identity of the enforcer, we have identified the probable key players responsible for issuing the order which resulted in Tremayne's death. We still have a way to go before any charges are laid anywhere in the world, but it seems likely none of those involved are Australian citizens. It appears, if and when there is an ultimate end to this story, it will be played out either somewhere in Asia, or possibly somewhere in South America."

"This is almost impossible to take in. While I thought I was ready for whatever our research might uncover, I don't think I had envisioned anything like this."

"Not surprising; and I can understand how difficult it must be for you. But, there is a little more I could share with you, if you think you can handle it."

"Of course I can handle it. I haven't come this far to be left wondering about any aspect of his life, no matter how insignificant – or shocking – it might be."

"While what I said about his drug trafficking connection being the possible root cause of his death, some grey areas are associated with that. Nevertheless, that remains our preferred thinking at the moment. We are still investigating those 'grey areas'. So far, we have discovered some suggestion that, during his time in the Middle East, Tremayne became involved in other activities as well. There is evidence to suggest he became a player in human trafficking operations being run out of that area. Until we confirm a few things, we can't be quite sure whether it was a problem with his drug trafficking activities, or something related to his human trafficking involvement that ended up with Tremayne being killed."

I was shaking my head as Taylor finished speaking. It was not entirely in disbelief, but also in disgust ... so much disgust at so many things: disgust that those responsible might never be brought to justice; disgust that Tremayne became involved in something which probably ruined many lives. Above all, I was disgusted that, in one of his many personas, his disregard for life allowed him to become a taker of lives.

Later that night, I found some solace in the fact our research and today's gathering brought closure and relief for a number of people whose lives our mystery man had devastated. And, I gave thanks I hadn't known the facts Inspector Taylor shared with us this evening until after our meeting with those families. Perhaps this is one chapter of the story they don't need to know … not now, and not until they have time to recover from what we shared with them today. …And, hopefully, before Kate brings out that damned book of hers.

*****

After another four days of the odd casual meeting with family members slotted in between accompanying Kate on research trips, it was time for me to head home. Kate came to Heathrow to help me while away the hours I had to be there before my flight was due to depart. She seemed a bit tense, and I didn't think it had anything to do with my leaving. I soon found out the reason.

"I don't suppose I need to tell you Dan and I have established something of a relationship. It has a possibility of developing into something long-term and permanent. How would you feel about my moving into the cottage when I return? I want to stay close, but I think we both need our freedom; need to be free to lead our lives as we want without being concerned about the impact on the other one. Dan and I will be spending whatever time we can together, and the cottage would work well for us. That aside, with me out from under your feet, you and Connor will be able to get on with your lives together without me looking over your shoulder."

"What do you mean about Connor and I having a life together?"

"Oh, come on, Lisa. If you haven't already worked out how Connor feels about you, then it's time you bloody well woke up. For as long as I've known him, Connor has carried a torch for you, but he would never do anything to interfere in your life, or would impact on your marriage. That's all changed now. You are no longer married … never were as it turns out, not legally anyway. This is your chance to have a real-life, and a real marriage. Don't… mess … it … up."

Of course Kate could move into the cottage. I couldn't think of a better arrangement, and I was thrilled to have the Kate-and-Dan relationship confirmed. But, the Connor thing…? Well, I had a long flight home to think about that. Somehow, I didn't think it would require too much thought. And, I was looking forward to having him waiting at the airport to drive me home.

The long flight gave me time to reflect on my time in England and all that happened there. Most noteworthy was the change we witnessed in Roslyn Williams. Gone was the aggressive, aloof woman of our initial encounters with her, to be now replaced by a more chastened and normal human being. The whole event, and the truths encountered, were difficult for her to comprehend and accept, but she was coming to terms with all of it.

Another significant outcome from the trip was seeing an unexpected side to Tremayne's personality. Although it appears the way he treated his 'wives' was of no consequence to him, he took his responsibilities to his offspring seriously. Marrying women from substantial backgrounds, whose parents could support them when he moved on, seemed the mainstay of his life's plan. But, he needed money not only to finance his many 'lives', he also need to support his children until they reached their majority. That's where Roslyn and I came into the plan … well, more so Roslyn than me. While we produced no children, we did contribute to his child-support coffers. In hindsight, I must have been an extreme disappointment to him on that front.

*****

And then I was being met at the airport by Connor as arranged. Conversation was light on the drive to the farm. On opening my front door, I lifted the veil on another of his hidden talents. The man can cook! A stew was simmering on the stove, and it was delicious. Over dinner, we both relaxed sufficiently for deep and meaningful discussions afterwards.

"Connor, I'm sorry, but I have to rescind my offer for you to move into the cottage." I saw him struggle, but not quite manage to mask his disappointment. "Kate and Dan – Inspector Taylor – will be moving into it when they return from overseas."

"I understand. By the sounds of things, it might not have worked out anyway. Thanks for the heads-up. I'll look around for somewhere else before Dad returns."

"You won't have to look too far. I was hoping you might consider moving into this house with me." Before I had time to think, I was having the life almost hugged out of me.

"I don't want to just live in the house with you. Will you think about… Will you marry me?"

"Quite possibly… But, there is something I want to clear up first. When you came back from down south to live at the farm, your father suggested you came home to heal a broken heart; something to do with an impending marriage that didn't happen. I suppose I need to know…"

"There never was an impending marriage; not even an engagement. On one of my trips home, I brought a work colleague and close friend with me to see this part of the country. She and Dad hit it off straight away and had many long conversations, which I thought were about farming in the tropics. A few hints Dad dropped in phone calls after I returned to work had me curious. Long story short, it seems my friend believed we were more than friends, and gave Dad to understand she might soon be joining the family. It was never going to happen … and it didn't. From my point of view, it wasn't that kind of friendship. But, I already had made up my mind to chuck it in and come home to help Dad. It was easier for him to believe I came home to heal a broken heart, than for him to accept I had come home to look after him. So, I let it stay that way."

"I'm not sure what to say … except I won't be enlightening him any time soon. Thank you for sharing that with me."

"Lisa, there was a time – a long time – when I struggled with a broken heart. It started the moment you married Tremayne. There never has been anyone else but you for me."

*****

Two weeks later, it was my turn to be waiting at the airport for Kate's flight to arrive. She stayed on in the UK to complete her research before returning to deal with her work commitments here. Inspector Taylor and his Scotland Yard colleagues left London for destinations unknown a couple of days before Kate boarded her flight home. She confirmed Taylor had not yet returned to Australia.

After my 'talk' with Kate at the airport and on the drive home, clearing Tremayne's things out of the cottage was my first priority. I had plenty of help. Thanks to the continuing heavy rain, there was nothing much to do on either of our properties, so Connor spent his days – and most nights – at my place. I'm not sure how his father will react to these developments when he, and his lady friend, return home next week.

My life seems to have taken on new meaning over the last couple of weeks. And, I can't imagine anything better than having Kate and her Dan, and Connor share it with me. A lot of things have taken on a new perspective. Not the least of those is my diminished interest in Inspector Taylor's investigation into the death of the man I married, the man *known by any other name* by so many other people.

The End

Also by the Author

Revenge is not Enough
Harbour Plaza: built on dreams
On the Way to Istanbul
An Unsuitable House
A Land Too Far
Paradise Interrupted
Unwelcome Mail

About the Author

KAYLA DANOLI spent her early years traipsing around Australia and then Europe with her parents, and then completed her tertiary education in England before returning to Australia. There were a variety of jobs in various parts of Queensland before eventually making her way towards the coast. She now lives in a small coastal town on the Queensland coast where she works part-time on a charter vessel.

In the early days after settling in that small town, to fill in her spare time, both when at home and while on cruises, she started scribbling down her ideas for stories. These days, she writes whenever time permits. Her *Harbour Plaza* series, previously released in 2015 as monthly eBook episodes, was updated, extended and released in 2016 as the *Harbour Plaza: built on dreams* compilation. *Revenge is not Enough,* also released in 2016, was her first full-length novel.

By Any Other Name is Kayla's eighth full-length novel.

Discover more about Kayla and her work by visiting

www.eaglemountbooks.com.au/kayla-danoli

or contact her at

admin@eaglemountbooks.com.au